BITTER BETRAYAL

Philip Janvrin passes many a sleepless night in his prison cell reliving the day he was arrested for drug smuggling. And so, when he is suddenly and mysteriously released, he cannot believe his luck. But as Philip is immediately delivered into the hands of Gregory Sorel, colleague of his brother Peter, and head of a Special Intelligence unit at the Foreign Office, he soon learns that a price must be paid for his freedom.

Some months ago, whilst on a special assignment, Peter Janvrin disappeared without a trace. More than anxious to know if his colleague is dead or alive, Gregory Sorel enlists the reluctant Philip to pose as Peter – to whom he bears a startling resemblance. And so Philip takes on a new life and waits for the puzzle of his brother's disappearance to become clear. But as the shadowy world of Peter Janvrin begins to emerge, Philip finds that he must struggle not only to make sense of every day but also to stay alive . . .

Skilfully plotted, compelling and assured, *Bitter Betrayal* further establishes Palma Harcourt's reputation as one of our finest spy writers.

PALMA HARCOURT

Bitter Betrayal

HarperCollins*Publishers*

HarperCollins*Publishers*,
77–85 Fulham Palace Road,
Hammersmith, London W6 8JB

Published by HarperCollins*Publishers* 1993
2 4 6 8 9 7 5 3 1

A catalogue record for this book is
available from the British Library

ISBN 0 00 224187 0

Typeset in Linotron Plantin
at The Spartan Press Ltd, Lymington, Hants

Printed in Great Britain by
HarperCollinsManufacturing Glasgow

ONE

The prison governor sat at his desk and stared into space, his brow creased in a frown. Charles Sinclair was a big, heavy man with a bovine face that made people misjudge him, for in fact he was intelligent, conscientious and sensitive to others – especially those in his charge. These qualities, however, were not always helpful, and today he would have been glad of a less demanding temperament.

If he had been asked to describe his present feelings in one word, he would have replied, quite quietly, that he was annoyed. But this would have been an understatement. He considered that he did his job competently – even very competently – so that it was natural he should object to external interference. But, as he waited for Philip Janvrin to be brought to his office, he knew that he was worried as well as angry, though he couldn't have explained why, unless it was his dislike of any sequence of events that savoured of mystery. And the man who had called on him that morning *had* been both mysterious and enigmatic.

The visitor had been in his early thirties, a slight figure with soft fair hair and spectacles. If it had not been for his Savile Row suit and his obviously hand-made shoes, the governor, adept at sizing people up, would have put him down as a minor civil servant, a bank clerk or possibly a social worker of some kind.

'Good of you to see me at such short notice, sir,' the man had said pleasantly enough, though there had been no trace of subservience in his manner. 'First of all, may I suggest you read this letter, and then perhaps we can talk.'

Recalling the telephone call from the Home Office which had made the appointment, the governor had some premonitions about the contents of the letter. He was however unprepared for the total authority it conveyed.

'This letter is to introduce Gregory Sorel,' he read. 'I trust that you will do precisely as he suggests and give him every assistance

7

in your power. The matter is important and urgent.' Over the personal signature of the Home Secretary, there was no doubt that this was an order that the governor would have no option but to obey. He had concealed his feelings and made the best of it by demanding that Sorel should produce some identification.

'So what can I do for you, Mr Sorel?' he had asked blandly after he had been satisfied.

Sorel had wasted no more time. 'You have in your charge a certain Philip Janvrin, convicted of drug smuggling seven years ago. Even with remission he would in the ordinary course of events still have several years to serve. I want him released at six o'clock tomorrow morning. I will meet him and take charge of him, though he will no longer be a prisoner.'

'You want him released – just like that? May I ask why?'

'Er – it would oblige the Home Secretary – sir.'

'And I'm not entitled to any further explanation?'

'That's correct, sir.'

'But what do I tell Janvrin? Good behaviour?'

'Has he behaved well?'

'Yes. He's been a model prisoner. At first he was very morose and withdrawn, as was only to be expected. We watched him carefully, just in case he should contemplate anything dramatic, but he soon settled down. At present he works in the prison library, and he seems as happy as anyone in his circumstances can be.'

'Good! Now, what else can you tell me about him? What about visitors? Correspondence? Any special chums among the other inmates?'

'No, to all those questions. In the early days of his sentence people did come to see him – mainly members of his family – but he refused to meet them, so they stopped making the effort. The very few letters he gets he tears up as soon as he has glanced at them. He writes none at all. As for what you call "special chums", the only person who's made any real contact with him is the Roman Catholic padre who comes here once a week to hear confessions and say Mass. You know that Janvrin's a Papist?'

'Oh yes. We know about his background.'

This had been a somewhat cryptic comment, Sinclair thought, and it had disturbed him at the time; in retrospect, as he reviewed his conversation with Sorel, it still disturbed him. And this was not the only point that concerned him – and had concerned him over the years.

Why, he wondered for the umpteenth time, why on earth had Philip Janvrin, younger son of Major General Sir George Janvrin, educated at Ampleforth and Christ Church, Oxford, a clever boy with every advantage, decided to attempt to smuggle a large quantity of heroin into the UK?

This was the question that the defending barrister had repeatedly asked at Janvrin's trial, but no satisfactory answer had ever emerged. It had been established that he had never been known to take drugs, or shown any interest in the drug scene. He was not in debt. There was no evidence that he was being blackmailed. He was a practising Catholic, and until his detention at Heathrow his reputation had been unblemished.

But the evidence against him had been damning and seemingly unanswerable. The governor had asked Sorel if any new facts had come to light, but had been assured that the verdict remained valid. As far as the authorities were concerned, there was no doubt that Philip Janvrin had been – and remained – guilty as charged.

That had been the end of his conversation with Gregory Sorel, apart from some administrative arrangements for Janvrin's release through, they agreed, the governor's own private entrance. Sorel had impressed on the governor, to the latter's annoyance, the need for confidentiality, and the need to let as few of the staff as possible know what was happening and warn them not to talk out of turn. The other prisoners – Janvrin's cell-mates, for example, could merely be told that Janvrin had been taken ill. As far as Sorel was concerned, his visit had never taken place. He – Sorel – would explain all to Janvrin when he met him in the morning.

A sharp tap at the door roused Charles Sinclair from his musing. He sat up straight and composed his features. His voice was level as he gave permission to enter.

'Thank you, Dobson,' he said to the prison officer who had brought in the prisoner. 'You can leave us for now, but tell the Chief I'll want to see him – and you – when you've taken charge of Janvrin again.'

'Sir!'

The governor waited until the door shut behind the officer before he pointed to a chair. 'At ease, Janvrin, and sit down.'

'Thank you, sir.'

Philip Janvrin was thirty, but looked older. A tall man – he was an inch under six feet – he was too thin for his height, and his pasty complexion, the result of too little air and exercise, tended to spoil an otherwise pleasant face. Dark-haired and blue-eyed, he had once been an attractive man, but seven years of prison life had given him a bearing of quiet submission that would have better suited someone twice his age. Whatever crime he had committed, the governor could not help feeling sorry for him.

Sinclair said, 'Janvrin, I have news for you.'

'Yes, sir.'

'You don't sound very interested.'

'I'm sorry, sir.' Janvrin's smile was surprisingly sweet. 'Should I be?' Then his expression changed, became anxious. 'Is it bad news? My brother?'

'No, Janvrin, nothing like that! This concerns you personally.' The governor hesitated, wishing he knew how the man would react to what he was about to hear. There was nothing for it but to be blunt. He said, 'Janvrin, you are to be released tomorrow morning.'

For a moment Philip Janvrin stared at the governor, unable to believe what he had been told. Then a spasm – almost a convulsion – seemed to spread through his whole body, though he still didn't speak. He looked sick.

'Janvrin, are you all right?'

'Yes – thank you, sir. But why? Why? It must be much too soon.'

Sinclair paused. He hated to lie to those in his charge. Then he said, 'Put it down to your good behaviour, and the fact that prisons are overcrowded.' He went on hurriedly, 'But it's good news, surely? Unexpected, of course, but once you've taken it in . . . ' Sinclair continued his monologue until, exasperated by the lack of response, he said, 'Janvrin, are you listening to me?'

'Yes, sir. You were saying I was young. I should put the last few years behind me and make a fresh start. I was luckier than many people. I was well-educated and – '

'Quite!' Sinclair controlled his irritation. 'You realize that it won't be easy to adapt? Life in prison is inevitably deadening. The outside will seem strange to you. You'll have to take responsibility for yourself – ' The governor paused, wondering how true this would be, in view of Sorel's visit. 'Anyway, there are many avenues which, because of your record, will no longer be open to you. And there will be temptations.' Conscious that he was mouthing platitudes, many of which would probably prove inapplicable in these odd circumstances, he stopped and sighed. 'Janvrin, while you've been here you've chosen to cut yourself off from your family and friends, but I have every hope that now – '

'No!' It was the first time the prisoner had shown any real animation. 'I no longer have a family. My mother's dead, as you know, sir. Not that it would have made any difference had she still been alive; my father, who disowned me long ago, wouldn't have allowed her to make me welcome. As for my sister, she's eight years younger than I am, and I wouldn't know her if I met her in the street. Anyway, she and her husband live in Australia. That leaves my brother Peter. We were very close, very alike – so much so in fact that we were sometimes taken for each other – but he's married and there's his career in the Foreign Office to consider. Apart from the fact that it might cause a rift between him and our father, it simply wouldn't be fair to saddle him with an ex-con, and I don't intend to.'

It was a long speech, and Charles Sinclair could think of no rebuttal that might be effective. Clearly Janvrin had made up his mind. In spite of his quiet manner he was, the governor thought, a formidable young man.

'Then there's nothing more for me to say. You'll go straight to the hospital wing and spend the night there. You'll be off in the morning.' The governor stood up and held out his hand as Dobson, for whom he had rung, came in. 'Wait outside while I speak to this officer. I don't expect we'll be meeting again. I wish you luck, Janvrin. Goodbye.'

'Goodbye, sir, and thank you.' At the door Philip Janvrin turned and smiled once more. 'I've enjoyed working in the library, sir,' he said. 'I shall miss it.'

*　　*　　*

For some minutes after Philip Janvrin had gone, and while he waited for Dobson to return with the Chief Officer, Charles Sinclair continued to stare at the door. He had no reason to reproach himself. He had done his best to warn Janvrin – as he would have done with any other convict about to be released – that after so many years in prison he would find life on the outside full of hazards. But, even to his own ears the warning had on this occasion sounded unreal – even unnecessary. He was not happy about it.

He knew why. He was disturbed by his curious meeting with Gregory Sorel, and the unexplained circumstances that surrounded the request – order – for Janvrin's release without delay. He had been duty bound not to mention Sorel to Janvrin, but he regretted the undertaking he had been forced to give. In a way, he somehow felt that Janvrin should have been put on his guard against Sorel – though why this should be he didn't know. He had no cause to distrust Sorel; Sorel's credentials had been impeccable, and he had carried out his task with meticulous courtesy. Nevertheless . . .

He thought for a while. Then realizing that, in spite of his promise about confidentiality, he had to go some distance towards satisfying his curiosity, he lifted the receiver of his private phone and tapped out the number of a friend who was highly placed in the Civil Service. He explained the situation, as briefly as he could. The friend called back some hours later. Sinclair found what he had to say less than reassuring.

There was no official in the Home Office called Gregory Sorel, but a man by that name apparently worked in a security section of the Foreign and Commonwealth Office, run by one Brigadier Dermot Aubyn. Little was known about him, or his section, and inquiries were not encouraged.

'There are plenty of ex-cons around,' the friend continued, 'so Sorel must want this particular chap, and no other. Why, I can't imagine. And, if you take my advice, Charles, you'll forget the whole thing. You don't owe Philip Janvrin anything and, from what I could gather, Sorel could be bad news. It seems that he and his boss are very much a law unto themselves. Certainly they aren't subject to the same constraints as lesser mortals like you or me. So keep out of their way if possible and, whatever you do, don't try to take a hand in whatever game they're playing.'

Charles Sinclair had thanked his friend, and promised to take his advice and forget the whole episode. But it was a promise not easy to keep.

Meanwhile, as the prison governor brooded over a seeming mystery that was not his direct concern, Philip Janvrin, oblivious of the interest being taken in him, was trying to come to terms with his impending release. He found it almost impossible to accept, either mentally or emotionally. It had come too suddenly, too unexpectedly.

Originally, when he had been sentenced to twelve years imprisonment he had thought of it as a lifetime. He would be in his thirties, almost middle-aged, before he was free. In the meantime he would have to exist and the only way to do that, he realized after a few months, was not to look ahead. So he refused to contemplate the future and lived in the present, enduring each day as it came. And now the future had been forced down his throat.

Two factors had combined to save him from a mental break-down during the past seven years. One was his work in the prison library, monotonous and undemanding though that was – had been. He had meant it when he told the governor that he would miss the library. It had given him an opportunity to be alone in a comparatively congenial atmosphere, a blessed respite from the confines of his cell with its three other inmates. Until his imprisonment he had never appreciated how vital his privacy was to him.

The second, and probably the more important factor, that had helped to preserve his sanity, had been his religion and the encouragement of Father Malory, the Jesuit priest who visited the prison every week. It was through him that Philip had learnt, among other things, of the marriage of his brother Peter to Zara Beaumont – a friend from childhood of both the Janvrin boys – and the subsequent birth of their son, Patrick. Writing a brief note to the priest, he wondered if he would ever see young Patrick.

These thoughts of his family, especially of Peter, saddened him. Though he was three years younger than Peter, he had always loved and admired his more extrovert brother, and it had seemed right that Zara should marry him. Dear Zara. He remembered her with affection. He had been in love with her too once upon a time.

Nevertheless, he ruminated, he had no regrets about his final decision to cut himself off from all of them. He was still convinced that it had been the wisest course to take. And, in a sense, he had not initiated the process. His father had been responsible for that. His father had said that he had disgraced the family, and he deserved the sentence he had received. This was the main reason why he had accepted the outcome of the trial and had not appealed, in spite of urging by his lawyers, his mother and Peter. Even when his mother had died there had been no attempt at reconciliation. On the contrary. The lawyer who had written to inform him of her death had said it was his father's express wish that he should not ask for permission to attend her funeral, permission which the prison governor would probably have granted.

Staring out of the barred window of the hospital wing at the neat flowerbeds below, Philip Janvrin sighed. It had all been so long ago, in another lifetime. Useless to brood on it now, he knew. He must force himself to think of the future, a future inevitably different from the one he would once have chosen.

He turned away from the window. He must get ready for bed. He was to be called at five the next morning. He had not been allowed to return to his cell, and his few personal possessions had been brought to him, together with his civilian clothes and the original contents of their pockets.

The whole concession was unprecedented, he guessed. And why? Whatever the answer, it was clear that at the very least tomorrow would be a momentous day.

He found it difficult to sleep. For the first time in years he was alone at night, for there were no other prisoners in the ward, and the silence lay heavy around him. He missed the snores, the snuffles, the muttered swearing, the occasional weeping of those who had shared his cell. And he felt unnaturally clean. He had been allowed a long, hot bath and permitted to wash his hair, put on clean pyjamas and get into a fresh-smelling bed. What was more there was a proper lavatory a few yards away along the corridor which he was free to use. He got up twice, not because it was necessary, but just to make sure that this adjunct to civilization was still available to him. He wondered what he would be like in the real world, if he behaved in this fashion while he was still inside; he tried to laugh at himself, but found it hard to do so.

And as sleep continued to elude him he could not keep his thoughts away from that day at Heathrow Airport that had changed his life. He had been returning from a holiday in Europe with Peter. They had both been in high spirits; it had been an excellent three weeks.

For Philip it had been a significant three weeks, too. Though he had as yet told no one, not even Peter, he had made up his mind what he wanted to do now that he had come down from Oxford with the First Class degree for which he had hoped. In a way, he had known that it was a decision he had already made. His easy acceptance of Peter's casual admission that he and Zara were lovers had merely confirmed it.

They had collected their bags from the carousel and had been about to make for the exit when Peter said, 'I must go to the loo. You go ahead, Philip, and see if you can spot Mother. I'll be as quick as I can.'

Philip had made for the 'Green' channel and had strode along confidently. He had never had trouble at Heathrow before, and didn't expect to be stopped. He had almost reached the exit when a customs officer called him back. He had been asked to open his bag. His dirty clothes, his toilet articles, the bottle of brandy he had bought for his parents, the perfume for Zara, had all been spread out on the bench. It wasn't much, but he and Peter had been travelling light.

The customs officer had turned the bag upside down and shaken it. 'Anything else – sir?' the man had asked.

'What – what should there be?' He was sure he had looked guilty.

The customs officer had produced a small knife – a sharp Stanley knife – and had slit the lining at the bottom of the bag. Exposed had lain the thin plastic bags, filled with white powder.

'A little matter of these – sir. Heroin, do you think?' He had

15

called another officer to witness his find, then said to Philip, 'Please come with us.'

The memory was so vivid that, as in the distance a clock struck three, Philip Janvrin found he was sweating with fear.

TWO

'He should be coming out any minute,' said Gregory Sorel. 'It's almost six.'

'He's not got much of a day for it,' said the other man in the Rover, as a sudden shower of rain beat down on the car's roof. Generally the weather was overcast and gloomy – scarcely appropriate for the occasion.

'All the better, Hamish – at least for our purpose. Make him think twice about rejoicing in his new-found freedom – and more likely to jump at anything he's offered.'

Hamish Constant laughed doubtfully. He was in his early twenties, not long down from university and a new recruit to the Section, just out of training. He had never worked with Sorel before and, though he wouldn't have admitted it, he was a little scared of his superior.

'And if you're thinking I'm a heartless bastard,' Sorel continued, 'forget it. Philip Janvrin was part of a drugs chain. He may have been comparatively small fry. He may not have used the stuff himself. He may have just done the courier bit for kicks, or money. He may have been unlucky to be caught. I don't know how he came to be caught, and I don't care. But in my opinion anyone who brings heroin into this country deserves what he gets.'

Constant was silent. He couldn't disagree with Sorel. He held no brief for anyone involved with hard drugs. Nevertheless, he felt a sneaking sympathy for Philip Janvrin. When the judge had passed sentence on him, Janvrin had been the same age as he himself was now, Constant reflected. Twelve years – a lifetime. Now reduced to seven – though there was a catch.

Sorel yawned. He had been up since five, after a late night, but weariness wasn't the reason for the yawn. Gregory Sorel was bored. He hated playing a waiting game, and it seemed that waiting games were an inescapable part of his present job. He wished also that he had someone with him who was more

17

experienced than Constant. He had studied Janvrin's file and listened carefully to the prison governor's comments, but in fact he knew very little about this man whom they had come to meet and who could be so important to them. He and Constant had rehearsed their approach, and he could only hope that Constant would co-operate with some expertise.

Another squall of rain battered the car, and ran down the windows to obscure the view of the small door in the prison wall – the governor's private entrance. Then the storm eased, and they saw the door open. For a moment two figures were visible, one short and square and in uniform, the other tall and thin. They shook hands briefly. The taller figure slipped into the miserable grey street as a distant clock began to strike. The door shut behind him. Philip Janvrin was a free man.

And Sorel nodded his head in satisfaction. At least the prison authorities were on time. He approved of such efficiency.

Philip shivered. It had been August when he was arrested at Heathrow and he had been wearing thin slacks and a summer jacket. On this wet and chilly day in May, even with a raincoat on top, it was an inadequate garb. Head down, carrying the brown paper parcel which contained his few belongings, Philip started up the road. He scarcely noticed the Rover.

'Mr Janvrin!'

It was so long since anyone had addressed him as 'Mister' that Philip stopped in surprise. He stared at Sorel who had got out of the car and was holding open the rear door for him. To his knowledge Philip had never seen the man before, or the other man in the driving seat.

'Come along. We'll give you a lift.'

Philip was wary. Having said that he did not want anyone in his family to be informed of his release, he had not expected a reception committee – and these were strangers. Why had they met him? How did they know when and where to meet him? Instinctively he distrusted them.

'Who are you?'

'Friends, I assure you, Mr Janvrin.' Sorel sounded sincere and forthright. 'Come along, there's a good chap. This is a beastly day for standing around in the open.'

Still Philip hesitated. The easy assumption that he would do as he was asked was beginning to annoy him. He had spent the last seven years of his life obeying orders without question. He saw no reason to continue now. He was about to say he would prefer to walk, when another sudden burst of rain came sheeting down. The temptation to take shelter was overwhelming, and what had he to lose?

'Okay.' Deliberately Janvrin handed Sorel his brown paper parcel and got into the car ahead of him. 'You seem to know who I am,' he said as Sorel followed, to sit beside him on the rear seat. 'Perhaps you'd introduce yourselves.'

'Certainly. My name is Gregory Sorel, and my companion is Hamish Constant. Foreign and Commonwealth Office.'

They gave him their identity cards, and he studied each in turn. The photographs seemed to correspond with their faces and, as far as he could tell, the cards looked official. Then an unpleasant thought struck him.

'If this concerns my brother, Peter,' he said coldly, 'you can forget it. I haven't had any contact with him for years, and it's not his fault he's got a brother who's an ex-con. It would be grossly unfair if his career should be – '

'Hold it!' Sorel held up an authoritative hand. 'Mr Janvrin, you malign us. Isn't that so, Hamish?'

'Of course.' Constant twisted in his seat to smile at Philip. 'We're not in that sort of business.'

'All right, I accept that. But then what kind of business are you in? What do you want with me?' demanded Janvrin.

'Mr Janvrin, I'll be perfectly candid – as far as I'm allowed,' Sorel said hastily, to forestall any injudicious comment from Constant. 'We want to talk to you about a job that you could possibly do for us. We can't tell you precisely what it is at present, but we can tell you a certain amount about it. I suggest we go and have breakfast together.'

Philip hesitated, considering. Then he said, 'Thanks, but I've already had breakfast, so if that's all you've got to say I'll be on my way.'

'You're not interested? Not even curious?'

'Not particularly,' Philip lied.

Of course he was curious. How could he fail to be intrigued? He couldn't imagine what job he could possibly do for anyone in the

FCO, at least not any job that was legal. And, ex-con though he might be, his qualifications – a history degree and some experience in a prison library – didn't seem to him much use for any illegal employment. He couldn't blow a safe or pick a lock or handle a firearm.

'Why not have a second breakfast? Then we'll drive you to wherever you want to go,' Sorel urged persuasively. 'There's no one expecting you, is there?'

It was not really a question. They had done their homework well, Philip thought, and at length he said, 'Okay. You can buy me a second breakfast if you like, but I very much doubt if it will do you any good.'

'That's a risk we'll gladly take.' Sorel sat back in his seat, at ease at last. 'Off you go, Hamish,' he ordered. 'I'm hungry, even if our friend here is not. So far, at this ungodly hour of the morning, all I've had is a cup of coffee.'

Although Philip had been to London frequently, to parties, to shows, to stay for weekends, he was not really familiar with the city, and when Constant drew up in front of a block of flats he couldn't have said whether he was in Kensington or Islington or anywhere else. He had the impression they had been going round in circles, though Constant had sworn loudly about one-way systems, which could have been to blame for the seeming detours.

Sorel produced a key and led them into the anonymous hall of the block. They went up two floors in a lift, and Sorel opened the door opposite. He took Philip's raincoat and flung it over a chair in the smaller but again curiously featureless hall of the flat. Constant, following them, put down Philip's parcel that he had brought up from the car, and disappeared in the direction of what, from the smell of eggs and bacon emerging from it, was clearly the kitchen. Sorel directed Philip into a sitting-room.

It was an uninteresting room, with the impersonality of a hotel, though the furnishings were not unpleasant. There were no books, no photographs, no ornaments. The only concession to a sign of occupation was a vase containing spring flowers placed in the centre of a round table that was laid for a meal for three. Philip noted that Sorel and Constant had fully expected him to accept their invitation to breakfast.

20

Almost at once Constant returned with a tray on which were a pot of coffee, hot milk, orange juice and toast; butter and marmalade were already on the table. He was closely followed by a short, fat woman in a cook's white apron, carrying plates of eggs and bacon. Each held two eggs, two rashers and fried tomatoes – a good deal more generous than prison fare. The woman made a point of not looking at Philip and withdrew without speaking.

'Let's sit down,' Sorel said quickly. 'We can talk while we're eating.'

'Right.' To his surprise Philip realized that he also was hungry. He had been too excited to eat more than a little of the breakfast that the prison had provided. 'You can start the talking, Mr Sorel.'

Sorel talked, with occasional interpolations from Constant. Philip listened, but realized that he was little wiser when they had finished their duologue. Apparently he was being offered a job which would last for two to three months. It would be well paid, and there would be a bonus at the end if he completed the task successfully. He would then be given good references and help to get further employment, or to train for any specific work or profession he might have in mind. It was, as Sorel said, an excellent offer – especially for an ex-convict.

'But what's the catch? There must be some catch,' Philip said at length. 'Perhaps several catches.'

To his surprise Sorel agreed at once. 'You're quite right. First, we're talking about a confidential assignment, which is why even this conversation must never be mentioned to anyone. Next, you'll have to sign the Official Secrets Act. That means that if you're ever tempted to sell your story to the newspapers or talk to anyone about it, you'd better think again. So watch it – or you'll be back in gaol.'

There was a vicious air – almost an air of satisfaction – about the way Sorel spoke, and Philip felt his dislike as if it were a physical blow. He sensed that Sorel had mentally added 'where you belong' to his last remark. But when Sorel continued his bland manner had returned.

'Secondly, I must warn you that it *might* – just might – be dangerous. But, in addition to the material and immediate advantages you'd gain from it, you'd also, to employ a cliché, be helping to pay off your debt to society. As a practising Christian, that aspect of the offer should surely appeal to you.'

'I thought I had done that in the last seven years,' said Philip mildly.

'Mr Janvrin, in my opinion you could never repay it fully.' Sorel's voice was soft. 'However – '

'Any other snags?' Philip asked sharply. He was getting annoyed by Sorel's attitude. 'Is what you're suggesting legal, for example?'

'Part of it could be on the borderline,' Sorel admitted with surprising frankness, 'but we'd make sure that if you were called upon to do anything illegal it wouldn't count as a black mark against you.'

'What on earth do you mean by that?'

'We mean that you wouldn't pay any penalty for it,' Constant said. 'You'd have diplomatic immunity.' He laughed as if he had said something funny.

Sorel was not amused. He glared at his colleague before turning to Philip. 'That's about all we can tell you at this stage, Mr Janvrin, but it's a generous offer which in your position you'd be sensible to accept.'

'Is that a threat, Sorel?'

'Certainly not! But you're an intelligent man. You must realize that life won't be easy for someone coming out of prison after seven years, and those who've done time for drug offences find people particularly short on sympathy.'

It was the same warning that the governor, Charles Sinclair, had given him, Philip thought as he slowly buttered his last piece of toast. And they were right, damn it; it was not going to be easy. Nevertheless, every instinct urged him not to commit himself to Sorel. He still didn't trust the man, or the reason for the extraordinary and obscure offer that had been made.

'Is that why you picked me for this job? Because you thought I'd be in no position to refuse?' he asked.

'To some extent, yes.'

Again Philip was surprised by the candour of the reply. 'And were there any other reasons? After all, there are plenty of ex-cons around.'

'We made inquiries about you, and you seemed to fill the bill.

You're intelligent, young and in fair shape. You don't come from a criminal background, and you know how to behave.'

'Greg means you wouldn't balance peas on your knife.' Constant grinned.

'I see – or rather, I don't see. But it's irrelevant. Thank you for your offer, gentlemen, but the answer's no.'

'You refuse?'

'I refuse. I've no idea of any details of this project, or job, but I want no part of it. As far as I can tell, it stinks. At least if I've learnt nothing else in prison, I've learnt to recognize a bad smell when there's one around.'

Constant would have continued the argument, but Sorel shut him up. As promised they drove Philip where he asked, which was Baker Street Station. They didn't offer to shake hands when they dropped him in the station forecourt, but they wished him luck and Sorel gave him a card with a telephone number on it.

'If you change your mind, Mr Janvrin, give me a call.'

'I shan't change my mind. Goodbye.'

'Goodbye,' they replied in unison, but as the Rover's door slammed behind Philip, Sorel said urgently, 'Watch him, Hamish! Watch him!'

Sorel was hurriedly pulling a holdall from under the front seat and extracting a navy blue raincoat and a tweed hat of the kind worn by fishermen. He struggled into the coat, found a pair of spectacles in its pocket, and jammed the hat on his head. His appearance was transformed.

'It's okay,' Constant said. 'He's not gone into the station. He's waiting to cross the Marylebone Road. It looks as if he's going down Baker Street.'

'Right. Follow us if you can, but for God's sake don't be obvious about it. If you lose us, go back to the office.'

Sorel didn't wait for a response. He was out of the car, and could see that the lights at the intersection of the Marylebone Road and Baker Street were changing. He sprinted out of the station, dodging umbrellas and splashing through puddles. In spite of the rain the junction was as busy as ever. Buses, cars and vans streamed in each direction along the divided highway, and pedestrians thronged the pavements.

23

Neither the bustling crowds nor the weather were disadvantages to Sorel. He had no trouble keeping Philip in sight; nor did he need to worry about being spotted by him. Philip was much too occupied coping with the unaccustomed traffic and the jostling people to bother about being tailed, even if the idea had occurred to him.

Sorel watched Philip make his way down Baker Street, and turn purposefully into a Barclays Bank. Sorel hastily crossed the road, found a convenient shop doorway and took shelter in it. He waited, never letting his gaze stray for more than a couple of seconds from the bank's entrance. Customers entered and departed. Philip Janvrin remained inside; whatever business he had there was taking a considerable amount of time.

At last, however, Philip emerged. It was impossible at this distance for Sorel to tell if he looked satisfied or despondent. Leaning into the rain Philip continued to walk south to the next set of traffic lights, where he abruptly turned right and started to walk fast.

Once more Sorel followed, cursing the rain which was now trickling off the brim of his hat into his collar. He wondered how much longer this pursuit would have to continue. The sight of Constant driving slowly past in the comfort of the Rover didn't improve his temper. He knew he could have chosen to drive and let Constant plod through the puddles, but he didn't trust him not to lose Janvrin.

He was thankful when Philip reached Gloucester Place and turned right again. At least this meant that Constant could follow them northwards up this one-way street. Philip seemed to be peering at the house numbers as he walked. Eventually he found what he sought because he ran up the steps and rang the bell. A woman appeared at the door. There was a brief conversation and Philip went in. Some minutes later the notice which said 'Room to Let' was removed from the front window.

Sorel hurried down the road to where Constant was parked. 'Get on the phone,' he ordered. 'Janvrin's gone to ground, at least for the moment. We need watchers. We'll have to wait here till they come.' He bent and wrung out the bottoms of his trouser legs. 'Damn Janvrin! Why couldn't he have agreed at once? This is such a bloody waste of time, and we don't have much time to spare.'

THREE

Philip Janvrin sat on the edge of the narrow bed, his head in his hands, despair in his heart. Tomorrow he would have to leave this ugly little room with its stained carpet, the cigarette burns on the table and the smell of disinfectant that came from the bathroom along the passage. He had been there two weeks.

They had been weeks of frustration – frustration that had begun in Barclays Bank in Baker Street. The bank had not been busy and he had chosen a cashier who, he hoped, would be understanding. He had explained that he had an account with Barclays in Oxford, but required some immediate cash. No, he didn't have a Visa card but he had offered a cheque with a confident smile and when asked for some confirmation of his identity, had produced his driving licence. The cashier had directed him to a seat in a waiting area, and disappeared to telephone the branch in Oxford.

From the moment he had seen her returning he had known that something was amiss. She had pushed his cheque back across the counter to him, and he could remember the exact conversation that had followed.

'I'm sorry, Mr Janvrin, but we can't cash this.'

'Why not?'

'It's a dormant account, Mr Janvrin.'

'So what?'

The girl had hesitated. Then she had said, 'Mr Janvrin, they have traced your account, but – I'm not really supposed to give you this information. However, even if it wasn't dormant, there's not enough money in the account to cover this cheque.'

'But there must be!'

During his last year at Oxford his godmother had died and he had inherited a thousand pounds. He had paid it into his account and had never touched it. It had to be there, plus the odd few pounds left over from the allowance that his father had given him.

'It's a mistake,' Philip had said. 'The number of my account's

25

on the cheque. Did you – did they get it right? And my name? Janvrin. Philip Janvrin.'

'I'm afraid there's no mistake, Mr Janvrin. The balance of this account is now just six pounds and thirty pence, and in the circumstances – '

'What circumstances?'

'Well, even if there were enough in the account, as it's been dormant, with no deposits or withdrawals for several years – more than three years, in fact – you'd have to go to Oxford and identify yourself properly and sign some papers before they could do anything to reopen the account.'

Remembering the encounter, Philip shivered. The cashier had begun to look at him curiously, even suspiciously, and for a moment he read her thoughts; she was wondering if he had stolen the cheque book and driving licence or found them somewhere, if perhaps she should tell the manager and get him to call the police.

Philip hadn't argued any further. He had picked up his worthless cheque, mumbled some thanks and fled. He had been three-quarters of the way down Baker Street before he realized that he had no idea where he was going, and he couldn't walk about aimlessly in the rain. He had to find shelter, a room, some cheap room somewhere.

There was no possibility that he could follow his original plan and try the small hotel where he had stayed two or three times with Peter years ago. He couldn't afford it. Indeed, he soon discovered that he couldn't even afford the 'cheap' and nasty room he had lighted upon. He had of course been aware that prices had soared while he had been out of circulation, but the knowledge had made no real impression on him in the security of prison – a security to which he almost wished to return.

There had been little opportunity for Philip to think seriously about his future before his sudden release. He had decided to spend a while in London, acclimatizing himself to freedom, buying a few clothes and trying to get a job. He had been under no illusion that his godmother's money would last for long, but he had thought that at least it would give him a breathing space.

26

He had counted on this, and it had been a bitter blow to learn that the money had inexplicably disappeared. His situation was desperate. Without that money to cushion him, he hadn't been able to buy a half-decent suit or have his hair cut respectably, or get rid of the aura of prison that he believed still clung to him. Even his raincoat was a plastic affair, not the good Burberry he had had at home.

Home? Idly he wondered what his father had done with his personal possessions, his books, his golf clubs, his old fiddle, his record collection. Probably given them to charity, he thought. And his room? Had that been stripped so that there was no longer any reminder of him in the house?

Philip lifted his head and sat up straight. He would *not* succumb to self-pity. He must take some positive action. But the choice was limited. It had been made abundantly clear to him when he signed on at the employment exchange – or 'Job Centre', as it now seemed to be called – that no one wanted to employ an ex-con with no references and no relevant qualifications. In fact, this was not precisely true. He had been offered two jobs, one washing dishes in a sleazy restaurant in Soho, and the other driving a van for a man who didn't bother to pretend that his business was honest. He had turned down both. Now he almost regretted them.

Tomorrow he would be out on the street, homeless and nearly penniless. He hadn't the money to pay for another week's rent, and his landlady whom he had met in the hall had already reminded him that it would be due the following day. He had told her he would be leaving, and she had expressed neither surprise nor regret. Lodgers came and went; providing they paid, she didn't care.

So what remained? Philip had telephoned Father Malory, the priest who had been so kind to him in prison. Father Malory had given him the name and address of a Catholic organization which took in men down on their luck, but Philip didn't want charity, and anyway this would only be a short-term solution.

Nor would he take the priest's advice to pocket his pride and appeal to his father or his brother. He couldn't imagine his father welcoming home the prodigal son. Peter was different. Peter, he knew, would never turn him away, and for a minute he was tempted. But he had made the decision to cut himself off from Peter and Zara years ago, and he couldn't go back on it now. It was not merely pride on his part. They had their own life, and it would not be right to disrupt it.

And after all, there was an alternative, and if he, as an ex-convict, couldn't do what he really wanted, it hardly mattered what he did do.

Hamish Constant, a broad smile on his face, came into Sorel's office. 'Philip Janvrin has surfaced,' he announced. 'He's just phoned. He's prepared to consider our offer.'

Sorel gave no sign of relief; he had backed his judgement against that of Brigadier Aubyn, his boss, and he had been vindicated. But there had always been the possibility that Janvrin would go whining to his old dad, or perhaps a former girlfriend who would take pity on him, or – what would have been worse – the shit might have turned to some of his pals in the dope business. Still, Sorel was not going to admit these thoughts to Constant. 'Thank the Lord for that!' he said. 'I've got bored with waiting.'

'I wonder what made him change his mind,' Constant said. 'He was so positive he wasn't having any part of us.'

'Who knows?' Sorel shrugged. 'Perhaps he found the going too tough on the outside. We can ask him. But we must treat him gently, Hamish. This is only the first step, remember. He could still change his mind.'

'I know. Anyway, he said he would be waiting on the steps of the George Street entrance of St James's, Spanish Place, after the noon Mass tomorrow morning, and we could pick him up there.'

'Right. You do that, and take him straight to the house. I'll meet you there, and we'll have a late lunch. It'll give me time to do some shopping for him.'

'What about his watchers? Shall I call them off?'

'No–o, not until you get him to the house. I doubt if he's trying to trick us – he's given no sign that he was aware of being tailed – but there's no point in taking unnecessary risks.'

'Okay. Anything else?'

Sorel hesitated. They needed to win Janvrin's confidence, and he had to admit that Hamish, in his innocence, was more likely to do that than he was. But innocence was akin to ignorance. 'No, except be sure to guard your tongue,' he replied sharply. 'To any questions, just say he'll be told everything in due course.'

*   *   *

In the event, the warning was scarcely necessary. Philip showed a minimum of curiosity. He greeted Constant as if he were a casual friend who was giving him a lift, and asked no questions as they drove out of London. Constant, not Philip, began to find the silence trying.

'You must be glad to be out of prison,' he remarked at last, thinking he couldn't fail to learn more about Philip Janvrin – more than he had already learnt from the dry files – if he could only persuade him to talk.

'Obviously prison's an experience you've never had.'

'Well – no.'

'I don't recommend it, Mr Constant.'

'Hamish, please. We'll all be on first name terms now. It's simpler.'

Philip raised an eyebrow, but made no comment. Once more the silence between the two men lengthened. They had turned off the dual carriageway, and were driving more slowly through the Sussex lanes before Constant spoke again.

'Have you been in touch with your family, Philip?'

'No!' The answer was curt.

'What about friends? Haven't you told anyone you're free?'

'No one except Father Malory, the prison padre.'

'Will he be surprised if he doesn't hear from you for some time?'

Philip turned his head to stare at Constant. 'Am I about to go into some kind of purdah?'

'Not exactly,' said Constant and, remembering Sorel's warning, added quickly: 'Everything will be explained soon.'

'Good!'

'What about us, Greg and me? Did you tell anyone that we were – interested in you?'

'I did not, Mr – Hamish, and no one's going to miss me, so I'm completely at your service, if that's what you want.'

'That's great,' Constant said, but he hadn't missed the irony in Philip's comment, or the vague implication of reluctant consent in the remark. Nevertheless, he had gained some useful, if negative, information to pass on to Sorel, and he was pleased with himself.

Five minutes later the car turned through a pair of wrought-iron gates into a short tree-lined drive, which led to a fair-sized house. It was not a thing of beauty. What had once been a small neo-Georgian manor had apparently been architecturally ruined by some eccentric millionaire. The house now sprouted twin towers, and an extra wing had been added which was balanced by what appeared to be stabling and garages.

'The inside is a great improvement on the outside,' Constant said as he drew up before the front door. Then he realized that his choice of words might seem inappropriate to someone recently released from prison. 'We – we find it extremely comfortable,' he added weakly.

Sorel, who had been awaiting their arrival, came out to greet them. 'I'm so glad you decided to come, Philip,' he said, taking the parcel containing Philip's belongings from him. 'You had a good trip down? Not too much traffic, I hope?' He didn't wait for answers. 'I'll show you to your room, while Hamish parks the car.'

Philip said nothing. He could think of nothing to say. The situation was bizarre. He was being received like a member of a weekend house party, or a guest at one of those expensive country hotels where the owner makes a point of treating visitors as personal friends. But somehow Gregory Sorel didn't fit either role – the host of a house party, or a hotel-keeper.

Sorel led the way across a marble-tiled floor and up a wide staircase. He opened a door and motioned to Philip to enter first. The room was of a good size and furnished in great comfort with a deep carpet, a three-quarter bed, two armchairs, a television set in one corner, and a table that held magazines, newspapers and a bowl of fruit. Fitted cupboards lined one wall.

Philip walked over to the long windows which looked out on an expanse of well-tended lawn ending in a wood. He opened the windows and stepped out on to a small balcony. The air was cool and fresh, and he breathed deeply. It was the first moment he had really enjoyed his freedom. Whatever was to come, he thought, this was better than being behind bars or in a cardboard box on the Embankment or in some shop doorway.

Behind him, Sorel said, 'I don't want to hurry you, but lunch will be waiting. If you'd like to wash your hands there's a bathroom through there, and you'll find a few things in the cupboards. Fifteen minutes, say? Just come downstairs. The dining-room's on the left.'

'Thanks.'

The bedroom door closed behind Sorel, and Philip, half disbelieving what was happening to him, went into the bathroom. This was tiled in blue from floor to ceiling, and boasted bath, shower cubicle, washhand basin and bidet. Large and small, the fluffy towels matched the décor. The floor was cork. But what surprised Philip most was the array of expensive toiletries and the silk dressing-gown hanging behind the door.

And back in the bedroom he found on shelves in the cupboards half a dozen shirts of the right size, a cashmere sweater, a change of underclothes, socks, ties and two pairs of pyjamas. In addition, a jacket and a pair of slacks were hanging above slippers and some suede shoes. Philip would have liked to change, but there clearly wasn't time and, shaking his head in bewilderment, he went downstairs.

In the dining-room, the long table which could have seated fourteen with ease had three places set at the far end. As Philip came in he found Sorel and Constant by the door. They made a fine palaver of forcing him to glance through the Official Secrets Act and witnessing his signature to a lengthy statement. Philip suspected that they were trying to impress him.

'Now let's eat,' Sorel said when Constant had removed the documents. 'It's cold, I'm afraid. I hope you don't mind.' He had reverted to his role of considerate host.

'Not at all,' said Philip. For the last couple of days he had been living on hamburgers, and not many of those. 'But when are you going to tell me about this so-called assignment? Even that signature doesn't commit me, you know.'

'We'll discuss it over coffee. Meanwhile let's try to get better acquainted with one another.'

Philip made no objection, though it soon became obvious that the process of getting better acquainted was to be one-sided. In fact, he found himself being subjected to a mild interrogation. He was asked what sports he played, if he could swim or drive a car or ride, if he knew anything about firearms or unarmed combat, if he was interested in racing. The questions were a curious medley, and he sensed that only some were important. He also sensed that on the whole his answers were not totally satisfactory.

31

He didn't care. He was enjoying the best meal, hot or cold, that he'd eaten for years. There was smoked salmon, a variety of cooked meats, a mixed salad, French bread and cheeses, all accompanied by a white wine. He had had no breakfast and only a meagre supper the night before, and he would have welcomed a second lunch. But, conscious that Sorel was watching him, out of pride he ate sparingly and drank sensibly.

The table was cleared and coffee served by the same short, fat woman who had cooked breakfast for him in the London flat the day he had been released from prison. Her name, according to Sorel, was Ada. Philip accepted her presence without surprise. Indeed, cheered by the food and mellowed by the wine, he felt that nothing could surprise him. He was quite wrong.

Gregory Sorel's next words shattered his tranquillity, and dispelled any euphoria he might have felt.

'Philip,' Sorel said as Ada shut the dining-room door behind her and the men were left alone, 'it's time I told you what we want of you.'

'Yes?'

'We want you to find Peter, your brother.'

FOUR

Philip was shaken. 'Find Peter? You mean he's – he's missing?' He knew it was a stupid question, but Sorel's statement was unthinkable. His time in prison had made him more aware than most of the dreadful dangers that individuals faced in today's world – assault, kidnapping, murder; he had met some of the villains. But surely not Peter. 'I – I don't understand.' He sensed that in some curious fashion Sorel was enjoying his discomfort.

Sorel said blandly, almost casually, 'Peter's disappeared.'

'But I still don't understand. When – and where?'

'Let me explain,' Sorel went on. 'Peter was paid by the Foreign and Commonwealth Office, but he was not what is known as a career officer. He was in a special section, involving intelligence work. Last month he went to Amsterdam on an assignment. The day he was due to fly home he checked out of his hotel, took a taxi and – disappeared.'

Sorel paused, expecting questions, but Philip remained silent. Over the years, as his cell-mates changed, he had learnt that he lost nothing by remaining silent and listening if others were prepared to talk. Besides, he needed to collect his thoughts and assess what seemed to him on the surface an incomprehensible situation.

Sorel continued. 'Of course, we've made all the usual inquiries – the hotel, the taxi-driver, the police, the airport.'

'With great tact and discretion.' Constant grinned nervously. 'Our chap pretended to be a detective keeping an eye on an errant husband.'

'But no luck.' Sorel again took up the tale. 'It seemed that Peter had simply vanished – and still seems so. We've considered the possibilities. We couldn't believe he'd defected – obviously the first thought of suspicious bastards, like people in our line of work. Apart from any other considerations, we know that Peter has always been fond of his creature comforts, and in the present state of what was once the Soviet Union he'd have

33

had to be out of his mind – or under great pressure – to make such a move voluntarily. But, you ask, need he have gone voluntarily? Well, he might have been kidnapped, but there's no obvious reason why, and there have been no ransom claims of any kind, either for money or a *quid pro quo*, such as an exchange. That leaves murder, of course, but you'll be glad to hear that so far his body's not been found, so we must hope that somewhere he's alive.'

'There is an outside chance that he got fed up with everything here and is living the life of Riley in South America, for instance,' said Constant, 'but Greg believes that's too remote a possibility.'

'So that's the position,' said Sorel, ignoring Constant's intervention.

'You haven't mentioned Peter's family – his wife,' Philip said, as the two men looked at him for some response. He hadn't wanted to ask about his father or Zara but in the circumstances the question was inevitable.

'They don't know that Peter's disappeared.'

'What? But surely Zara must know?'

'She and Peter are separated. They've been living apart for the past two years. She and the boy are staying in the country with your father, while Peter has a flat in London. They don't often meet, though their relationship seems quite amicable.'

'I see,' said Philip, trying to absorb yet another unexpected development.

'And you've no idea at all what's happened to Peter?' he asked suddenly and suspiciously. He stared from Constant, who refused to meet his eye, to Sorel, who smiled ruefully. Then he added, 'It may seem strange to you as I've deliberately not kept in touch with him, but I'm still very fond of my brother.'

'That's why we hoped you'd be prepared to help us,' Sorel said smoothly, too smoothly in Philip's opinion.

Philip thought for a moment. Then, 'So you *do* believe he's alive?' he demanded.

'No. *I* don't.' Again Sorel spoke almost casually, as if Peter's life were a matter of little concern.

'Then what the hell – ' Philip controlled his temper with difficulty.

'I may be wrong, Philip. My boss doesn't agree with me, for one,' Sorel said quicky. 'Even if I'm not, we need to establish

34

Peter's death, if only for the sake of his wife, his son, his father. And what about you? Don't you want to know?'

'Of course, but – ' Philip knew he was being out-manoeuvred. 'But why do *you* want to know so badly?'

'I've told you that when he went missing Peter was in the middle of an assignment for us. I'm not at liberty to tell you what that assignment was, but you can be assured it mattered – it was important for a variety of reasons. So, quite apart from the fact that he was a colleague and we don't like each other getting hurt, we need to know why he was prevented from returning to London, and how or by whom. You can understand that, surely?'

'Have you consulted the people with whom Peter was – was negotiating, if that's the word? Or are they suspect?'

'No, they're not suspect, and we've been able to find out that what you term the negotiations were successfully completed. Incidentally, the other parties to the – the negotiations don't know that Peter has disappeared.'

'Surely – ' Philip interrupted.

Sorel raised a hand. 'I know what you're going to ask. We've made arrangements. Another colleague has taken over Peter's casework, and it's been given out that Peter caught one of those slow-developing viruses some time ago while on duty in the Far East and is now seriously ill. However, this deception has already gone on for too long. We believe that it would be inadvisable to continue with it for more than another week or two.'

'Then what happens if – if Peter's still not found?'

'We hope that by then, Philip, you will be ready to take his place.'

It was a daft scheme, absolutely mad, Philip thought, and he hadn't hesitated to say so. He had also maintained that it wouldn't – couldn't – work, but Sorel had been very persuasive. In the end Philip had promised to consider the proposition and to give them an answer when they met for drinks before dinner. But, here he was, bathed, changed into the new clothes that had been provided for him and prepared to go downstairs, but still undecided.

On the face of it he knew that he had little choice. If he refused, Constant would drive him back to London the next morning and he would face the same appalling situation that he had exchanged for relative luxury. Perhaps they would let him keep the new clothes he was wearing. They might even offer him some small remuneration, which shamefully he would accept. But that wouldn't be much use – merely a temporary relief.

And, what was more important, he would always blame himself for not trying to help Peter – and Zara and the boy – when he might have done. Sorel had admitted that the scheme was one of desperation and it might be dangerous, but he had stated categorically that it could be successful. Peter and Philip were very alike in appearance – any differences could be explained away by Peter's supposed illness – and there would be two weeks to prepare and brief Philip for the role he was to play.

'At worst,' Sorel had said, 'we ought to get a line on those responsible for Peter's disappearance. I don't see how they can ignore the sudden surfacing of a brand new "Peter", and what's more a new Peter who is being accepted as such. And at best, this might enable us to trace Peter and bring him home safely.'

Then why was he hesitating? Philip asked himself. Sorel had warned him there could be some danger and he realized that they probably considered him expendable, but that wasn't the reason. If he could help Peter, he should, as Peter would certainly try to help him were their positions reversed. He even had the added selfish incentive which Sorel had promised – that when he had played his part, they would do their best to give him a fresh start – money, and a job; it was surprising what a little influence could do, Sorel had remarked.

Philip rose from the armchair and went across to the window. He gazed out across the lawn to the distant trees. It was a view, he thought, of which he would never grow tired, but to acquire it – or something like it – one would need money or influence and probably both.

At last he was realizing why he hesitated. He did not like being manipulated, even exploited. If he had been asked in a straightfor-ward fashion – in the presence of Charles Sinclair, say, whose discretion could surely be trusted, even by 'suspicious bastards' – he would have done whatever he could for Peter's sake even if he had known he would have to return to prison afterwards to serve out his sentence.

But Sorel and his chums had failed to appreciate that simple fact. They had used their power – and it must have been considerable – to spring him from prison. Almost certainly it was they who had stolen – or at any rate deprived him of – his godmother's money, a sum that was rightfully and legally his. Heaven knew what else they had done. He did not trust them. There was an odd, illogical element in their story, though he couldn't put his finger on it. And there were many unanswered questions, such as why did Sorel dislike him so much and why did Constant sometimes appear embarrassed.

Well, it would be interesting to see. After all he had nothing better to do and nothing to lose, and if he could help Peter . . .

Squaring his shoulders, Philip went downstairs.

During the next fortnight one extraordinary experience followed another, as far as Philip was concerned. Even his early weeks in gaol and his initiation into prison life did not equal them.

The first day began with a physical examination. After an excellent breakfast that Ada had brought to his room, Constant came to collect him.

'You're in for a few surprises now, Philip,' Constant greeted him. 'Some pleasant, some not so pleasant. I must warn you that this hideous-looking supposedly country residence isn't quite what it seems. First, you're to see Dr John.'

Dr John proved to be a medical doctor, though there were no certificates on the walls of his clinic to verify the fact. He was a man in his forties, white-coated, a stethoscope around his neck, a nurse in attendance, and he was efficient. As soon as Constant had gone he pointed to a screen and ordered Philip to strip. He then proceeded to give him a routine but thorough examination – weight measurement, heart (including an ECG), lungs, reflexes, the usual tests and so on. From time to time he referred to some papers on his desk and grunted, though it wasn't clear to Philip whether he was pleased or displeased.

'That's fine,' he said at last, indicating that he was finished and Philip should get dressed. 'Thank you.' He gave a small, tight smile of dismissal. He was lifting a telephone receiver as Philip left the room.

Philip refrained from inquiring about the verdict; doubtless he would know in due course. He was almost relieved to find

Constant waiting for him in the corridor. He had been wondering what he should do next.

'I'm your shepherd for the day,' Constant said. 'Now we're off to the gym. I hope you're in good shape.'

'Not very,' Philip admitted. He was beginning to like Hamish Constant. 'I've not had much chance to keep fit lately.'

Constant grinned sympathetically. 'Then I expect you're in for a lot of hard work.' He opened a door and gestured Philip into a large brightly lit room. 'Here we are.'

The gymnasium was well-equipped. There was a vaulting horse, rings, an exercise bicycle, a punchball and a treadmill, together with the usual dangerous-looking assortment of machinery equipped with weights and springs and levers – a free-weight bench and a pull-down machine and body-building equipment of that kind. Two men were circling each other on a judo mat, and two others were fencing. Philip inspected the scene somewhat dubiously.

There was an electronic ping as one of the fencers scored a hit. They stopped, took off their helmets and shook hands. Philip was mildly surprised to see that the taller man was Gregory Sorel; Sorel had given him the impression of being a cerebral rather than a physical type.

Sorel brought his companion over to Philip and introduced him. 'Philip, this is Gervase, who'll make sure that you're in as good a condition as possible before you leave here. He's already been assured by Dr John that you're fit enough to face what he intends to put you through.'

Gervase, a short, dark, Italianate character, was looking Philip up and down. 'You can obviously do with some work-outs, Philip,' he said pleasantly. 'But that sort of thing's for later on. We'll go easy on you today. Hamish will show you where to change. Then we'll see how fit you really are.'

An hour later he was shaking his head sadly. 'You're going to have to work like hell, Philip. If we had six months it would be fine, but with just two weeks God knows what we can do. Why have you let yourself get into this state?'

'I didn't have much choice, Gervase.'

'No. Sorry. I suppose not.' He shrugged as he apologized. 'Still, one can't do the impossible. Let's go along to the pool. You claim you can swim. Twenty-five yards breast stroke with your head

38

well up?' But it was said not unkindly, and when Philip demonstrated that, though hopelessly out of practice, he was a fine swimmer, Gervase was loud in his praise.

From then on the day improved. After a meal carefully designed to put on weight Philip spent the afternoon watching television and reading papers and magazines. This he found enjoyable, though it brought home to him the narrowness of his life in prison, where the staple current reading matter was the tabloid press.

Tea was followed by a gentle jog around the grounds with Constant. Philip saw several people but was not introduced to them and he asked no questions. Drinks and dinner – again a special meal for Philip – were served by Ada in a small room where he was joined by Sorel and Constant. During dinner they started to brief him on his brother Peter, his work, his habits, his likes and dislikes. He was given a short list of Peter's friends, one or two of whom were already known to him.

'Inevitably our knowledge of Peter is incomplete,' Sorel said. 'Indeed, we suspect that you may appreciate some aspects of his character better than we can. Anyway, he was a popular guy. He knew a lot of people from a variety of backgrounds, from the arts to racing. He was a keen racegoer. It's a subject you'll need to learn about. But Peter was a very private person too. I worked with him for years, but I wouldn't claim that we had a really close relationship. You'll just have to do your best, Philip. Plead your recent illness, avoid difficult situations, try not to compromise yourself and deal with what comes as best you can.'

It sounded good advice, Philip thought, but not easy to follow. However, he had enough immediate problems. The most pressing was to keep his eyes open and he was thankful when Sorel suggested he should go to bed. He slept dreamlessly for eight hours.

The next few days followed much the same pattern. The morning exercise routines became increasingly strenuous and were combined with instruction in self-defence. Gervase kept his word and worked Philip to the limit of his endurance. In the afternoons there was study of current affairs, racing, what was known of Peter's friends and acquaintances, details of his flat in

Kensington, his club, his favourite restaurants. This would be followed by a swim or a game of tennis, and after dinner more study, which included brushing up Philip's French and German. During one of these sessions Philip raised a question that had been bothering him.

'You say that Peter and Zara have been separated for a couple of years,' he said. 'What about girlfriends? They could be a real problem.'

'The point has occurred to us, naturally,' Sorel replied. 'We know of no serious – entanglements, shall we say? If we're wrong you'll have to play it by ear, as they say – though perhaps "ear" isn't quite the right word.'

'I see,' said Philip unhappily.

There was some variety in the routine. One day he was photographed and, later, equipped with driving licence and passport and other personal papers that Peter might be expected to possess. Several times he was allowed to drive a car, similar, so he was told, to Peter's, and he learned the latest Highway Code. He was also taken to what he had thought to be stabling; this turned out to be a weapons range and, somewhat against his will, Philip was taught how to handle a handgun. Ironically, he had a good eye and proved an apt pupil.

By the end of the second week, with his hair cut like Peter's and his eyebrows trimmed a little, the similarity to his brother had increased considerably, and he was as ready for his role as could be hoped for in such a short period of training and briefing. Excellent food and plenty of sleep had made him put on weight, and he was in vastly better physical shape than when he had left prison. He actually felt well. Admittedly he was beset by doubts as to how long he could successfully masquerade as Peter. But he had pushed to the back of his mind his distrust of Sorel. He was more confident than he had originally thought possible, and he was determined to do his best for Peter's sake, and for Zara's and little Patrick's.

FIVE

'Goodbye for now, and good luck, Philip – Peter.' Constant held out his hand. 'I liked the real Peter. He was always kind to me. He never scorched me with sarcasm whenever I made a mistake. And I do make some,' he added ruefully, grinning.

'Thanks.' Philip shook the proffered hand.

The two men were standing on the pavement in front of a large block of flats opposite South Kensington Station. Constant had driven Philip up to London from the 'safe house' in Sussex. As Constant got back into the car and drove off, Philip watched his departure with regret. Sorel, he remembered, had neither wished him luck nor offered to shake hands.

Philip picked up the bag that lay at his feet, an old rather battered suitcase that Sorel had provided for him. Liberally covered with a variety of airline and hotel stickers, it contained the clothes he had worn during the last two weeks.

He paused for a moment before, shrugging his shoulders, he thought, 'Now for it.' Then he pushed his way through the unlocked outer doors and crossed the spacious hall to the bank of lifts. Everything was in place, exactly as he had been briefed. He pressed the button for a lift.

'Good-morning, Mr Janvrin, sir. Nice to see you home again. Been on your travels, have you?'

For one awful moment Philip panicked. Then he forced himself to turn around. Sorel had impressed on him that the best way to arouse suspicion was to appear surreptitious.

'Hello, Baker,' he heard himself say, recognizing the head porter from one of the many photographs of Peter's contacts he had been shown. 'Yes, I've been abroad, but some bug I got in the Far East caught up with me and I've had weeks in hospital.'

'Sorry to hear that, sir.' Baker, a man in his fifties who had once been an army sergeant, looked Philip in the face. 'Yes. If you don't mind my saying so, you don't appear at your best at the moment.'

Philip swallowed his relief and managed to grin. Baker had accepted him; he had passed his first test. Sorel had been right: people mostly saw what they expected to see.

The lift arrived, and Philip refused Baker's offer to help him with his suitcase. As he was carried up to the sixth floor he leant against the wall of the lift cage, thankful to be alone. This was merely the beginning, he reminded himself. There would be more rigorous tests to come.

The lift stopped, the doors opened, and Philip collided with a smartly dressed woman who was about to enter. They apologized mutually, but it was she who addressed him by name. He hadn't the faintest idea who she was, though he was supposed to have been briefed on those who were to be his near neighbours.

Philip's hand was shaking as he fitted the key into the lock of flat Number 63. Sorel had provided him with duplicates of the set of keys that had been found in Peter's office safe, including one for the flat. He opened the door slowly and let himself in, feeling rather like a shabby thief, in spite of or perhaps because of the fact that this was his brother's home.

Leaving his bag in the long, narrow hall he rejected the idea that he had no right to be there. He knew that the place had already been thoroughly searched by Sorel's minions, and he need have no qualms about intruding on Peter's privacy. He set himself to explore the premises.

This took very little time. There were two bedrooms – one furnished as a study – a bathroom, a kitchen and a twenty-five foot living-dining room. The pictures on the walls were modern originals, the carpets and curtains clearly expensive, the furniture comfortable and carefully chosen. There were a lot of books and cassettes, a large television set with a video recorder and an elaborate music system. The study was efficiently equipped, with a computer, fax and an answering machine attached to the telephone. In the bedroom was a three-quarter size bed and a second phone.

Philip opened cupboards and drawers. These were well stocked with suits, slacks, jackets, shirts, sweaters, sports clothes and underwear, all of the best quality. There were arrays of ties, socks, silk handkerchiefs and two dozen pairs of shoes in various styles. In the hall cupboard, apart from a set of golf clubs and three tennis racquets, were a cashmere overcoat and a couple of Burberry raincoats. Even the kitchen had its share of tinned and frozen delicacies, and the wine rack was full. Philip found hard liquor and a box of Havana cigars in the living-room.

Throwing himself into an armchair, Philip laughed aloud. After seven years of a poverty that was often degrading, the fortnight at the 'safe house' hadn't prepared him for such a degree of opulence as this, but Peter had always been extravagant. Then one obvious point struck him – nowhere in the flat was a single photograph on display. Somehow sobered by this thought he got up and went into the kitchen. There was no fresh food, but he made himself a scratch meal from a can of soup, sardines, Ryvita and tea; he couldn't cope with the seemingly complex coffee machine.

After lunch he unpacked his bag. He knew that he ought to go shopping. It was what Peter would have done after he'd been away for some while. But for the moment Philip couldn't face the prospect. He had studied a street map of the district. He knew the names of the shops and their owners, but he didn't feel up to meeting them, not yet; and there was always the possibility that he might be accosted by someone with whom he was meant to be on intimate terms.

Besides, there were more things to be done in the flat. He must go through the mail that had been neatly piled on the table in the hall by Mrs Robyn who, he had been told, came in once a week to clean for Peter. Fortunately she was not due for a couple of days. He must listen for any messages there might be on the answerphone. He must go through Peter's desk and papers; Sorel's men might have ignored something that would make sense to him.

By four o'clock Philip had exhausted all he could do in the flat. Peter's mail had been uninteresting and had required no immediate action. It had included a bank statement, a couple of bills, a reminder from a dentist that he was due for a check-up, some magazines, an invitation to a cocktail party from a couple called John and Pamela May and another to the opening of an art show. The rest was junk mail. There were no personal letters.

Philip had torn up the junk and glanced through the magazines. The invitations had been out of date, but he had noted the names for possible future reference. He was mildly interested to see that Peter's current account had such a healthy balance; the Peter he

43

remembered had almost always lived on an overdraft or on the verge of one. But he had been told to pass all bills on to Constant. As for the dentist, he was someone to be avoided at all costs.

The contents of Peter's desk had proved even less informative than the mail. Presumably Sorel's men had done a thorough job. Nor was the answerphone of much use. There had been a fair number of calls, but scarely anyone had left a message. This became more understandable when Philip had played back Peter's request; Peter had said that if the caller would leave a name and phone number, he would get in touch when he returned from abroad, but the disembodied voice was authoritative and less than encouraging. To Philip it hardly sounded like the Peter he had known.

Of the four messages that had been left on the machine, one was from the woman whose party Peter had failed to attend. Another was a sharp reminder from the dentist's secretary. And the remaining two were from someone named Sylvia, who had not included her telephone number. Philip presumed that it was well known to Peter, but Sylvia's name hadn't been mentioned during his briefings, so her identity remained a mystery.

Then the telephone trilled and Philip jumped. He stared at the instrument on the desk with distaste. He had no wish to answer it, and had to force himself to pick up the receiver and say, 'Hello.' The caller – a man – asked for Mary, and when Philip said he knew no one of that name, the man apologized and rang off.

Philip shook his head in self-reproach, ashamed of his pusil-lanimity. If he were scared of such a simple response as answering the phone, he certainly was not going to get far towards finding those responsible for Peter's disappearance. And anyway, he rationalized, he *must* do some shopping.

Hoping that he wouldn't meet anyone who would claim acquaintance with him, he set off for the row of small shops in Bute Street, close by. His immediate need was for fruit, vegetables, milk and so on. And at once he came up against an unexpected problem. When he had not been at boarding school or Oxford he had lived at home – or been in prison. He had never had occasion to housekeep for himself, and he had no idea of quantities or amounts. Some things, such as milk, would be simple, but should he buy a pound or half a pound of butter? What was more, he had to realize that his knowledge of cooking was minimal.

He abandoned the idea of small stores and walked slowly down the Old Brompton Road until he found a self-serve supermarket, where he was able to inspect the goods and take what he wanted from the shelves. The girl at the check-out desk paid him no attention, and he was pleased until he realized that he had spent the best part of twenty pounds. This made a nasty hole in the hundred that Sorel had given him, and reminded him how out of touch he was with the basics of life such as prices.

And he knew that he had cheated. He was meant to be Peter, and should be behaving as Peter would on his return, shopping in his accustomed places and not skulking in the anonymity of a supermarket. Tomorrow he would do better, he promised himself.

He was shaving the next morning when he heard the front door open, and he hurried into the hall still clutching the razor. A dark-haired woman in her late thirties, carrying a basket, was shutting the door behind her. As she turned and saw Philip, she gave a small scream, instantly suppressed.

'Lord help us, Mr Janvrin. You didn't half scare me. I didn't know as you was home again.'

'Mrs Robyn!' Realizing who she was, Philip had recovered quickly. 'You scared me too. What are you doing here on a Thursday? Friday's meant to be your day, surely?'

'I'm going to spend the weekend with my daughter and my hubby suggested we get an early start tomorrow. You don't mind, do you, Mr Janvrin?'

'Not a bit.' Philip wished she would stop peering at him, and frowning.

She shook her head. 'You do look poorly, Mr Janvrin, if you don't mind my saying so. Not yourself at all.'

'I've been seriously ill, Mrs Robyn. I've been suffering from a strange bug that really laid me out.'

'What a shame! It comes of going to those foreign parts, I'll be bound. You must take good care of yourself now you're home again, Mr Janvrin.'

'I will, Mrs Robyn. I will.'

Philip retreated to the bathroom. He had been warned that Mrs Robyn was something of a character, but she was known to be sharp-witted, and Philip was glad to have tackled his first encounter with her so successfully. Later, when she waved him goodbye as, continuing to vacuum, she watched him leave the flat, he knew that she didn't suspect him.

This gave him confidence, which increased as he did a little more light shopping, this time in the local stores. Two or three individuals nodded good-morning to him, but none stopped to talk, and the shopkeepers were either too busy or too polite to question his appearance. Nevertheless, he made a point of explaining that he had been ill whenever he had an opportunity. In the end, he found that he had enjoyed his morning of deception.

Mrs Robyn had gone by the time he returned to the flat, but she had left him a note on the hall table. 'A young lady phoned, said her name was Sylvia and you'd know. You're to call her. Please find casserole in fridge. You can heat it up when you like. Yrs truly, E. Robyn.'

Grinning, Philip went into the kitchen. He put away his purchases and inspected the casserole. He estimated that it would provide him with two suppers, and blessed Mrs Robyn. He decided that on Saturday he would have dinner at *Les Oiseaux*, a small local restaurant that Peter was said to frequent.

But he would not be entertaining Sylvia who, he feared, judging by her perseverance, was Peter's current girlfriend – at least he wouldn't be dining with her if he could possibly avoid it. He didn't want to face her at present, especially with so many unanswered questions about the nature of her relationship with Peter. His confidence in his ability to deceive was not yet strong enough – and deception would certainly be impossible in bed, if the question arose.

He mixed himself a gin and tonic and took it into the study. He was pleased with his morning. He planned to go for a walk after lunch, to savour his freedom; he felt he deserved a little time to relax, to be himself, and he needed the exercise. First, however, he intended to phone the Mays, whose cocktail party he had failed to attend.

A woman's voice answered the phone. Philip didn't ask who it was, but said, 'Hello. This is Peter Janvrin.'

'My dear boy!' The reply was immediately effusive. 'How splendid that you're home again. You've been away just ages and we've missed you. When are you coming to see us?'

46

Philip, slightly overwhelmed by such a welcome, wondered if he had been sensible to contact Mrs May, but it was too late for regrets now. He repeated his story about the mysterious bug and his illness, and listened to an outpouring of sympathy.

It ended with, 'Peter dear, we're giving a small buffet on Tuesday. You will come, won't you? Eight o'clock.'

Philip yearned to refuse, but Mrs May was not a girlfriend. From her voice she was no longer young. And he had to start meeting people who knew Peter as well as the Mays apparently did. The difficulty was that some of them might know Peter a good deal better, and suddenly it occurred to him that the persistent Sylvia might be among the guests. However, he knew he must make an effort to enter Peter's life.

'I'd be delighted,' he said at last. 'Many thanks. Eight o'clock. Tuesday.'

Philip enjoyed his walk in spite of the hardness of London's pavements. He had adapted to the jostling crowds and the relentless traffic. His initial reaction that this was a strange world in which he had no part had been tempered. He still had a sense of unreality, but it was receding. If, after seven years of incarceration, he didn't exactly feel that he belonged, at least he didn't expect hostility from those he encountered. Oddly, taking on Peter's persona, however doubtfully, had helped.

On his return to the flat Philip made himself a pot of tea. He watched television and studied *The Times* and the *Independent*, which had appeared on the mat that morning, presumably thanks to Baker who knew Peter's reading habits. Later he had a drink and ate some of Mrs Robyn's casserole. He went to bed early, satisfied with his first full day impersonating his brother.

Shortly before midnight the doorbell of the flat rang. It rang again before Philip could reach the hall, still pulling on his dressing-gown, but he remembered to be cautious.

'Who is it?' he demanded.

'It's me, Baker, sir.'

The voice was hoarse and Philip didn't recognize it, but its urgency reached him. He undid the chain and opened the door. At once he was forced back into the hall by the shorter of two men,

47

who punched him in the stomach as the other kicked the front door shut behind him.

Philip stood no chance. Even if he hadn't been taken by surprise and hadn't temporarily forgotten the instruction on self-defence he had received at the 'safe house', it wouldn't have availed him now. The men were professionals. Being careful not to mark Philip's face, they systematically beat him up. It took less than five minutes.

They left him unconscious on the hall floor, and quietly let themselves out of the flat.

SIX

Philip regained conciousness slowly. He felt ill. He tried to get to his feet, but the hall revolved around him and he slithered to the floor again. However, his need to reach the bathroom was becoming urgent. He had no alternative but to crawl. After what seemed to him an interminable time – no more than a couple of minutes, in fact – he reached his goal and vomited violently into the lavatory pan.

For a while he sat there on the floor. He managed to wipe his mouth on some paper, and flush away his vomit. Gradually the nausea passed and, as he became conscious of the pain of his bruises, he yearned for bed. Once more he crawled on his hands and knees – he couldn't trust himself to walk yet – and the effort was worth it. He pulled his protesting body up on to the bed and drew the duvet about him. He lay and shivered, not because he was physically cold, but because he was mentally shocked. He wondered if he needed medical attention, but decided to wait at least until morning.

The shivering passed, and his mind began to function more normally again. Why? he asked himself. And who? Perhaps of more importance, was it Peter whom the two men believed they were attacking, or was it Philip pretending to be Peter? They hadn't spoken a word since they had entered the flat, so there was no way of knowing.

At length Philip abandoned the conundrum and slept. He was woken by the telephone, and as he reached for the receiver he saw that the time was six-thirty in the morning, and realized that, in spite of his pain, he had slept for almost seven hours. But who on earth would call him at such an hour as this?

'Yes?' he said weakly.

'Listen, Janvrin!' The voice was smooth yet belligerent. 'You've had your lesson. In future you'll do as you're told. You won't just disappear and leave us in a fucking mess. Try it again, *old boy*, and God help you!'

49

The line went dead. Philip put down the receiver. The voice had chilled him. It reminded him of a former cell-mate, one of the more compatible inmates who, in spite of his appalling record, was intelligent and soft-spoken. Somehow, without apparent effort, this villain had ruled the prison block; no one ever dared to oppose him or, if they tried, they regretted the attempt.

Shifting his position in bed Philip gritted his teeth to prevent himself from groaning. As feeling returned, he felt as if his body had been used as a punch bag, as indeed it had. But at least he had one consolation. He knew now that the attack on him had been intended for his brother Peter.

Nevertheless, the question 'Why?' remained, and if anything it was more puzzling. Philip hoped that Sorel might suggest an answer. He had been told not to make contact before the Monday, when he was to go into the office – Peter's office – unless an emergency arose, or what he had to say was important. The decision had been left to him, and now he didn't hesitate. Early as it was, he tapped out the number he had been given.

A sleepy voice said, 'Hamish Constant here.'

Philip spoke cautiously. 'Hello, this is Peter. I'm not feeling my best this morning. Could you drop in for a few minutes? There's no great hurry.'

'I see.' There was a pause, then Constant said, 'Of course. What about breakfast? Seven-thirtyish?'

'Splendid,' Philip said.

Philip had managed to wash and shave before Constant arrived, but was still in pyjamas and dressing-gown. He moved stiffly ahead of Constant into the living-room and sat down with care.

'You appear rather frail today, Peter.' Constant spoke as if amused, but he couldn't hide his anxiety.

'I not only appear frail. I am frail, my dear Hamish.' Philip tried not to sound waspish. 'And you'd be frail too if you'd been through what I have.'

'Sorry. Tell me.'

'Would you please get us some breakfast first? Just toast and coffee for me, if you would.'

'Right.' In a few minutes Constant had returned and, as he poured the coffee, he repeated, 'Tell me all.'

Philip did his best, and he found Constant a good and sympathetic listener. Nevertheless, it seemed to him that Constant, with his questions, was testing the accuracy of his story. He repeated that he was certain of the words spoken by his first caller that morning. He doubted if he would ever forget them.

Constant grinned apologetically. 'Okay. He didn't actually call you Peter, but he appeared to assume you were Peter.'

'Yes,' Philip said shortly. He sighed. 'May I have some more coffee?'

'Sure.' Constant was absent-minded. 'Do you want to see a doctor? We've got a discreet one on tap if you do.'

'No, it's not necessary. They were careful. The main trouble's bruising and stiffness, I'm sure.'

'Very well. It's odd,' Constant went on almost to himself. 'It doesn't make sense.'

'No.' Philip agreed. 'They seemed to blame Peter for disappearing, but how could they if they were responsible?'

Suddenly Constant cheered up. 'Anyhow, Greg will be pleased.'

'That I've been battered?'

'No, of course not.' But Constant was obviously disturbed by the question. 'That you're being accepted as Peter, and that you're getting some reaction. After all that's the objective of the operation, isn't it?'

'But is it reaction from the right quarter?'

'We'll – We'll have to see.' Constant was clearly still not at ease. 'Any other problems I can help with?'

'The main one is to know friend from foe,' said Philip drily. 'It's easy enough to classify my visitors of last night. And the dentist is a foe, though he may not realize it. My teeth certainly won't equate with Peter's records, which could be embarrassing. It's people like the Mays who worry me, and this girl Sylvia.'

'I'll find out what I can about them. Meanwhile I suggest you go to the Mays' party on Tuesday unless you hear from me. And as for Sylvia – ' Constant shrugged. 'Better avoid her, I'd say. If she is Peter's girlfriend, I doubt if you'd deceive her and she could cause trouble.'

'Right. I'll obey instructions.' Philip spoke lightly.

'Anything else?' asked Constant.

'There's the question of money. A hundred pounds won't go very far, and I daren't use Peter's bank.'

'We'd thought of that,' Constant said. He pulled out a thick envelope. 'This should keep you going. Send any bills to us, as we told you. And take care of yourself, Peter.'

'I'll do my best,' Philip promised.

'And how's our little drug-pusher today?' Sorel inquired as Constant came into the office.

Constant informed him. Sorel smiled broadly and made no pretence that the solicitude he expressed was heartfelt. But the smile was replaced by a frown when he began to discuss the telephone message that Philip had received that morning.

'It doesn't make sense,' he said, repeating Constant's comment to Philip. He was silent for several minutes. Then, 'Hamish, apply your mind, such as it is. How do you assess the situation?'

Constant shrugged. 'This mob seem to me to be crazy, Greg. We know they must have found out that Peter was trying to get the dirt on them or they wouldn't have attacked him in the first place, and they would never trust him again. So why were the guys who called on him – as they believed – last night merely instructed to beat him up and threaten him? Why didn't they waste him? They appear to have blithely accepted that Peter, having somehow managed to recover from the attack on him, should surface and continue business with them as usual. All I can think of is that whoever ordered last night's affair is as ignorant of the true situation as we are.'

Sorel was nodding. 'Yes. That is – an idea. Of course, none of this gets us very far, but I suppose we've been lucky. If they'd finished Philip off last night we'd have spent a lot of time and effort on him without achieving anything. Incidentally, what about his minder while all this was going on?'

'Useless, I'm afraid,' Constant replied. 'That block of flats is a warren of a place and people come and go continuously.' Constant hid his distaste for Sorel's indifference to Philip except as a pawn in the game. 'It's impossible to keep him a hundred per cent safe without a full-scale op.'

'But we might do a bit better than one per cent.' Sorel hated inefficiency. 'You didn't let him suspect that he's under surveillance or that his phone's bugged and therefore the names of Sylvia and the Mays weren't new to you?'

'Of course not. I said I'd find out about them if I could. What shall I tell him?'

'To stick to what you advised. The Mays are clean. John's a businessman with a good reputation in the City. Philip should go to that party. But we haven't got a line on this Sylvia yet. He'd better just string her along.'

'Okay.'

'Another thing. When he went for a walk yesterday he spent twenty minutes saying his prayers in the Brompton Oratory. He must cut that out. Peter was a Catholic, but he wasn't fanatical about it. For that matter, I've got my doubts about our Philip. Such devotion scarcely goes with dope smuggling, does it? I hope we can trust him.'

'I think he would do things for his brother's sake,' Constant said slowly, 'that he wouldn't do for us or for himself.'

Sorel snorted. He had no patience with woolly-minded colleagues who were ready to take a charitable view of heroin dealers. He hated Philip Janvrin with a hatred that left no place for forgiveness, however repentant the sinner might be – or pretend to be. If there had been any other means of achieving his purpose he would never have used this brother of Peter's.

'Philip Janvrin's a bastard, Hamish,' he said decisively. 'Don't let him fool you or you could land us all in the shit.'

For Philip the weekend that followed was comparatively uneventful. He stayed in on Friday, nursing his bruised and aching body. He had no visitors, and the only phone call was from Constant, who reiterated what he had said about the Mays and the unknown Sylvia. He also passed on the admonition that Peter was not excessively zealous about observing his religious duties, and Philip must follow his example. It was a fact that Philip had known from years back, and the warning made him smile ruefully.

By Saturday he was feeling considerably better. In the morning he wandered around the shops and made a few purchases. He didn't forget Constant's advice to take care, but his confidence was growing, and in the evening he went to dine at *Les Oiseaux*. The maître d' greeted him with enthusiasm.

'Mr Janvrin, how nice to see you again, sir. Your usual table?'

'Please.' Once more Philip repeated his spiel about his unfortunate illness, and duly received sympathy.

The meal passed pleasantly. Philip enjoyed the food and the wine, and found the atmosphere more relaxing than he had expected. All the waiters appeared to accept him at face value. The only embarrassing incident occurred as Philip was leaving, when a party of six, already merry with liquor, arrived. One of the men, who looked vaguely familiar though he couldn't place him, hailed him as Philip.

'Peter,' Philip corrected.

'Yes. Of course. My dear chap, I'm so sorry. How stupid of me.' He patted Philip on the arm. 'Peter. Of course. Old memory isn't what it used to be. I'd forgotten how alike you two brothers are.'

'Not to worry!' Philip did his best to respond to the man's mood. He didn't want to appear churlish. 'Enjoy your dinner.' With a wave of his hand he made a thankful escape among a chorus of good-nights.

It had been a tricky moment, but no damage had been done. Nevertheless, Philip was sweating a little as he left the restaurant. He knew that he had been caught off guard, that if the man had been sober, better acquainted with Peter and himself, or more persistent, the situation might have become fraught with difficulty. He accepted that such incidents must not be allowed to happen. He must not relax unless he was alone in the flat, the front door locked and chained, to be opened only after a cautious reconnaissance.

Even then there was still the telephone. It was trilling the next morning when Philip, having disregarded Constant's comment on Peter's sometimes less than enthusiastic approach to his religion, returned from Mass. The caller was the mysterious and determined Sylvia.

'Peter! At last! This is Sylvia. Where the hell have you been?' She had an attractive, if peremptory, voice.

'I've been ill, Sylvia. I got desperately ill while I was abroad,' Philip explained.

'I see.' She didn't sound very compassionate. 'But you've been back for days, Peter. I know, because I spoke to your Mrs Robyn. I left a message for you to call me. Why didn't you?'

'Because I'm still far from well, and it's been as much as I could do to cope with the shopping and looking after myself.'

'Oh, nonsense, Peter! It doesn't take a minute to phone. Frankly I don't know what you're playing at.'

'I couldn't help being ill.'

'I suppose not, but there are such things as phones, even in hospitals. Why the long silence? I simply don't understand you.'

'But then you haven't been as ill as I have.' Philip had decided to be more aggressive. 'I damned near died.'

'I still don't – ' Sylvia began, then seemed to change her mind. 'All right, Peter. When do we meet? Later today? Tomorrow?'

'No!' Philip tried to think quickly. He was aware that there could be pitfalls in whatever line he took. 'Next week – what about Wednesday or Thursday?'

'For heaven's sake, what's got into you? You can't play fast and loose like this or you'll regret it, Peter.'

'Wednesday or Thursday.' Philip ignored the threat – if it had been a threat.

'I'm not sure that will do. I'll have to see. Don't bother to phone me. I'll get in touch with you, Peter.'

And Sylvia banged down her receiver, causing Philip to wince. Thoughtfully he went through their conversation. He was none the wiser; she might be an innocent, a girlfriend angry at being neglected, or she might . . .

SEVEN

On Monday Philip took a taxi to what had been Peter's London office in a quiet square on the borders between Belgravia and Pimlico. From the outside the building looked like a private house, but the door was opened by a uniformed guard and there was an inquiry desk in the hall. Hamish Constant was waiting for him.

'The Brig wants to see you,' he said simply.

While he was at the 'safe house' Philip had been briefed on Brigadier Dermot Aubyn, formerly of the Irish Guards, so the man came as no surprise to him. Aubyn, even sitting down, appeared massive, like a strong and powerful bull of whom it was best to be apprehensive, though in fact he was soft-spoken. He greeted Philip pleasantly and gave him a preliminary appraising glance. Then, having waved him to a chair, he continued to regard him for a full minute before he spoke.

His first words were encouraging. 'Yes, the likeness to your brother – physically – is amazing. I'm not sure it would deceive anyone really close to you, but with this story of a serious illness to back up any minor changes you should get by in most cases. Are you finding the impersonation difficult?'

'Not necessarily, sir, unless I'm taken by surprise, and I'm doing my best to avoid any such situation. It's the seemingly small points that present difficulties. For instance, I've been invited to a supper party tomorrow night. I don't see how I can refuse, and I don't know if I should take my hostess flowers or chocolates – or nothing – not to speak of how I should treat any of the other guests who might know my brother.'

'Safest to take nothing. She could be allergic.' Aubyn gave a great belly laugh. 'I'd have thought this mysterious Sylvia was much more of a problem.'

'Yes. I can't go on avoiding her. I'm hoping Sorel may find out who she is – and something about her relationship with Peter – before I have to meet her.'

'Unfortunately we've had no luck there so far.'

'What about Peter himself, sir? Is there any news of him?'

'Your brother, no – no news, I'm afraid, but we must hope.'

Philip wondered if he had detected a fractional hesitation before Aubyn's answer or if he had imagined it. But there was no time now for any such speculation. The Brigadier, he realized, must have rung a bell concealed under his desk, for a minute later there was a tap at the door and Constant appeared. It had been a brief interview.

'Ah, Hamish! I've decided Philip should have another week's sick leave. There's no need for him to come into the office. But take good care of him. We don't want him beaten up again.' Philip reflected that the Brigadier could have been speaking about a horse or some other animal for which he had a use.

'No, indeed, sir.' Constant was apologetic.

'Off you go then, Philip-Peter, and remember it's in your own interests to help us. We valued your brother highly.'

'Yes sir. Thank you sir.' Philip responded automatically.

And as he got into the lift beside Constant he thought that if the Brigadier was less friendly than Constant – which was only to be expected – at least he had seemed neutral and not totally antagonistic like Sorel.

As if reading his thoughts Constant said, 'The Brig's a fair man. He won't let you down. Trust him. You'll be okay when – when all this is over.'

'Assuming I'm still in one piece.'

'Of course you will be.' Constant spoke with a forced heartiness. 'Whatever makes you – '

Constant's soothing manner made something snap in Philip's brain. 'Hamish!' he said. 'I want the truth.' He suddenly seized Constant by the arm and twisted it hard behind his back.

'For God's sake, Philip. You're hurting me.'

But Philip had learnt how to be brutal. 'Is Peter dead or alive? Answer me!'

But he had no time to persist. They had reached the ground floor and the lift doors were opening. Constant could shout for the guard. Instead, as Philip released his grip, he shook himself free and took several strides into the hall before turning.

'Why the hell did you do that?' he demanded. He rubbed his shoulder and upper arm. 'What got into you, Philip?'

Philip shook his head. 'I'm sorry.'

Constant grinned suddenly. 'Forget it. I tend to forget what a strain you must be under.'

'Hamish, I'll be candid. I don't mind being used, or rather I do, but I accept the fact, and I accept that you're not telling me – maybe you're not allowed to tell me – all you know about this business. But I do want one thing – the truth about Peter. Is he dead or not? And if not why does everyone speak of him in the past tense?'

'To the best of my knowledge he's alive, Philip. I swear it, and as far as I'm aware there's no reason to believe the contrary.'

'Thanks,' said Philip. But he hadn't found this rather pompous statement as reassuring as it was intended to be. It was clear that the blunt question had troubled Constant, and that his words had been carefully chosen.

By Tuesday evening, when Philip was due to go to the Mays' supper party, there had still been no phone call from Sylvia, and no one else had taken any interest in him. For this he was thankful, though he knew that his relief was illogical. His instinct for self-preservation, finely-honed in prison, made him desire to avoid danger and anyone who might be dangerous, but he would not find Peter – or Peter's enemies – merely by lying low.

In different circumstances, had he been free of any commitment on his brother's behalf, he could have enjoyed this brief period of inactivity. After all those years of incarceration it was a treat to go for a walk in the rain, to have a long hot bath when he liked, to do anything he wished – read or listen to music or watch television – to go to bed and get up when he chose. But he was not free and, with a threat of violence always present, he was beginning to find inaction stressful. In spite of his apprehensions, he was glad of the forthcoming party.

The Mays lived in a large flat in a luxury block overlooking Regent's Park. A white-jacketed houseman opened the door to Philip and escorted him to the drawing-room – spacious and elegant – where about two dozen people, each with glass in hand, were chatting in groups.

'Mr Peter Janvrin,' the houseman announced.

58

There was a momentary diminution in the sound of conversation. Then a woman in a purple dress, large-bosomed and thin-legged, advanced to greet him. She lifted her cheek to be kissed, then held him at arms' length and studied him.

'My poor Peter,' she said. 'You really have been ill. I thought you might have been making excuses for neglecting us.'

'As if I'd dream of doing that,' answered Philip disingenuously.

'Of course he wouldn't.' A silver-haired man who from his proprietary air was clearly John May had joined them and was offering his hand. 'Glad you could make it, Peter.'

'I'm glad to be here – in more ways than one,' Philip told them, referring to his supposed illness.

'Well, have a drink.' Mrs May gestured to a tray containing glasses of champagne that a waiter was offering. 'And come and meet our other guests. I don't think you know anyone here, but we've a surprise for you later.'

That he was not expected to know anyone was good news to Philip, but the promise of a surprise was not. In spite of Constant's assurance that the Mays were above suspicion he felt vulnerable in this opulent apartment. He allowed himself to be introduced to everybody, sipped champagne and made casual but careful conversation.

Finding himself beside John May he said, 'What is this surprise, John? An old friend I've not seen for ages?' It was a guess, but his thoughts had naturally focused on Sylvia.

May grinned. 'You've hit the nail right on the head, Peter. Don't tell Pam I told you but we're expecting Carella. She's coming on from a *vernissage* at that gallery of hers. Incidentally, she doesn't know that you'll be here, so there'll be a surprise for her too.'

'Thanks for telling me. I'll show all the astonishment that Pam would wish,' said Philip.

In the event his acting ability wasn't strained. Carella – Miss Carella Rindini, as announced by the houseman – made an entrance. She was a tall girl in her late twenties, and a striking beauty. She wore a full-length scarlet dress caught at the waist with a belt and slit up to the thigh on either side. She walked with easy confidence, like a model.

'My dears, I'm so sorry I'm late,' she said, embracing the two

Mays in turn, though the light musical voice turned the apology into a conventional phrase.

'You're just in time for supper. But we have a surprise for you first. Peter! Where are you?'

Philip murmured his excuses to the couple with whom he was chatting and came forward. He was not sure how he should greet Carella and hoped that she would give him a lead, but she stood absolutely still, staring at him.

'Hello, Carella,' he said and, when she didn't answer, added, 'Here I am, returned from the dead, as it were.'

'Peter! Peter!' Carella muttered.

Then her tongue came out and wetted dry lips. Simultaneously her eyes rolled upwards, her knees buckled and slowly – or so it seemed to Philip's amazed gaze – she collapsed in an ungainly heap on the carpet.

'Good God!' said John May. 'You expected Peter to be a surprise, Pam, but not such a startling one as this.'

'Don't be silly, John.' His wife spoke sharply. She knelt beside Carella and patted her hand. 'The poor girl can't be well. It's nothing to do with Peter.'

Philip was far from sure that Mrs May was right. He had seen the look of absolute horror on Carella's face when she was suddenly confronted with him, and possibly his remark about being back from the dead – which he had made in all innocence – hadn't helped. Of course, it could be his imagination, but . . .

He withdrew discreetly. One of the Mays' guests, a doctor, was examining Carella. She had only fainted, he was saying, and was already recovering, but as she opened her eyes and appeared to recall what had happened she began to cry. Pam May and the doctor helped her from the room.

The party resumed. Mrs May soon reappeared and supper was announced. Philip asked after Carella and was told that she had gone home. 'She works too hard and eats too little, like so many young women these days,' said Pam May. 'You must ring her up, Peter, now you're back. You used to be very fond of her.'

'Yes, I must,' said Philip, and wondered what Constant's reaction to this incident would be.

It had been a late night and Philip had been tired when he returned to his – or rather his brother's – flat. He forgot to set the alarm, with the result that he did not wake until ten. He showered, shaved and dressed and read the morning paper over breakfast. He had to phone Constant, but after that there was nothing, pleasant or unpleasant, in prospect. He considered how he would spend the day, how Peter on sick leave might spend the day.

He was still debating with himself whether or not to overcome his indolence and go out – to the Tate Gallery, perhaps, or for a stroll in Kensington Gardens – when someone pressed his buzzer in the hall below. He went to the entry phone.

'Yes? Who is it?'

'It's me, Peter. Can I come up?'

'Yes, of course.'

It was Wednesday, a day that he had mentioned to Sylvia, and Philip was pretty certain that he recognized her voice. He was waiting with the flat door wide open as the lift came to a stop at his floor. Nevertheless, he took care. Depending on who emerged, he ws ready to slam the door, put up the chain and call the porter. It was unlikely that anyone would come to attack him again in mid-morning, but he was taking no chances. Once had been enough. He watched, but it was only a tall dark-haired girl who stepped out of the lift and came, smiling, towards him. The lift doors closed behind her; there was no one with her.

Whether it was relief that the girl was alone and there was to be no hassle, or his supposed recognition of her voice or her casual manner, Philip momentarily let his guard drop. After she had lifted her face and he had kissed her lightly, he said, 'How nice to see you, Sylvia.' And at once he realized he had made a mistake; the girl was quick to recover, but for a split second her eyes had widened and she had tensed. 'Come along in,' he added.

He let her go ahead of him, and it was clear she knew the flat because she went straight into the living-room. But she wasn't Sylvia. So, who the hell was she? Somehow she seemed vaguely familiar, but he had no time to consider the question.

'Let me look at you, Peter,' she said. 'You've changed. You are thinner.'

'I got ill while I was abroad. I almost died, in fact.' The lie came easily by now. 'That's why I've been away so long. Incidentally, how did you know I was back?'

61

'I heard.' She didn't elaborate. She arranged herself carefully on a sofa. 'Peter, why did you call me Sylvia? It's not my name.'

'I'm sorry. It was a slip of the tongue.'

'Who is this woman Sylvia?'

'A friend of mine who's been trying to get in touch with me. I was about to phone her when you arrived, and she was on my mind. I suppose that's why I called you by her name.' I'm talking too much, Philip thought. 'Forgive me.'

'I suppose so, but remember – I'm Andrea.'

Philip made no response. The girl worried him. She had been studying him carefully, and now she was looking around the room. He braced himself for another question.

'What have you done with the Bridget Riley that used to hang over there?' She pointed vaguely.

'It's – it's being reframed.'

'Where?'

'A little place around the corner.'

'What about that yellow china cat you had?'

'What about it? For heaven's sake, Andrea, stop interrogating me. Would you – ' He had been on the point of asking her if she would like some coffee, but he remembered that he hadn't yet learnt to cope with Philip's complicated machine, and he knew instinctively that he couldn't offer her 'instant'. 'Tell me what you've been doing with yourself.'

'Oh, the usual things, parties, shows, weekends at the cottage. And of course our business keeps me busy. We've missed you, Peter. When are you going to Europe again?'

'I don't really know.' Philip tried to appear uninterested. The juxtaposition of Andrea's sentences had puzzled him. What was her – *our* – business? Why had *they* missed Peter? Why did her query about him going to Europe sound more than trivial? He said, 'I'm still on sick leave at present. It'll probably depend on my next check-up.'

'I see. We must just hope you get well soon, sweetie.'

Philip detected a certain acidity in the comment. He began to tell her about the bug he had caught, how ill he had been, how efficiently the doctors and nurses had treated him. He had been briefed with care, and it was a safe subject. It was also a subject that soon bored Andrea, and she said that she must go as she had a lunch date.

Philip saw her to the lift. He heard the metal grille on the inner door clang shut and listened to the whirr of the descending cage before he returned thoughtfully to the flat. He had not enjoyed meeting this Andrea. He was moderately sure that she suspected him of something, and he cursed himself for his carelessness in assuming she was Sylvia, and, worse, calling her by that name. It had been a poor start. It might have caused her to try to catch him out with questions about the Riley, for instance, or the yellow china cat; perhaps neither of these objects had ever existed.

And now he would have to admit his stupidity to Constant. He could imagine how caustic Sorel would be. Reluctantly he went into the study to phone.

'Sylvia and Carella and Andrea!'

'Not forgetting Mrs Pamela May,' Constant added.

Sorel looked at him in disgust. 'And possibly more to come. Peter seems to have had a whole harem of girlfriends. If only we had his little black book and could place them it would save a lot of time and effort.'

'We've got Carella's surname, and we know she's connected with some art gallery. Anyway, the Mays must have her address.'

'I'd prefer not to ask them. Nevertheless we'll have to track her down, if only because of her extraordinary reaction on being confronted with Janvrin – Philip – if Janvrin was the cause. And this girl Andrea never gave Janvrin a reason for her unexpected visit, did she?'

'No. Nor did she say how she knew "Peter" was back.'

Sorel was ruminative. 'I've been trying to remember. I've been in Peter's flat twice, perhaps three times, but always at parties. I've no recollection of a Riley picture, nor of a yellow china cat. Annoying. And of course Janvrin isn't trained, so we can't place much trust in his assessment of Andrea.'

'He's an intelligent man, Greg.'

'Intelligent? To go and call Andrea by another girl's name? Don't be a bloody fool, Hamish. It was a stupid give-away.'

'So why should you care, Greg?' Constant spoke with unusual sharpness; he was growing weary of Sorel's continued scorn. 'I thought the idea was that Philip should arouse interest by impersonating Peter, and so provide us with a lead to the villains.

As long as he does that, what does it matter if he betrays himself? He's just an ex-drug-pusher and disposable – at least in your opinion.'

Constant's voice trailed away. His colour was high. He had never spoken to Sorel in this fashion before. He waited to be consumed by the senior man's anger.

However, all Sorel said was, 'It was his intelligence I was questioning. Nothing else, Hamish. But you're right. I'd cheerfully see him in hell once he's done this job for us.'

EIGHT

At six o'clock on Thursday morning Philip was woken by the telephone beside his bed. He recognized the voice immediately. The caller was the man who had spoken to him in such chilling tones once before.

'Listen, you,' the voice said. 'Stop playing games. We don't stand for it. Just do as you're bloody well told or it will be worse than last time. Understand?' He gave Philip no chance to reply but banged down his receiver.

'No, I do *not* understand,' Philip said aloud, though there was no one to hear him. 'How the hell am I supposed to do what I'm told when I've not been told anything?' He could only assume that the message would have had some significance for his brother.

For himself, he recognized the reality of the warning, the threat. The previous assault was vivid in his mind; indeed the bruising had not completely healed, so that he still felt an occasional twinge of pain. He had no wish for another going over, 'worse than last time'. Nevertheless, action – apart from reporting to Constant – was impossible and, not wanting to appear unduly pusillanimous, he decided to postpone making the call until Constant would be in his office.

This proved to be a fortunate choice. Shortly before nine the phone trilled once again. This time the caller was Sylvia – and Sylvia in a seemingly conciliatory mood.

'You did suggest Wednesday or Thursday, Peter dear. I wasn't sure at the time, but it's all right. So dinner tonight. Meet me the usual place, at eight?'

Philip didn't pause, though he had no idea where 'the usual place' might be. His brief training at the 'safe house' had at least taught him how to deal with this kind of problem. Take the initiative – and take it immediately, he had been told.

'Eight's fine,' he said at once. 'But not the usual, please. I'll meet you at *Les Oiseaux*.'

'Why *Les Oiseaux* this time?'

'I like the place. The food's excellent. And it's convenient for me.'

'Close to your flat, you mean? Peter, if you're hoping to bed me down after dinner you can think again. We have an agreement, remember? No sex.'

'I wouldn't dream of such a thing,' Philip said truthfully.

'Oh no?' She laughed. 'See you tonight then.'

Constant was not only congratulatory but helpful. He promised that he would arrange for a watcher – someone Philip wouldn't know, but who would know him – to be at *Les Oiseaux*. The watcher would be able to identify Sylvia as Philip's companion and would trail her when she left him. With luck they would discover where she lived and who she was, and this would be an achievement.

Philip himself was to arrive at the restaurant half an hour early, and tell the maître d' that he was expecting a lady, so that she would be shown to his table and he would have no difficulty in recognizing her. The rest he would have to play by ear. But he must take his time about leaving, so that the watcher had a chance to go ahead.

As for the threatening phone call, Constant admitted that there was little to be done except take reasonable precautions. Privately he decided to warn Philip's minders of the possibility of another attack. He wished he could have told Philip about these minders, but he couldn't disregard Sorel's instructions, and Sorel believed Philip would act the part of Peter with more self-confidence and possibly more bravura if he remained unaware that he was under personal surveillance.

Sorel could have been right. At any rate, in spite of the fact that Constant could offer little reassurance, Philip, as always, found the contact comforting, and the prospect of dinner in a familiar restaurant, albeit with the mysterious Sylvia, less daunting after Constant's advice. Indeed, he looked forward to the evening, if not with pleasure, at least without great trepidation.

★   ★   ★

As Constant had suggested, Philip arrived at *Les Oiseaux* half an hour before he was due to meet Sylvia. He had booked his – or rather Peter's – usual table, to which he was shown by the maître d'. He explained that he was expecting a lady, and said he would wait to order dinner.

Because it was so early in the evening the restaurant was more than half empty, but by eight o'clock it was beginning to fill up. As it did, Philip amused himself by glancing round the room in the hope of spotting Constant's watcher, but he found no un-accompanied men; in fact the only single diner was a white-haired lady, probably in her seventies.

It was a quarter past eight, and Sylvia had still not appeared. Philip, pretending to study the menu, was reduced to watching the entrance anxiously. Nevertheless he nearly missed her appearance. A party of eight had arrived and it was not until a waiter had started to show them into an inner room that he saw a lone girl hovering behind them. The maître d' moved quickly, and seconds later she was being escorted to Philip's table.

Sylvia was a surprise. Although he naturally had no definite picture of her in his mind, Philip had imagined that she would be tall and slim, perhaps a little glamorous, like Andrea, like Carella Rindini, like all Peter's girlfriends he had met – and like Zara, Peter's wife. But Sylvia was different; she was small, a petite woman with a good figure, fair hair and, beneath outsized spectacles, cold blue eyes. She was not unattractive, but the adjective that first leapt into Philip's head was 'businesslike'.

Philip rose to greet her. The table was between them, so there was no opportunity to kiss her, and she didn't seem to expect any such gesture. She sat down and regarded him coolly. Philip made himself smile at her.

'How nice to see you, Sylvia. It's been a long time.' Her dress, he thought, was pretty, but it was the large diamond on her right hand that had caught his attention.

'It has indeed, Peter.' She regarded him thoughtfully. 'And I must say you don't look well.'

'That's only to be expected. I told you. I've been ill, desperately ill in hospital.'

'Where?'

'Abroad.'

'In Amsterdam, you mean?'

Philip hesitated, surprised at the girl's apparent knowledge of Peter's movements. Then, 'Yes,' he said again.

'Why didn't you let us know?'

Philip made no immediate response and luckily Sylvia was distracted by a waiter offering her a menu.

'What about a drink?' she said. 'I'd like my usual, Peter.'

Philip was prepared for this one. 'Not tonight,' he said. 'Tonight we'll have champagne – to celebrate my return to the land of the living.'

'Were you really as ill as that?' Sylvia sounded interested.

'Yes, I was. It was touch and go.'

'I believe you. But I'm not sure everyone would.' She leant across the table and scrutinized him closely. Then she nodded her head. 'Yes, you *have* been ill. I can tell. Poor old Peter! All the same, Tomas is far from happy about you. You let him down and that's one thing he doesn't appreciate. He's not a forgiving character, you know.'

'It wasn't my fault. I couldn't help catching a bug.'

'But you *could* help those weeks of silence when we didn't know where you were or what you were doing.'

The wine waiter bringing the champagne, and the waiter who wanted them to order, interrupted and gave Philip a minute or two's reprieve, but he could think of no more excuses. And the conversation they had been having had reached beyond his comprehension. He had never heard of Tomas; he wondered if Tomas could be the man with the chilling voice who had phoned him twice – but the evidence for this was meagre. And how did Peter relate to Tomas? There seemed to be a 'business' connection between them, in which Sylvia was involved. At least, he thought with some relief, it had become clear that Sylvia was not a romantic attachment as far as Peter was concerned.

'How is business, Sylvia?' Philip asked mildly as the waiters departed.

'Not good. You cost us a lot of money, Peter, and then this vanishing act of yours was extremely inconvenient. Incidentally, Tomas won't approve of you wasting your money on champagne while you owe him.'

'That's a pity, but let's enjoy it while we can,' Philip said, lifting his glass to her. '*Santé!*'

68

Sylvia shook her head, but she responded to his toast. 'You've not changed, have you, Peter? You always were a singularly irresponsible numero.'

'Do you really know me well enough to justify that comment?'

'Perhaps not, but you do seem to believe in a short life and a gay – no, I can't say that any more, can I – a colourful one, Peter. But take my advice – and be careful that it's not a *very* short one.'

It was not the kind of comment that was conducive to a happy and relaxed evening between friends. Friends? By now Philip was moderately sure that Sylvia had not personally known Peter that well, for she had shown no such suspicions as Andrea had. But there was some close connection between them. Philip wondered if he should take a risk in the hope of discovering more about Sylvia and Tomas. His opportunity came as they finished their main course.

'When are you going back to the Continent again?' Sylvia asked suddenly.

'That's what everyone wants to know – Andrea and Carella and the Mays,' Philip said with feigned exasperation, seizing the opportunity to mention the names. 'But I've no idea. As I've told them all, it depends on my health. At the moment I'm officially on indefinite sick leave.'

'Who's Andrea – and those other people?'

'Oh, just friends of mine.' Airily Philip dismissed them as unimportant, and Sylvia didn't persist. 'Actually I'm feeling much better, so I expect I'll soon be back to the old grind.'

'Good. Tomas will be glad to hear it,' Sylvia said coolly.

They had reached the coffee stage. Sylvia refused a second cup and looked at her wristwatch. Philip was anxious. During the meal he had occasionally tried to spot Constant's man, but without success. Now he purposely drew attention to himself as he summoned a waiter to ask for the bill.

And Sylvia said, 'I'll tell Tomas you're not yet a hundred per cent fit, but he'll expect you at Sandown Park on Saturday. You'd better be there, Peter.'

'Sandown Park?'

'Yes. It's *the* meeting of the week.' Sylvia laughed.

Philip was in no position to appreciate the joke, if it had been a joke. When he had been at Oxford he had had a friend who lived near Esher and, though he hadn't seen the friend for years and had even forgotten his name, he recalled being taken to a couple of race-meetings at Sandown Park. But that had been a long time ago.

'I'll be there, Sylvia,' he said, and thought that before Saturday he must get Constant to brief him more fully on the racing scene. 'Don't worry.'

'It's not me who needs to worry, Peter.' Sylvia was standing up and collecting her purse. 'Thanks for the dinner. I'll be in touch soon.'

'Half a mo.' Philip tried to delay her. 'I've not paid my bill yet. Wait for me.'

'No need. I'll get a taxi. 'Bye for now, Peter.'

Philip shrugged helplessly. There was nothing he could do to keep her without making his intention obvious. 'Goodbye, Sylvia,' he said. 'See you. Thanks for a good evening.'

He paid his bill, collected his change and said good-night to the maître d'. He didn't hurry. Sylvia had already disappeared. No one had followed her from the restaurant.

Philip walked back to the flat. It wasn't late, the streets were well lit and there were plenty of people about, so that he didn't feel unsafe. Nevertheless, he kept his wits about him until he was inside with his front door securely locked and chained.

He went into the living-room and flung himself on the sofa, feeling too restless to go to bed though he was tired. The evening had been exhausting, more exhausting than the Mays' party. In the tête-à-tête with Sylvia he had been forced to concentrate without appearing to do so, to watch every word he spoke and also to weigh what Sylvia was saying. He knew that first impressions were important but they could be deceptive, and it was up to him to judge.

The phone trilled. Philip pushed himself off the sofa and went into the study. Constant had promised to call him to hear about his evening with Sylvia and, it was hoped, to say that the woman had been traced to her home. But it was too soon for that, surely.

'Hello,' said Philip neutrally.

'Peter, it's Andrea.' They exchanged pleasantries and she said, 'I'm giving a small party on Sunday, drinks and supper. I know it's short notice, but Monique's coming over for a few days and – '

'Monique – ?' Philip thought it safe to query; there could well be more than one Monique.

'The Contessa.' There was the slightest question in Andrea's voice, as if she had expected Philip to recognize the name immediately. 'She'd love to see you, Peter. Do say you'll come. Sunday. Eight-thirty.'

'I'd love to. Many thanks.' But where, he wondered; he couldn't ask. Then he remembered that when she had been at the flat Andrea had spoken of a cottage. 'You'll be in town? You're not going to the country for the weekend?'

'No, no! We'll be at Suffolk House.'

'Great. I'll see you on Sunday. Thanks again, Andrea.'

With a sigh of relief Philip put down the receiver. It was not much – an Andrea of no known surname who lived somewhere in London in a place called Suffolk House – but perhaps Constant could do some detective work before the weekend.

As if on cue the phone went again, and this time it was Constant. He sounded tired and preoccupied, but he listened to what Philip had to tell him.

'Interesting,' he muttered finally, 'but somehow inconsistent. It's like a jigsaw puzzle with bits that don't fit – bits that might belong to another picture. I'll be around tomorrow evening, sixish, to discuss it with you and let you know what I've learnt. I'll get this Andrea of Suffolk House checked, too. Meanwhile you'd better brush up on your racing. Watch television in the afternoon. They'll be covering the Sandown meeting.'

'Right. I'll do my best.'

'Of course you will. So – '

Philip sensed that Constant was about to ring off, and hurriedly inquired, 'Hamish, what about Sylvia? Did you – ?'

'We lost her at Oxford Circus.' Constant spoke calmly, but he couldn't hide his disappointment and bitterness; Sorel had savaged him. 'Tell you tomorrow,' he added quickly, giving Philip no chance to ask further questions.

71

NINE

'Hi! Peter!'

Philip swung round. A man of about his own age was waving at him from across the street. Philip lifted a hand to wave back, and realized that he was holding a lettuce that he had just picked up from the display outside the greengrocer's. It was Friday morning and he was doing his weekend shopping while Mrs Robyn cleaned the flat. He half turned away, hoping the man would walk on, but, having waited for a gap in the traffic, he was now crossing the road to the shop, where Philip, caught in the midst of paying for his purchases, couldn't ignore him.

'My dear chap, it's been ages since I saw you last. How are you?'

It was indeed ages since they had met. Philip wouldn't have recognized the short, overweight figure with its heavy jawline and receding hair, but he had recognized the voice. He searched his mind for a name. Robert – Robert Fauvic. 'Fruity' Fauvic, who had been a contemporary of Peter's at Oxford and had stayed with the Janvrins on several occasions.

'Hello, Robert.' Philip put down his shopping bag and offered his hand. 'How are you?'

'I'm fine, but you don't look too hot, if you don't mind my saying so.'

Small blue eyes peered at him, and Philip gave a shortened account of his supposed illness. Fauvic was sympathetic. He suggested they should go and have a drink together and brushed aside Philip's excuse that it was too early. The pubs, he pointed out, had been open some time.

It was years since Philip had been into a pub; he hadn't had the courage to visit Peter's local by himself. But the publican greeted him as an old customer and a couple of obvious regulars, seated at the bar, nodded good-morning to him. Fauvic didn't appear to be known to them.

Philip went to sit at a corner table and, while Fauvic bought

72

their drinks, he tried to remember what he knew about the man. It wasn't much. After Oxford and a poor degree in English he had taught for a time in a preparatory school, but there had been some kind of a scandal . . . Philip couldn't recall any details. Nor had he any idea what Fauvic was doing now, or of any other facts about him that Peter might well have been expected to know.

'Here we are.' Fauvic put down their gins and tonic and seated himself beside Philip. There was a pause while they sipped their drinks, and then Fauvic asked suddenly, 'Have you seen Zara recently?'

'No–o.' Philip didn't want to talk about his sister-in-law, but at least the query suggested that Fauvic and Peter were not currently on particularly intimate terms, which was a relief. 'Actually, I haven't seen anyone apart from doctors and nurses for some weeks and, anyway, you may not know but Zara and I don't live together any more.'

'Oh, God! I'm sorry. I did know, but I'd forgotten.' Somehow Fauvic sounded less than convincing.

Philip wondered idly if Fauvic had a wife and, perhaps, children. 'But we're still on good terms, Zara and I,' he remarked.

Fauvic's next comment was somewhat odd for a mere, if long-standing, acquaintance. 'Zara can't be having much fun these days, poor dear,' he said, 'on her own, and facing the responsibility of looking after your offspring and your ancient dad – not to mention the estate. Must be hard on her. I suppose you keep in touch because of Paul.'

'Paul? Do you mean Patrick?'

'Oh yes, Patrick, of course. Your son. Silly of me. Slip of the tongue.'

Philip wondered. Had Fauvic been trying to catch him out? It didn't seem likely. But what was he doing in Bute Street? Was it coincidence that he had suggested coming to a pub, apparently unknown to him, but where Peter was known? Why all this slightly inconsequential concern for Zara? Philip knew that by now he was inclined to be suspicious of everyone, but in the circumstances it was a fault hard to correct. He told himself the chances were that his meeting with Robert Fauvic was fortuitous, and Fauvic was merely attempting to be sociable.

He said, 'And what have you been up to lately, Robert? Anything exciting?' He hoped it was an innocuous question.

'Frightfully dull, I'm afraid. I do a spot of journalism. It helps pay for the caviare, so to speak. My main job's editing educational books.'

It was not a subject about which Philip felt he could enthuse, or even discuss. He offered Robert the other half, and was glad when it was refused. They parted company outside the pub, Robert saying that they must lunch together soon and Philip agreeing with a false joviality.

Philip continued with his shopping and, by the time he returned to the flat and the meal that Mrs Robyn had prepared for him, he had done his best to dismiss his meeting with Robert Fauvic as unimportant.

Charles Sinclair regarded the prisoner standing before him with a jaundiced eye, and suppressed a sigh.

Robinson, known among his fellow-inmates as Crusoe, was an old lag. Now in his late fifties, a runt of a man with sloping shoulders, a balding head and a permanent nervous tic, he had been in and out of prison for the greater part of his life. He had tried most kinds of crime, from petty theft through housebreaking to being the look-out man for more serious villains. Time and time again he had been caught, usually because of his own inefficiency. Time and time again attempts at rehabilitation had failed. By now it was accepted that he was an incorrigible recidivist.

'You asked to see me, Robinson,' said the governor. It was every prisoner's right to make such a request.

'Yes, sir.' Robinson glanced sideways at the prison officer who had brought him to the office. 'But it's a private matter like.'

Sinclair nodded to the officer to leave them. He was not impressed. The matters about which Robinson asked to see him were usually 'private', but invariably of little substance – mere minor complaints. Sometimes Sinclair thought that the old lag enjoyed coming to talk to him as a change from the monotonous routine of prison life.

'Sit down, Robinson,' he said, not unkindly, 'and tell me what the problem is this time.'

'It's Janvrin, sir, the chap who's doing a long stretch for trying to smuggle dope.'

Sinclair opened his mouth, and shut it again quickly. He had nearly given the game away by replying that Robinson could have no conceivable cause for complaint against Philip Janvrin because Janvrin was no longer in the prison. 'Go on,' he prompted instead.

'Well, as you know, sir, yesterday was a visiting day, and the wife came to see me. Nothing extraordinary about that. She's always been very good, even when it was hard on her – '

'Get to the point, Robinson.'

Robinson looked hurt; the governor rarely spoke so harshly to him. 'She – she was all agog, sir!'

Sinclair, schooled to patience, checked the expletive that rose to his lips. With a wry sense of humour he admitted to himself that since the mention of Janvrin he too was 'all agog'. But it was useless to hurry Robinson, better to let him tell his story in his own way. And it was quite a story.

According to Robinson, Mrs Robinson – it was in effect a courtesy title since the marriage had never been blessed by church or state, though it had produced five children and lasted thirty years – had been having a gin and bitters in their local when a young woman had approached her and said she was prepared to pay a good sum for information.

Here Robinson had digressed to explain how suspicious his wife had been, and how she wouldn't have dreamed of doing anything in the least dishonourable, let alone illegal. But the woman had said that she was a girlfriend of Philip Janvrin's and, since she hadn't heard from him or of him for some while, she was worried. He hadn't answered her letters and she didn't like to visit him, but she wanted to be assured that he was all right – and if only Susie would inquire from her husband when she next saw him –

'How could Susie refuse?' concluded Robinson.

'How indeed?' said Sinclair, and refrained from asking how much Susie had received for her services. Instead he inquired, 'How do you suppose this girl knew that Mrs Robinson's husband was in the same prison as Janvrin?'

'I don't know, sir. The point's worried me.'

'What did you tell your wife, Robinson, when she asked you? And I want the truth.'

'That I hadn't seen Janvrin for a week or two, but I'd heard he'd been sent to the infirmary.'

'You've heard nothing else?'

Robinson looked uncomfortable. 'There was a rumour he'd been released, but it didn't make sense like, not with his offence and so much of his stretch left to go.'

Charles Sinclair cursed the prison grapevine. 'Did you mention that rumour to your wife – hint at it, even?'

'No, sir.' Robinson was shrewd, and he sensed that for some reason which he didn't understand he had provided the governor with some information that was interesting. 'I hope I did right coming to tell you about this, sir,' he whined.

'Absolutely, Robinson, if you wanted to do so.' Belatedly Sinclair did his best to make light of the incident, and pressed the bell under his desk to summon the officer who would be waiting in the outer office. 'Your wife was sensible and so were you. There are too many stupid rumours flying around this place. You quash them if you get the chance.'

'Yes, sir. Thank you, sir.'

The governor nodded his dismissal, but it was a full five minutes after Robinson, accompanied by the prison officer, had departed before he roused himself and reached for his telephone. He tapped out the number Sorel had given him. To his surprise Sorel himself answered at once. Sinclair explained why he had called.

'I do hope I've not wasted your time,' he said rather acidly as he came to the end of Robinson's story, to receive no immediate response.

'Far from it,' said Sorel. 'Sorry. I was thinking. I'm most grateful to you, sir. Did you get a description of the young woman who accosted this Mrs Robinson?'

'No.' Sinclair hadn't thought of it. 'I didn't want to suggest to Robinson that his tale could be significant,' he prevaricated. 'The man's not altogether reliable.'

'Ah!' With one syllable Sorel made it clear that he guessed this was an excuse. 'Perhaps you could let me have Mrs Robinson's address. I think the lady warrants a call.'

'My secretary will get it for you. One moment.'

'Thank you, sir.'

And while he waited Sorel smiled to himself. He was beginning to get some action at last. Anyone who would go to the length of making inquiries about Philip Janvrin was almost certainly more than casually interested in his brother, Peter.

★   ★   ★

Philip spent Friday afternoon watching racing on television, with a copy of *Sporting Life* and the *Racing Post* and a collection of relevant books and pamphlets beside him. He would have enjoyed the afternoon if he had not been conscious that the next day he would be at Sandown Park in a situation that would be strange, if not alien, to him, and would require him to keep all his wits about him if he were to behave as Peter would and not make a fool of himself.

Constant arrived a little after five. He was cheerful, but his elation seemed rather forced. He made Philip go through the events of the previous evening again, and questioned him closely.

'You're pretty sure that Sylvia accepted you as Peter, and believed your story about having been ill?'

'As far as I can tell, Hamish. But it appeared to worry her – annoy her is probably more accurate – that Peter didn't get in touch, ill or not ill. There was – is – clearly some kind of business relationship between Peter and Sylvia, and this Tomas. Is it conceivable that it's to do with horseracing in some way?'

'Possibly. It's not exactly encouraged in our line of work, but Peter never made a secret of the fact that he gambled a bit on the gee-gees.' Constant shook his head.

'Hamish, if Sylvia did accept me and my story, doesn't it prove that she had nothing to do with Peter's disappearance? After all, if she had, she'd know perfectly well what had really happend to him.' Philip spoke diffidently; he couldn't understand why this argument had apparently not occurred to Constant. 'Her connection with Peter could have been quite innocent, a business matter, unrelated to his work.'

'She could have been playing very clever, Philip, leading you on to believe just that – that she was not involved with Peter's – Peter's disappearance.'

'Perhaps.' Philip was doubtful.

'I've no doubt she was convincing, but how did she know Peter had gone to Amsterdam? It's not the kind of thing he'd have told anyone. What's more, last night she knew she was being followed when she left that restaurant and deliberately lost her tail. It wasn't an accident. The girl tailing her is good, but on this occasion Sylvia was better. She's no wide-eyed innocent, Philip.'

'The girl tailing her – was she in the restaurant? I didn't see anyone – '

'With her companion, yes. Two were less conspicuous than one. Besides the man had to see you safely home. We're not all that flush with staff. You never suspected?'

'That I was being watched? No!'

Constant grinned. He had made his point about Sylvia, and Sorel had agreed that it was time for Philip to be told he had a minder. Then Constant became earnest again.

'Philip, your man confirmed what we already guessed. You're being watched, not just by us for your protection, but by someone else. A chum of Sylvia's?'

'I wouldn't know. I got so used to being watched in prison that it's not something I'd notice, I suppose.' Philip couldn't keep the bitterness from his voice. 'Incidentally as you're keeping such a careful eye on me you'll know I met an old friend – an old acquaintance – in Bute Street this morning, and had a drink with him in Peter's local. He used to know Peter much better than he knew me, and he took me for Peter.'

Philip explained Robert Fauvic, and mentioned the fleeting doubts that had crossed his mind about some aspects of Fauvic's conversation. Constant was interested and made notes, but he agreed that it was foolish to suspect everyone. Nevertheless, Constant reminded him, it was essential not to drop one's guard.

Something in Constant's voice alerted Philip. 'You've learnt something then?' he asked quickly. 'About Peter?'

Constant wished that Philip was not such a complex mixture of swift intelligence and naïveté. He hesitated before replying. Then he said, 'Not directly, no. But there are some definite signs that the people – whoever they may be – who were responsible for Peter's disappearance are sniffing at the trap you've set for them.'

'You mean that you and Sorel have set for them. That's an unhappy metaphor, Hamish, when you're talking to the cheese.'

'I – I'm sorry.' Constant appeared genuinely embarrassed. 'What I'm trying to say is that someone isn't taking you and the story of your illness at face value. There's the fact that you're being tailed and – and that you've aroused curiosity. There have been inquiries.'

'What sort of inquiries?'

Constant regretted his remark; he couldn't tell Philip of Sinclair's phone call. He shrugged. 'This woman, Andrea, for one. She doesn't trust you. Incidentally, she's a Mrs Bernhardt

Manheim and she and her husband live in Flat 6, Suffolk House, which is a block of mansion flats in Marylebone. She works part-time in an art gallery, the *Galerie Lamoye* in Bond Street, where her sister who is – surprise! – Carella Rindini, also works. That's why Andrea reminded you of someone you'd met. Bernhardt himself is a businessman – a fixer of deals, an arranger. But there's nothing known against any of them.'

'Nevertheless, Carella takes one look at me and faints. Then presumably she tells her sister to come and inspect me. Odd, don't you agree?'

'Yes, I do, but odd incidents sometimes have simple explanations. If Carella had been close to Peter, and was suddenly confronted by a stranger who looked like Peter, sounded like Peter, but was – different – in some indefinable way, she might have passed out. But it's a definite fact that Andrea doesn't trust you.'

'So you said earlier. How are you so sure?'

'It's like this – '

Constant had run into Mrs Robyn as she left at the end of her morning's work. She wasn't to know that he had been waiting for her. She had greeted him as one of Mr Janvrin's friends. She had met him when he was ostensibly keeping an eye on Peter's flat while Peter was away, and had accepted him. Constant knew it would be useless to ask her about the Bridget Riley – she wouldn't know a Riley from a Rembrandt – but the yellow china cat was a different matter.

'Mrs Robyn, I wonder if you'd help me,' he had said in the hall. 'I want to buy Mr Janvrin a gift for his return. I thought I might replace the yellow china cat he used to have. Do you remember what it was like?'

But Mrs Robyn had denied all knowledge of any yellow china cat.

'So you see, my dear "Peter",' Constant concluded, 'this operation's starting to pop.'

'Good,' Philip said, and suddenly thought of the peace of the prison library, which had been a haven from so much that had revolted him. He had no wish to be back there. However unacceptable, his present life was an improvement on that. But it was only temporary. He sighed. What he really wanted was as unattainable as it had been since the day the jury had, fairly enough, found him guilty, and the judge had pronounced his sentence; and it always would be unattainable now.

Misreading his expression, Constant said, 'There's still a long way to go, Philip.'

TEN

Philip Janvrin's first thought when he woke on Saturday morning was that it was going to be a stressful weekend. On Sylvia's orders, he was due to go to the races at Sandown Park in the afternoon, and on the following day, Sunday, Andrea had requested – if 'requested' were the right word – his presence at her supper party to renew his acquaintance with some foreign Contessa. He wondered which of these events would represent the greater strain. Both, he suspected, would have their problems.

He dressed with care. Most of Peter's clothes, though they fitted too loosely on his spare frame, he had found comfortable, but unfortunately this did not apply to the checked suit and the brown trilby that he guessed Peter would have worn on a racecourse. Indeed in one of its pockets he discovered a numbered coloured slip, obviously from a bookie, which proved that Peter didn't always pick winners.

Philip exchanged the suit for cavalry twill trousers and a jacket. The weather forecast was for sunshine with an occasional shower, so he topped them with a light raincoat. The trilby he decided to forget; it was years since he had worn a hat. With a field-glass case slung over his shoulder he considered his appearance in the bedroom mirror. The very picture of an eager racegoer, he decided, though a great deal would depend on what Sylvia and this Tomas would expect him to look like.

Shortly before twelve he left the flat and went to collect the car. There was no garaging for residents on the premises, and Peter had kept his Rover in a lock-up in a nearby mews, for which he paid what seemed to Philip an exorbitant rent. He had already inspected the car, which was immaculately clean and obviously well-serviced, and had even taken it out on the road to accustom himself to the feel of it. The only slightly surprising fact was that Peter should have driven such a sedate saloon – something considerably more *sportif* would surely have been in character.

London traffic was particularly heavy at noon on a Saturday and, in spite of his trial effort, Philip drove with extreme care until he reached the outskirts of the city and the motorway. Here he began to relax, and even to enjoy himself. He assumed that he was being followed, and that one of Sorel's minions would be following the followers, but for the moment he disregarded them; he was doing precisely what he had been told to do. He turned on the radio and, as he drove towards Esher, listened with pleasure to part of *Carmen* – an opera which, in what seemed another lifetime, had always been one of his favourites.

He arrived at the Sandown Park racecourse early, though the car park was already starting to fill. Since it was not a day of major racing he had no difficulty in buying a pass for the Members' Enclosure, which was what Constant had advised, and, having attached the small cardboard label to his lapel, he bought a racecard and went towards the grandstand and the bar. He ordered a gin and tonic and some sandwiches. He ate and drank slowly, while he made a show of studying form. He wanted to make the meal last. Constant had suggested that this was the most likely place for him to be accosted.

But it seemed that Constant had been wrong. No one spoke to him, and as the bar emptied before the second race of the day – the two o'clock had caused little interest – Philip decided he could stay there no longer. He tried to remember Sylvia's exact words. He was sure she had said that this was *the* meeting of the week but according to *Sporting Life* and the *Racing Post*, there was no featured race at Sandown that afternoon. If anything, the meeting taking place at York was more important. He didn't understand, but then there was a great deal that he didn't understand.

According to Sylvia, Tomas expected Peter to be at Sandown, and God help him if he wasn't. So here he was, but what on earth was he expected to do? Philip tried to put himself in Peter's place, assuming that this was merely a pleasant day at the races. He left the Members' Enclosure, and wandered down to the parade ring to watch the horses being led by their 'lads' – many of them 'lasses' – around the track inside the rails, while groups of their connections – a word whose meaning Philip had just learnt – waited in the centre of the ring. A couple of men nodded to him

82

and wished him good-day, but whether or not this was because they recognized him as Peter he had no means of knowing.

He was beginning to feel a little conspicuous when the jockeys appeared in their bright silks. The horses were led from the track to the centre of the ring and, after their riders had exchanged last-minute words with their trainers and owners, were mounted. Then they proceeded in single file, some sedately, others very much on their toes, along the Rhododendron Walk – which, Philip had gathered, was one of the features of Sandown Park – to be freed on the course to go down to the starting stalls.

The threatened rain hadn't materialized, the sun was shining and Philip, caught up in the colour and excitement of the scene, hastened to the stand to watch the race. He hadn't bothered to place a bet, but he had made a guess as to the winner, and felt a glow of pleasure when the horse he had chosen almost at random came home by five lengths.

The next instant the glow had faded. Suddenly he had become aware of a hand fumbling inside his raincoat pocket. He acted instinctively. Before the hand could be withdrawn he had seized its wrist and turned to confront the potential pickpocket.

'Steady on, Peter,' the hand's owner said. 'You're hurting, old son. You don't know your own strength.'

He was a man of medium height, thin, with hollow cheeks, pointed features and sandy hair. He made Philip think of a fox, and in his mind he christened him 'Foxy'.

'Sorry,' Philip replied automatically.

Foxy massaged his wrist, and glared at Peter. 'So you should be. You damn well hurt me.' He sounded aggrieved. 'All I was doing was giving you a little present for the girlfriend. Make sure she gets it, Peter. Intact. And don't try the disappearing act again. I've had to do a good deal of your work and it's not really my line. I don't like it.'

'Sorry,' Philip said again, 'but it wasn't my fault.'

Foxy peered into his face. 'No, you do look as if you'd been ill.'

Philip resisted the temptation to step back. Foxy's breath smelt of a mixture of whisky and garlic; it was not a happy combination. He gave what he hoped was an ingratiating smile.

'Any other instructions?' he risked.

'Don't come the sarcy with me!' Foxy was indignant.

Philip, who had had no intention of appearing sarcastic, was at a loss. This meeting with Foxy seemed to be a minefield. And worse was to come.

Foxy said, 'Put a monkey on Box of Chox in the three-forty. On the nose. With Blinkers, natch.'

'Okay.' To give himself time to turn this racing jargon into English that he could comprehend, Philip pretended to study his racecard. A monkey, he knew, was five hundred pounds. On the nose meant to win and not each way. But five hundred pounds! He certainly didn't have that kind of money. He looked around at the various bookies' boards across the fence in Tattersalls Ring. And, if he had, he wouldn't put it on an outsider.

'Thirty-three to one!' he said.

'That's right. Double carpet. A nice little bet.' Foxy grinned. 'See you after the race.'

Even if Philip could have thought of an excuse there was no time to halt Foxy's departure. He made off, leaving Philip with an appalling problem. He couldn't bet money he didn't possess. And he had no idea who Blinkers might be. Presumably an on-course bookmaker, but he hadn't seen the name painted at the top of any of the boards when he was looking at the odds. He made another and more careful search, but found no Blinkers. He wondered what would happen if he failed to meet Foxy when Box of Chox had either won – or more probably failed to win – his race. The prospect was daunting.

'Hello, Peter. You look worried.'

'Hello.' It required an effort to smile. The last thing he wanted at that moment was an encounter with another stranger whom he was supposed to know.

'Aren't you going to kiss me?' she said, holding up her face and, as he bent towards her, added in a whisper, 'It's all right. I'm one of Sorel's people.'

She was in her mid-forties, Philip guessed, a pleasant if nondescript woman in a sensible suit and well-polished brogues, her round face bereft of make-up. She looked like everyone's maiden aunt, and Philip found her presence wonderfully reassuring.

'Let's take a stroll down to the rails,' she suggested, taking his arm. 'We can watch the next race from there, and you can tell me about the trouble.'

As they leant companionably on the rails and watched the horses go down to the start Philip reminded himself to guard his tongue. He had no idea how much the woman – she had given her name as Mary O'Donovan – was in the know. She had addressed him, and continued to address him as Peter, even when no one was standing close by, but this could merely have been an intelligent precaution.

As if she were reading his thoughts, she said, 'You don't have to tell me anything you don't want to, but I'm here to help you if you need me.'

Philip hesitated no longer. 'I certainly do need help,' he said. 'I've been instructed to put a monkey on an outsider called Box of Chox in the three-forty – to win, too. I'm to use a bookie with the unbelievable name of Blinkers. I can't see anyone called that, and anyway I haven't got five hundred pounds.'

Mary O'Donovan laughed. 'I'm sure that's not an insoluble problem, though I don't fancy Box of Chox myself. He's an outsider, as you say, and he's got an apprentice jockey up. However, mine not to reason why. First, the money. I shouldn't think you have to worry. My guess is that you'll find you have an account with this Blinkers. Secondly, as to who he is, I suspect that's a nickname of some kind – many of the bookies have them. I'll make some inquiries. You meet me near the Tote in Tattersalls Ring fifteen minutes before the start of the race and, with any luck, I'll be able to point him out to you. Anything else?'

'No. And thanks a lot.' There were questions he would like to have asked, of course, but he didn't think it advisable to voice them.

'Goodbye, then, for the moment.' And with a nod of her head Mary O'Donovan left him.

The rails near the winning post filled up as the next race became due. Philip, people on either side of him, put his hand in his

85

raincoat pocket to reassure himself that the present he was presumably to give to Sylvia was safe. He wondered what it was, and if the character with the foxy face could conceivably be Tomas.

Then the ground shook beneath his feet as fifteen two-year-old horses thundered past on the other side of the rails, but so close that he felt he could have touched the nearest. 'C'mon, Lester! C'mon!' A grey-haired man standing beside him shouted, dancing up and down in his excitement. Philip couldn't help grinning and the man, turning to him, said, 'I always have a fiver on Lester – greatest flat jock ever. Were you on him?'

'No such luck,' Philip said.

He was tempted to ask this seeming expert what he thought of Box of Chox's chances in the three-forty, but the man was already moving off, either to collect his winnings or place another bet, or because large drops of rain were beginning to fall. Philip went in search of an early cup of tea, but by three-thirty he was in his place, waiting for Mary O'Donovan. The shower had passed and the sun was shining again.

Mary O'Donovan arrived a few minutes later as Philip was starting to worry that she might not come. She was pink-cheeked and slightly out of breath, but she gave him an encouraging smile. 'Success,' she said. 'Your bookie's real name is Blenkinson and he trades with his son as his clerk. See – he's the one with a red face, dark hair, moustache, natty blue suit and a vulgar tie. His name's on the blackboard behind him.'

'I've got him.'

'Good!'

'Many thanks – ' he started, but she merely squeezed his upper arm and was gone. Philip felt a sense of loss. He wished she had stayed to watch him lay his bet with Blinkers, even though she wouldn't have been able to help if he made some stupid mistake. In the event, the process couldn't have been simpler.

He approached the red-faced bookie, waited his turn and said, 'A monkey to win, Box of Chox. On account.'

Blinkers showed no emotion. 'Sixteen and a half grand to five hundred. Box of Chox,' he said to a weedy youth beside him, adding a number. 'On account.' He handed Philip a bit of blue pasteboard.

Hurriedly Philip made way for the punter behind him. He could scarcely believe that it was so easy to part with five hundred pounds that one didn't possess and, in the unlikely event that Box of Chox was first past the post, win sixteen thousand and five hundred pounds. It was absurd.

Of course there was a catch. It was quite clear that he, or rather Peter, was being used in some curious fashion – a fashion that was almost certainly illegal, and probably not concerned with his official duties. And that gave rise to a personal – and worrying – question: just what extra-curricular activity was Peter involved in, and how serious was it? Peter had always liked money, or rather what money could buy, and sometimes had not been over-scrupulous. Unbidden there came into Philip's mind an incident that had occurred many years ago.

He had been thirteen and Peter sixteen. They had been on holiday with their parents and their young sister in Brittany. He – Philip – had found on the beach a wallet stuffed with francs and had at once suggested taking it to the *gendarmerie*; he had not been altogether altruistic because he had hoped for a reward. But Peter had laughed at him – the police would merely keep the money and there would certainly be no reward – and Peter had had his way. He had insisted that Philip should share the francs with him, and Philip had reluctantly agreed.

Why should he have suddenly thought of that incident now, Philip wondered? It had no bearing on the present problem. They had been children then, happy and carefree. Now . . . Slowly he made his way to the stands, from which he proposed to watch Box of Chox make his effort. As to what happened after that, win or lose, he would have to wait and see.

To his surprise Philip found that he was nervous. The horses had gone down to the start, but there was some kind of delay; one of them had spread a plate. But at last they were all in their stalls. Then they were off. Watching through his glasses, Philip was dry-mouthed as, in the final straight, Box of Chox came to the front, edging ahead of the favourite. The crowd was roaring. The horses swept past the post, a photo finish.

'Let's go and collect our winnings, Peter.'

Philip turned sharply. Foxy was standing beside him. 'Didn't you hear? It's a photo finish.'

'What do you bet old Chox will have lost? A tenner?'

'No!' Philip was having no side bets with Foxy, least of all a bet that Foxy was probably guaranteed to win. And a thought occurred to him. The bet had been placed on an account. Surely the winnings would be credited to the account, rather than handed over in cash.

He was pondering this mystery, when Foxy seized his arm impatiently. 'Come on,' he said. 'What's the matter with you? Blinkers'll be ready. It's not like you to be slow collecting, Peter.'

'Sorry! I – I felt a bit giddy for a moment,' Philip lied.

'Poor old you!' Foxy sonded genuinely sympathetic. 'Tell you what, when we've got the dibbins I'll stand you some champers. Unless you think you should push off home.'

'I think perhaps I had better, but thanks.'

Foxy didn't argue – it had been his suggestion – and Philip followed him through the crowd, thankful that he would soon be speeding towards the privacy of his flat. Some aspects of Peter's life were comparatively easy to simulate; he and his brother had been so much alike. Others were almost impossible, and today had seen many of those. The day, in fact, had been a strain. What was more, in a way that he couldn't completely explain, it had been extremely disturbing.

'Meet you by the Tote,' Foxy said.

'Okay!' Philip said.

He was approaching Blinkers' stand when a voice announced over the public address system that Box of Chox had won by a head. The applause was muted; it seemed that few punters had backed the outsider. Warned by Foxy, Philip was not surprised at the outcome of the race. Nor, evidently, was Blinkers. As Philip passed over his ticket Blinkers handed him without a word two identical packets of notes enclosed in elastic bands.

Philip nodded his thanks and returned to Foxy, who held out his hand. 'My half, Peter,' he said. And when Philip gave him one of the packets, 'Ta, I've earnt it.' He grinned broadly. 'Off you go home now, and take care. See you.'

'Goodbye,' Philip said. The last thing he wished for was to see Foxy again.

Philip drove back to London, garaged his car and returned to the flat. He counted the money that Blinkers had given him. It was exactly half his – or rather someone else's – winnings on Box of Chox. Foxy had claimed the other half; indeed, Foxy said that he had earnt it. Philip wondered how.

He put the money to one side and inspected the packet that Foxy had slipped into his raincoat pocket. It was about the size and shape of a paperback book, wrapped in fancy paper and securely taped. There was no possibility of opening and repacking it without this being evident.

The phone rang. The caller was Sylvia, and she wasted no time. She said, 'Peter, I'm in your local. Please come round *at once*. I'm in a hurry.'

'All right.' Philip didn't quibble. Glad that, thanks to Robert Fauvic, he knew the local, he thought it would be to his advantage if Sylvia saw him greeted as a regular by the publican; it might help to consolidate his persona as Peter and allay any suspicions that Sylvia might have.

'I'll be there in five minutes,' he said at once.

He was as good as his word. He found Sylvia sitting on a banquette in the corner of the pub, a glass of Cinzano on the table in front of her. He bought a gin and tonic for himself and went to sit beside her.

'Any trouble?' she asked.

'No. I think one could say it was a successful day.'

'That's as it should be.'

'I have a present for you.'

Sylvia showed no surprise. 'Pass it to me then. And the money. Don't make it obvious or the old fools over there will think you're paying off a whore.'

Philip slipped the package on to Sylvia's lap. She in turn put it, without a second glance, into the large handbag she had beside her on the banquette. Then, below the table she held out her hand for the money.

'Don't I get a share?' Philip asked.

'No! Not until you've paid off what you owe Tomas.' Sylvia

shut her bag with a decisive snap, finished her drink and stood up. 'You've done well today, Peter.' She spoke like a schoolmistress encouraging a poor pupil. 'Next weekend will be Longchamp. Let's hope you'll be as successful there.' And with that information she left him.

ELEVEN

Sunday was a curious day for Philip – a day during which his moods swung between pleasure and something akin to desperation. The weather was wet, windy and cold for June, which gave him an excuse to stay in, listen to some of Peter's cassettes, read and relax. He would have liked to go to Mass, but Sorel had again warned against a too conscientious practice of his religion and he felt bound to comply. Nevertheless, the absence of any responsibility was delightful.

However, he was still smarting at intervals from his conversation with Sorel the previous evening on his return from the races. Sorel, rather than Constant, had answered the phone when he called to relate his experiences, and it seemed that Sorel had already received a report – and an unfavourable report – presumably from Mary O'Donovan. In any case he listened in silence to Philip's story and then began to speak angrily and sarcastically.

According to Sorel, Philip had behaved inefficiently at Sandown. Peter wouldn't have wandered around the racecourse looking worried; Peter would have been eager to bet on every race; Peter would have been sociable at the bar and drunk champagne; Peter would not have left before the last race, as if bored by what had been an excellent meeting.

To add to this ineptitude, Sorel had raged, Philip had then calmly handed over the packet Foxy had given him to Sylvia without letting the authorities have a chance to examine it. Experts could have opened it, and it could have been X-rayed. If Philip had imagined that Foxy – Mary O'Donovan had identified him as Frank Pringle, a one-time assistant trainer of dubious character, often to be found at the races – had been sending Sylvia a genuine 'present' he was out of his mind. Was he being purposely stupid? Or did he, an ex-con, think he could live the comfortable life that his brother had lived, without doing his best to earn the privilege?

Philip's dislike of Sorel, which he knew was more than reciprocated, was growing. He yearned to tell Gregory Sorel to stuff the job and then walk out on him, regardless of the consequences. But he knew that he couldn't. Peter had to be found, alive or dead, for the sake of the family.

And to top it all, there was this supper party at the Manheims' to be faced – a party which he expected to dislike intensely and – much worse – a party which, unless he was constantly on his guard, might lead to his impersonation of Peter being shown up for what it was. But the choice was not his. In the present circumstances, there was no excuse, however valid, that Sorel would accept for a refusal to attend.

Philip's expression was grim as he went to get ready, though by the time he had bathed and dressed and was about to leave the flat his mood had changed again. His bouts of contentment and irritation, which had been with him all day, gave way to a single-minded determination to show the wretched Sorel that, ex-con though he might be, he was not to be despised.

He took a taxi to Marylebone. Suffolk House was one of those blocks of London mansion flats that appear unprepossessing from the outside, but inside are luxuriously appointed and run with seeming smoothness like the best of hotels. A uniformed porter let him into the building and a uniformed maid opened the apartment door to him, just as Andrea came into the hall.

'Peter dear, welcome! Welcome! It's such ages since you've been here.'

'Hello, Andrea. Yes, it's nice to be here again.'

They embraced, and she drew him into a large and opulent drawing-room which reminded him of Pam May's. Indeed, the two parties were not dissimilar, though this was smaller and more intimate. Everyone here was expensively dressed. Everyone was sipping champagne. Everyone looked elegant and was – or appeared to be – totally at ease. The most notable difference was that of age. No one at the Manheims' party was much over forty, with one notable exception – a silver-haired woman with a thin, aristocratic face, sitting in an upright chair towards one end of the room.

Looking around further, Philip recognized Carella Rindini, Andrea's sister – the woman who had fainted on seeing him at the Mays' – and, with a slight shock, Robert Fauvic. Philip couldn't believe that this was chance, that Fauvic was a casual acquaintance of Andrea and her husband. Nor could he now believe that his meeting with Fauvic on Bute Street the previous Friday had been accidental. He swallowed his surprise.

A fair-haired blue-eyed man, handsome with chiselled features, had come forward, hand outstretched in welcome. 'Delighted to see you, Peter.' He had a slight German accent.

It wasn't difficult to guess that this was Bernhardt Manheim. 'And to see you. It's been too long.' Sometimes Philip felt that he was a parody of his brother.

Manheim's handshake was firm. 'Yes, we understand you've had a rotten time lately. Too bad, Peter. Let's hope that's all behind you.'

'Bernhardt!' It was a half-amused, half-plaintive cry from the woman in the chair. 'You're monopolizing Peter, when I'm sure he's come here especially to see me.'

Manheim laughed. 'My dear Monique, don't be so impatient. He's about to join you.'

'Of course I am.'

Philip hadn't needed this by-play to guess that the lady was the Contessa of whom Andrea had spoken as someone who was in London for the weekend and was eager to meet him. With an apologetic grin at the Manheims he went across to her.

'My dear Peter.' She held out a long thin hand, the skin white, the nails scarlet, the palm turned down. 'How lovely to see you again. But I'm afraid you don't look your old self.'

Feeling a little foolish, Philip bent over her hand and brushed his lips against it. As he straightened himself he was surprised to meet hard blue eyes which now held no sign of caring or affection, and he wondered if her remark had any special significance. Then she twisted her hand around and her fingers clutched his tightly. He didn't like to pull his hand away, and had to suffer her seeming to massage each finger as she questioned him with what he sensed was false concern.

But she couldn't hold on to him for too long. A maid was offering him a tray containing flutes of champagne, and the Contessa was forced to release his hand. Turning, he was lucky enough to find Carella Rindini standing nearby, and he seized the chance to demonstrate his familiarity with Andrea's sister.

'Carella, how are you? Are you better?' he asked over-anxiously, and added to the Contessa, 'The other night the poor sweetie fainted at the Mays' party.'

'Who are the Mays?' the Contessa inquired.

It was Carella who answered. 'Rich business people. They're rather dull, but they buy from the gallery so I visit them occasionally.'

'You caused quite a stir, collapsing like that,' Philip said.

'It was stupid and embarrassing. I'd been working terribly hard preparing for a *vernissage* and I'd had nothing to eat all day. But it didn't mean anything.'

Although Carella dismissed the incident as trivial the glance she gave Philip was far from friendly, and he wondered how Peter would have reacted. Behind him a heated conversation was taking place in German. Though his German was rusty, he found he could follow it with comparative ease. A man and a woman were discussing the merits of two painters of whom he had never heard. It was not a conversation he wanted to join. But the Contessa was talking earnestly to Bernhardt Manheim and Carella had walked off, leaving him momentarily alone, uncertain what to do. Peter, he was sure, wouldn't have been so indecisive, but – to whom should he choose to attach himself? He didn't trust any of them, or rather he didn't trust his ability to deceive any of them.

As he hesitated, he was hailed by Robert Fauvic, who solved his immediate problem by leading him aside from the main group of guests. 'What luck meeting you here, Peter,' he said.

'Quite a coincidence.'

Fauvic either didn't notice the sarcasm, or chose to ignore it. 'I was going to phone you. I wanted to suggest lunch next week. How about it?'

'I – I'm not sure. I'm going to Paris. There's a big race-meeting at Longchamp at the weekend, and I've an interest in a horse. Incidentally, I had a good day at Sandown on Saturday. I was on an outsider – Box of Chox, he was called.'

'I see,' said Fauvic slowly. 'But what about early in the week – say Tuesday or Wednesday?'

Philip had been watching Robert Fauvic carefully and he could have sworn that the references to Sandown and Box of Chox and Longchamp meant nothing to him. Fauvic was no great actor. He couldn't hide the fact that he was ill at ease in Philip's company, even though he seemed to seek it out, and he would never have been able to conceal his feelings had he known of Box of Chox's win at Sandown.

'Tuesday would be fine,' Philip said at length. 'Many thanks, Robert. When and where?'

'Twelve forty-five, at the Garrick.'

'I'll be there.'

At that point Andrea clapped her hands and said that supper was ready. Everyone filed into the dining-room, which was long and narrow. The table sat fourteen. Philip was at Bernhardt's end, with the Contessa on his left and a pretty plump girl on his right.

As Philip started to drink his soup the pretty girl turned to him and introduced herself. 'I'm Anne-Marie Remington,' she said. 'You won't remember me, but we met ages ago. I was a friend of your sister's.'

'You were a friend of Meriel's?' True or not, Philip was encouraged. He had been briefed on his sister and hoped she would be a safe subect. 'Are you still in touch with her?'

'We exchange cards at Christmas. That's all.' Anne-Marie gave a small shrug. 'You know how it is when you don't see someone for a long time?'

'Yes, of course.'

'How is she?'

'Fine. Expecting a baby later this year. Actually I don't often hear from her myself. We were never very close. She's a lot younger than – than – ' Philip stumbled. He had so nearly said, 'than *Peter* and me.' Dear God! And he had thought this was a safe subject. 'Than I am,' he finished lamely.

'You had a brother too, didn't you?'

Philip was prepared for this one. He could lie with impunity. No one could expect him to tell a pretty girl, met casually at a party, that his brother was serving a long prison sentence for drug dealing. 'Philip's in South America,' he said. 'He's been there some while. But what about you? What are you doing these days?'

'Nothing much.'

She was getting married in September, and preparations for the wedding were keeping her busy. She nodded with pride at a good-looking young man who was sitting further down the table on the other side. His name was Tony and he worked for Bernhardt Manheim, which explained Anne-Marie's presence at the party.

95

By now the soup plates had been removed and the main course served. Politeness demanded that he turn to the lady on his left, the Contessa. Fortunately she seemed content to do most of the talking, though she glanced at him curiously now and again. She spoke of her apartment in Rome, her palazzo in Venice and her various travels. She didn't probe and Philip, listening carefully in the hope of gleaning some information about her, found no difficulty in responding.

The main course was followed, continental-style, by a salad and cheese. Manheim had gathered to himself the conversation at his end of the table, and he held forth on the problems of doing business in Europe – apart from anywhere else – when there were different languages, different laws, different customs and currencies. Even the different time zones added to his problems, he claimed.

'You can't do much about those – the time zones, I mean,' someone said.

'Sure we could, with a little good will – at least in Europe. As it is, it's surprising we ever achieve anything.'

There was a murmur of agreement. Bernhardt Manheim, Philip thought, was a man to whom the much overworked word 'charisma' applied. It was easy to imagine him arranging deals that would suit all parties.

Suddenly Philip was distracted by the Contessa's hand seeking his as the plates were cleared for the final course. 'I'm admiring your signet ring,' she said.

'But you've seen it before.' Philip, though wary, was on safe ground; his signet ring and Peter's were identical. 'It's the family crest.'

'Of course, Mr Janvrin.' She laughed at him and changed the subject, leaving him to wonder if there was any significance in the way that she had addressed him.

Dinner ended without formality. They all returned together to the drawing-room, where coffee and liqueurs were served. Philip saw the Contessa speak briefly but earnestly to Andrea. Then Andrea came across the room to perch on the arm of his chair.

'I've hardly seen you this evening, Peter,' she said. 'How are you? Feeling more like your old self?'

'Thank you, yes, Andrea, especially after that delightful meal.'

'And Monique's charming company?'

96

'That would enhance any occasion for me.'

Andrea laughed. 'Monique's always been very fond of you too, Peter, ever since that time you stayed with her in Venice. She often talks about what she calls your English sang-froid over that accident.'

'It was a long time ago.'

'But not something one would forget.'

Philip, feeling himself on a quicksand, gave what he was sure was a foolish grin. He had no adequate reply. He was not aware that Peter had ever been to Venice, stayed with the woman Monique or had an accident there. Indeed, were these facts? Or where they meant to test him?

Fortunately Andrea seemed happy to receive no direct answer. She patted Philip on the shoulder and went to speak to Anne-Marie. The rest of the evening passed without incident and at midnight, to Philip's relief, the party broke up. He refused a lift from Tony and Anne-Marie, and took a taxi back to the flat.

By the following evening some of the problems had been solved, at least to the satisfaction of Gregory Sorel. For Philip, however, the outcome promised to be daunting.

He had been summoned to Peter's office, where he had spent the day. Sorel and Constant had met him there and listened carefully as he described the Manheims' party – Sorel's manner had been cool, but no further reference was made to what might have been called the Sandown débâcle – and he was then told to wait while Constant set in motion some necessary inquiries. These took some time. Philip drank innumerable cups of coffee, had a sandwich lunch and yet more coffee. It was five o'clock before Constant came to collect him.

'Some progress,' he said. He jigged from one foot to the other. 'Hurry yourself. Greg's opened the drinks cabinet.'

'You mean there's good news – of Peter?'

'No! Philip – ' Constant was about to add something, but changed his mind. 'Let's go. Greg doesn't like to be kept waiting.'

Damn Greg, Philip thought, but he followed Constant to Sorel's office, which was as sparsely efficient as Peter's. However, laid out on the desk were a bottle of whisky, Perrier and three glasses.

'We have reason to celebrate?' Philip couldn't resist the question.

Sorel regarded him coldly. 'Never mind celebrations. First, I must tell you that I owe you an apology. We had an agreement that you would do your best to bring this affair to a satisfactory conclusion, and I would do my best to assist you. I have to admit I've fallen down.'

'Does it matter?'

'I dislike inefficiency in others, and I see no reason to excuse it in myself.'

Pompous ass, thought Philip. He asked, 'Are you saying you should have guessed that Miss Remington might be at the party and you should have warned me she was an old friend of Meriel's? Or that Peter had stayed with the Contessa in Venice?'

'No. I was not aware until today that Anne-Marie Remington had been at school with your sister, or that Monique Scribini – who incidentally is a genuine Italian Contessa – had a palazzo in Venice, or that Peter had visited her there. One can't be omniscient.'

Sorel poured three generous measures of Scotch, added a little Perrier and pushed glasses across the desk to Philip and Constant. He sipped his drink. He didn't seem to want to continue.

Philip became impatient. 'So what on earth was it you should have been aware of, but weren't?'

Sorel said, 'Peter has lost the extreme tip of the little finger of his right hand. I suspect this happened in the accident to which the Contessa referred. You said she seemed to take a particular interest in your hands.'

'I see.' Philip absorbed this information and its implications. 'Then they – they know definitely that I'm not Peter. What will they do?'

'It's impossible to guess,' said Sorel. 'But the point is that things are moving. I must tell you now that someone has been making inquiries about *Philip* Janvrin. Therefore we must assume, as you say, that they know who you are and will try to discover why you're impersonating your brother. However, it works both ways. I believe we now have a definite lead to those responsible for – or at least implicated in – Peter's disappearance, which is what we've been seeking. Though I must admit I don't understand how Sylvia and Tomas fit in with the Manheim lot, if they do. In fact, we still have a fair way to go.'

But I, thought Philip, have served my main purpose. I'm no longer indispensable.

TWELVE

No other course appeared open for Philip, but to continue with his impersonation of Peter – and see what happened. Sorel admitted that the risk to Philip had increased, but maintained that it was not much greater than had originally been envisaged once the cat was set among the pigeons, so to speak, or the trap baited for the mice. He promised to do his utmost to ensure Philip's safety, but Philip had no faith in his words. He knew that he had served Sorel's primary purpose – there was no secret about that – and he guessed that from now on the going would be rough and, if he came to grief, Sorel wouldn't give a damn. But he accepted the situation.

In no circumstances, however, could lunch at the Garrick be called rough. Philip arrived at the club on time. He knew that Peter was not a member, and thus was not surprised when the hall porter asked him to wait until his host came to collect him.

Fauvic greeted him with enthusiasm, and led the way into the big comfortable lounge. 'What will you drink?' he asked at once. There was a dark Scotch on the table at which Fauvic had been sitting. 'The same as me?'

'All I'd like is a glass of white wine, if you don't mind, Robert.'

'Of course I don't mind, my dear chap. But why suddenly so abstemious?'

'My insides are acting up a bit.' It wasn't strictly true, but Philip had realized that, after all those years of abstinence, he couldn't sustain what had emerged as Peter's apparent level of drinking. 'It's that wretched bug I had.'

Fauvic was duly sympathetic. He ordered the wine that Philip had requested, and another Scotch for himself though his current glass was not empty. They talked casually, mostly about politics and, as Fauvic's speech became blurred, Philip suspected that this was his third drink – if not his fourth. The suspicion was confirmed when Fauvic stumbled several times on the elegant staircase that led up to the dining-room. Philip would dearly have liked to know why Robert Fauvic was in such need of Dutch courage. He hoped that the reason might become clear over lunch, but he was disappointed.

By the time they were sipping coffee in the smoking-room, Philip, bored with Fauvic's increasingly intoxicated company, decided to try some leading questions of his own. He said, 'Robert, tell me honestly. Do you trust Bernhardt Manheim?'

'I – I trust him? What on earth do you mean?'

'Well, you work for him, don't you? You must know something about his affairs.'

'Work for him? Why do you say that? I – I do odd jobs for him sometimes, yes. But no more than that. I don't know anything about his business.' Fauvic, suddenly sober, stared hard at Philip. 'Why do you ask?'

'What sort of odd jobs?' Philip pressed him.

'Various things.' Fauvic showed his irritation. 'You shouldn't be so curious, Peter. But I'll tell you one thing. The Manheims don't like being crossed so, if I were you, I'd make sure I kept on the right side of them.'

This unexpected warning startled Philip into silence, as Fauvic pushed aside his half-drunk coffee and consulted his watch. It was obvious that he had no wish to continue a conversation of this kind concerning his relationship with the Manheims. Presumably he had achieved whatever he had hoped to achieve during the luncheon, but Philip still couldn't imagine what his aim had been.

Hastily Philip decided to try one more gambit. As they descended the stairs, with Fauvic clinging tightly to the banister, he said, 'By the way, Robert, I wonder if you can help me. I met an ex-girlfriend the other day. I remembered her perfectly, but I can't for the life of me recall her surname and I want to give her a ring. Her first name's Sylvia.'

'Sylvia? No. Means nothing to me.'

Philip described in detail the Sylvia with whom he was acquainted, but Fauvic continued to shake his head, and he was convincing. For Philip, however, it was but a small victory; he had discovered that Robert Fauvic didn't appear to know the mysterious Sylvia who gave Peter instructions concerning racing. This meant little. Sorel, if told, would probably point out that Fauvic could well be unimportant in the hierarchy of the villains who were being sought. As such, his knowledge could well be limited.

'Too bad,' Philip said. 'Anyhow, thanks for the lunch. I must reciprocate soon.' They were outside the Garrick by now, and he hailed a taxi. 'Can I drop you anywhere, Robert?'

'No thanks. Goodbye, Peter.' Fauvic hurried off, unable to hide his relief at getting away.

As Philip entered the flat he could hear the telephone trilling. He kicked the front door shut behind him and ran to the study. It was Sylvia, from whom he had been expecting a call.

'You're all set to go to Paris for the weekend, Peter?'

'Yes. I go Friday evening and return Sunday.' Philip had fixed it with Sorel, who had organized travel and hotel arrangements. 'It's not exactly an official trip – I'm still on sick leave – but I'll be staying at my usual hotel. Remember?'

'Of course. Fine. You'll be contacted as normal with your instructions.'

As normal, Philip thought; I hope I discover just what that means. But he decided to equal Sylvia's briskness. 'Sure. Anything else?' he said.

'Not at the moment. But follow the orders exactly. You understand, Peter?'

Philip didn't answer. For several minutes, while he talked to Sylvia, he had been staring at a clean, empty space on the desk. Then suddenly he had realized that it shouldn't have been empty. It was where the answerphone normally sat. But the answerphone had been pushed to one side. He could make out the slightly dusty marks around the edges of its original place. Clearly it had been moved, but by whom? It wasn't Mrs Robyn's day for coming to clean.

'Peter! Are you there, Peter?'

'Sorry, Sylvia, I thought I heard my front-door bell,' Philip extemporized quickly. 'But not to worry. I took in what you said. I'll be at Longchamp when necessary, and in the meantime you'll know where to find me.'

He said goodbye to Sylvia with relief, but for a full minute he didn't move. He let his gaze wander around the study. He could see nothing else out of place, and he wondered if perhaps Constant had been in the flat; to his knowledge, apart from Mrs Robyn, only Constant had a key. But why should Constant have visited the place when he knew Philip was lunching with Robert Fauvic?

Reminded of Fauvic and the lunch at the Garrick, he realized that though it had apparently served no purpose it had at least kept him out of the flat for a couple of hours. Philip began a more thorough inspection. At the end of it he was in no doubt that the flat had been searched – professionally searched – in his absence.

There was very little disturbance, but Philip was a tidy man. He knew that he wouldn't have hung up a suit jacket with a flap half in and half out of a pocket. Nor would he have unfolded one of Mrs Robyn's meticulously ironed shirts and attempted to refold it. There were other, small indications too. Philip smiled wryly as he thought that only a librarian, even an amateur one such as he had been, would have noticed that two books had been misplaced on a shelf.

As soon as he had completed his inspection, Philip phoned Constant. 'I've had a visitor while I was out,' he said. 'Nothing stolen. No mess.'

'Really?' Constant drew out the word into its different syllables. 'Interesting. I'll be along for an early tea, Peter, and I'll bring a pal.'

In the event Hamish Constant was there within half an hour. He was accompanied by a small, grizzle-haired man carrying a large briefcase, who looked as if he might have been an overworked porter in a seedy hotel. Constant introduced him as Stan. Stan nodded at Philip, but didn't speak or offer his hand. Instead, he placed his case on a table and opened it. Philip caught a glimpse of some complicated-looking electronic equipment, before Stan glanced meaningfully at Constant.

Constant picked up his cue at once. 'We'll wait in the kitchen, Stan,' he said. Again Stan nodded and Constant, taking Philip by the arm, urged him towards the kitchen where he put on the kettle. Then, 'Tell all,' he ordered.

Philip told him of the seemingly pointless lunch at the Garrick with Robert Fauvic, the phone call from Sylvia – whose name Fauvic had apparently failed to recognize – and his sudden realization that the answerphone had been moved which had led to his certainty that the flat had been searched.

'But why, Hamish? Why? What did they hope to gain?'

'Assuming the lunch was a put-up job to be sure of getting you out of the way, I'd guess the purpose of the search was to find corroborating evidence that you are not Peter Janvrin. The Contessa may not have been a hundred per cent positive about the tip of your little finger.'

'What sort of evidence might they hope for?'

'Maybe some clothes of a size different from Peter's. That wouldn't be proof of your real identity, but would certainly help to substantiate their belief that you aren't Peter. Or if they'd been really lucky and struck gold there might have been some documents – a driving licence or a passport, say – in the name of *Philip* Janvrin. It was worth a try.'

'Well, there wasn't anything of that kind for them to find – thanks to you.'

'Thanks to Greg Sorel. You may not like him, Philip, but he's a master of this kind of thing – tradecraft, as we call it – especially where details are concerned.'

Philip didn't comment. The kettle had boiled and he busied himself making tea. Constant started to speak about Longchamp and the annoying fact that the mysterious Sylvia still remained untraced. They were interrupted by Stan.

'If you'd like to move into the lounge, sir,' he said, 'I'll do the kitchen. The place is as clean as a whistle so far, and I don't expect it to be any different here. I don't think the gentleman has to worry about bugs.'

'Good,' said Constant. 'We didn't expect any, but it's nice to know. What about the phone?'

'It's not been tampered with, but any expert calling would be pretty certain the line was being tapped. It's those damned engineers and their shoddy workmanship.'

Constant grunted. 'Pour yourself a cup of tea,' he said to Stan as he ushered Philip into the sitting-room.

'Can't be helped,' he added, ' – if they know your line's being monitored, I mean. It may make them think, but it doesn't prove anything.'

'So what happens now?' Philip asked after a pause. 'I continue to wait and see?'

'Yes. I'm afraid that's about it.' Constant wriggled in his chair.

'Just – just take as much care as you can. We'll do our best, as Greg promised, but – '

'Hamish, I'm not a fool! Don't treat me like one!' Philip drew a deep breath and controlled his temper. 'Your best isn't all that good. If someone can come in and search this flat without you knowing, your watcher can't be up to his job. The phone could easily have been booby-trapped or a bomb planted. In which case, I wouldn't be sitting here now talking to you. And you might not be here either – remember that.'

'I know. I realize it. However, as I said before, we don't have unlimited staff and resources. The minder chose to watch you, not the flat.'

'So he guessed wrong? Too bad?'

'Yes. We can't give you complete protection. You must know that. We did warn you, Philip.'

'You did.' Philip sighed. 'I've no reason to complain, I suppose. But it's not easy being a kind of decoy duck.'

He sat back in his chair, contemplating. Then he said, 'Hamish, what do you really think will happen next? What should happen next – in theory? If you've arrived at any theories.'

'If our opponents sit tight and do nothing there could be a stalemate.' Constant spoke slowly, as if considering the situation. 'But we hope their curiosity will be too strong for them, and they'll try some action – maybe next weekend in Paris. It would most probably be directed at you in person.'

'And if they don't?'

'Greg will try to force their hand and make them act.'

'How will he do that?'

'I've no idea. He doesn't share all his contingency plans with me.'

'But either way I'm likely to be wasted?'

Constant hesitated. Then he said flatly, 'Yes.' He gave a sudden grin. 'But it's not inevitable, you know.'

Once Stan had completed his work at the flat Constant showed no inclination to linger, and the evening stretched before Philip. Constant had urged him to go out to dinner or to a club, not sit at home and brood. Peter, Philip guessed, would have phoned a girlfriend and taken her to a disco or a theatre or a concert and thence, in all likelihood, to bed. But he had no inclination for any such activity. He didn't want company.

On the other hand, he was restless. He would have chosen to go for a long walk over Hampstead Heath or – closer to the flat – in Kensington Gardens or Hyde Park, but he was put off – not by fear for his own safety as much as by the fact that he would be followed and watched. Shadows would intrude on his thoughts.

It was simpler to stay where he was, have a drink, make himself a light meal and read up everything he could about Longchamp, which was a racecourse very different from Sandown Park. At least he wouldn't have to deal with Blinkers or his equivalent, since there were no bookmakers in France, and all betting was done on the Pari-Mutuel system – the equivalent of the English Tote. Of course Blinkers himself could be there in a private capacity, and so might Foxy Pringle and Mary O'Donovan – and possibly even Box of Chox. Philip smiled wryly. He had little hope that the weekend would bring nearer the objective he shared with Sorel and Constant – finding Peter, or at least discovering what had happened to him. As to the future . . .

The persistent trill of the telephone roused him, and conscious that, deep in thought, he had failed to notice it at once, he hurried to the study. He gave his number.

'Peter! Peter! Thank God I've got you! I've been trying for ten days, but your office was as cagey as usual. All they'd say was that you were abroad. Even your boss, Greg Sorel, wouldn't be more specific.'

And when he didn't answer at once. 'Peter! This is you, isn't it? It's Zara.'

Philip swallowed hard. He hadn't needed to be told who she was; he had recognized her low, rather husky voice immediately though it was a long time since he had heard it.

'Yes, it's me, Zara. What is it?' He spoke sharply, more sharply than he had intended, but he had been thrown off balance by her sudden call. It had never occurred to him that she might phone 'Peter', though he realized he should have known it was a possibility. 'What do you want?'

'I'm sorry to bother you, dear husband.' There was ice in Zara's voice now. 'Obviously I've called at an inconvenient time but, like it or not, you still have a family. And Patrick's been injured, seriously injured. He had a bad accident on his bike. It's his head and his back, and for a time we thought he wouldn't – ' She choked. 'Anyway, he improved and they've let me bring him home. Now he's quite a lot better and he's started to ask for you. Peter – Peter, you must come. I've never asked anything for myself, God knows, but – ' Her voice broke. 'Please come!'

'I can't.'

'Why the hell not?' Zara was suddenly and justifiably furious. 'Don't tell me it's your precious work. You always used to make that an excuse. I'm not a fool, Peter. I know you've got a – a demanding job, but so have other men. Sorel for one. But he doesn't neglect his family.'

'Damn Sorel!' Philip said through his teeth.

It was a meaningless remark. He was damning not Sorel, but the situation. He could not go home. Zara would know at once that he wasn't Peter, his father would turn him out of the house, and his humiliation would be no help to Patrick. Besides, Zara would demand an explanation, and how could he explain? Perhaps, he thought bitterly, he could refer her to Sorel, of whom she had such a high opinion.

'Peter, are you listening? I'll say it again. Patrick – is – ill – and he needs you.'

'Yes, I'm listening. I understand. I'm sorry about Patrick, Zara, but I cannot come to see him. I'm going abroad tomorrow. Goodbye.'

Philip put down his receiver. He couldn't endure any more useless argument. As he did so he heard, or imagined he heard, Zara say that she didn't believe him. He wasn't sure. He sat, staring at the telephone, waiting for her to call back. But the instrument remained silent.

THIRTEEN

Friday, the day that Philip was due to go to Paris, arrived without further incident. As he was to be away for the weekend he had no shopping to do, so he took a bus to the West End, spent the morning in the National Gallery and had lunch in a pub. He made no attempt to spot his tails.

It was three when he returned. He met Baker, the porter, in the hall, and told him he was leaving for Paris on an evening flight but would be back on Monday at the latest. He went up in the lift, let himself into the flat and was shutting the front door behind him when he heard a slight noise that seemed to come from the bathroom. He froze.

Mrs Robyn should have been long gone, her duties completed. The bathroom was a strange place for an ordinary sneak thief. There was only one conclusion, and it was not pleasant. Fleetingly Philip wondered if he should let himself out of the flat, and leave as quickly as he had come. He could phone Constant and appeal for help. His bag was packed and there was plenty of time before he needed to set off for Heathrow.

Then, as these thoughts crossed his mind, Philip heard the sound of the lavatory being flushed and water running as if someone was washing his hands. Philip sighed with relief. Of course, it was Constant; only Hamish would make himself at home to this extent. And he reproached himself for his moment of near panic.

But it was not Hamish Constant. The bathroom door opened and a young woman emerged. Philip, who had been starting to move down the hall, came to a sudden halt. He had recognized her instantly, the tall narrow-shouldered figure, the long face, straight corn-coloured hair and grey eyes that so often looked as if they were viewing a faraway scene. This was Zara. He had known her all his life and always thought her beautiful, though her beauty was not orthodox.

'Peter!'

The hall was shadowed, and Zara had been expecting her husband. Philip stood still and let her approach him. He was sure that she would recognize him and, in this at least, his judgement was accurate. Zara stopped within a yard of him. Her eyes widened and her mouth fell open.

'Philip? Philip! What are you doing here?'

'I'm staying here.'

'With Peter? Or isn't he here? Was it you who spoke to me on the phone last Tuesday?'

'Yes. It was me, Zara.'

Philip knew that in highly charged situations conversation was usually ordinary to the point of banality. Nevertheless, meeting Zara like this after so many years – Zara, with whom he had once been briefly but desperately in love – struck him for a moment as being on the edge of farce. Then, as he saw the lines on her face and the streak of grey in her hair he realized that the only emotion he felt for her now was affectionate pity.

'Philip, what's happening? I don't understand.'

Philip managed to smile. 'My dear Zara, I'm not surprised. I don't entirely understand either. It's a complicated business. Let's go into the sitting-room and I'll try to explain.'

It was a bright sunny day, and in the clear light he could see blue circles under her eyes. She looked tired and drawn and he remembered that Robert Fauvic had said she was having a hard time. He wished it hadn't been he who now had the task of breaking to her the news of Peter's disappearance, but whatever Sorel might expect, he was not going to lie to Zara.

To put off the moment, he said, 'How's Patrick?' He waved her to a chair and sat down opposite.

'He doesn't seem to improve. That's why I'm here. I thought if I could talk to you – to Peter, I mean – I could persuade him to come home for a day or two. Patrick keeps on asking for him, as I said. And the doctors say his presence could make all the difference – the difference between Patrick being apathetic and wanting to get well.'

'I'm sorry.'

'Oh God! Philip, there are so many questions I want to ask, and you said you'd explain – but first, where is Peter?'

109

'I don't know, Zara. Nor does his office. Peter went abroad on some assignment. He had completed it and was on his way to the airport when he disappeared. That was a couple of months ago. His office is – is afraid for him.'

Zara wet dry lips. 'And you? How do you come into it, Philip? I – I thought you were still in prison.'

'So I should be, but . . . '

He gave her the bare bones of the story, and she listened intently, Patrick forgotten for the moment. At last she said, 'Poor Peter! I'm not altogether surprised, Philip. I've always known that the outfit Peter worked for was – was unconventional, to use an ambiguous word. Of course he told me a lot of lies to cover his official activities – not to speak of his personal ones.' She added the last few words with some bitterness. 'But I knew his work was important and not without danger. It was what suited him. You can't imagine Peter in a dull job, can you?'

'No, I can't,' Philip agreed.

'He may not have been the most faithful of husbands, but . . . '

'Zara, don't speak of him in the past tense. Peter's people aren't exactly communicative, as you know, but as far as I can gather there's a good hope that Peter is still alive. That's why I have to go on impersonating him – so as to get some lead on where he might be.'

'It could be dangerous for you.'

Philip shrugged. 'To be candid, I tried to avoid undertaking it, partly because I thought it wouldn't work, but – '

'And is it working, as you call it?' Zara interrupted.

Philip hesitated. 'That's something I can't discuss in detail, Zara. But yes, things are happening. Anyway, I discovered after a few weeks of liberty that life for a penniless ex-con isn't easy. My only alternatives were accepting the authorities' offer to help find Peter, or face a cardboard box on the Embankment.'

'You could have come to me. I'd have helped, Philip. Peter would have wanted me to help. You know that. He was terribly upset when – when you were convicted and given such a long sentence. He'd have done anything he could, but you refused to appeal, and then you didn't want to know us any more.'

'Zara, that's all past and done with.' Philip didn't want to talk about it. 'I've made my choice and, whatever happens, I don't have to go back to prison. So I'm grateful. Peter doesn't owe me a thing.'

'Okay.'

Zara didn't argue. She suppressed a yawn. She was tired; she had had very little sleep since Patrick's accident and, after driving up to London today, determined to force Peter to come home with her, she had been shocked to find not her husband, but Philip. For a moment she shut her eyes.

'Zara, are you all right?' Philip was anxious.

'Yes. Sorry, Philip.' Zara managed a smile. 'I suppose I couldn't have a cup of tea and a piece of toast, could I? I missed out on lunch.'

'Of course you can. Stay there and I'll get it.'

Before she could dissent Philip was on his feet and making for the kitchen. He was thankful for a few minutes to himself. He put the kettle on and bread in the toaster and prepared a tea tray. Time was passing. Soon he would have to catch a taxi for Heathrow. He hadn't yet told Zara that he was off to Paris.

She was standing by the window when he returned to the sitting-room with the tea, and before he could speak she said, 'Philip, I've been thinking. I've a favour to ask of you, a big favour, but it's not for me. It's for Patrick.'

'I'll do what I can, Zara.'

'I know you will. You were always kind, even as a child, much kinder than Peter was. Oh God, Philip, I don't understand. I've never understood that heroin business. Why, Philip? Why? Were you tricked somehow?'

'Forget it, Zara! It was a long time ago, and I've paid my debt to society, as they say.' Philip was impatient. 'What is it you want me to do for Patrick?'

'I want you to come home with me now, today, to go on pretending you're Peter, to deceive Patrick into believing that the Dad he keeps on asking for is at last there by his bedside.'

Philip stared at her in amazement. He could scarcely believe he had heard aright. It was a preposterous suggestion. Even had he been willing to do as she asked, circumstances made it impossible, and in any case he was not willing.

'Zara, you're crazy.'

'No, I'm not. You must have already deceived a lot of people, so why not Patrick? He doesn't know Peter terribly well. We can say you've been ill, which is why you didn't come earlier. It's a good excuse if he should question you. But I'm sure he won't. He's still under some sedation, and you're so like Peter in appearance. He'll accept you, all right.'

'Aren't you forgetting something, Zara?' Philip asked coldly. 'Or rather someone? My father! Patrick might not recognize me, but Father most certainly would – as you did yourself – and he'd kick me out of what may be Peter's home but is no longer mine.'

'You don't know?' Zara's voice was tight.

'Know what?'

'Father is – is almost blind. His sight has been deteriorating for ages. I can't tell you the medical details, but he's consulted all the experts and there's nothing to be done.'

Automatically Philip poured her a second cup of tea. As he passed it to her he saw that a toast crumb was sticking to the side of her mouth. For a moment that crumb took him back to his childhood, his gentle mother, his autocratic father, and the Beaumonts, Zara's parents, their nearest neighbours in the country, who were rarely at home, but left their daughter in the care of a succession of nannies and the family next door.

Somehow he couldn't imagine his father going blind, getting increasingly dependent on Zara. Nor could he imagine his father welcoming back the prodigal son, the ex-convict, the drug-pusher, however much Patrick might be in need of a pseudo-dad.

'I'm sorry,' Philip said formally. 'With Peter – away – it must make life difficult for you.'

'I try to face up to one crisis at a time. My present priority is Patrick. I can't help Father or Peter at the moment, but Patrick I can. I must. Philip, *you* must. Please.'

'Zara, I can't. Even if Father couldn't see me properly I'm sure he'd sense I wasn't Peter. Anyway, it's vital that I catch a flight to Paris in a couple of hours. I should be leaving here right now or very shortly.'

'You sound just like Peter,' Zara said, with contempt in her voice. 'Perhaps there's not much to choose between you.'

'I'm sorry,' Philip repeated. 'But I'm not going to Paris for fun.' He started to collect the tea things on to the tray. 'Zara, I'm going as part of the job – in the hope of getting a lead on Peter.'

'My son's more important to me, more important than anyone.'

Philip nodded his understanding. Poor Zara, he thought. He looked at her pityingly. He reflected once again that there was a time when he had been desperately in love with her, but that had been long ago and it hadn't lasted. He picked up the tray.

'So you won't come, then?'

'No, Zara. There's no point. It wouldn't work.'

'It might. It's worth trying. It could make all the difference to Patrick's recovery.' Her voice broke. 'Philip, won't you change your mind?'

Philip smiled sympathetically, but didn't answer and, as he left the sitting-room for the kitchen, he saw Zara bury her face in her hands. He washed up the tea things, conscious of the loud tick of the clock on the window-sill. In twenty minutes he would have to leave if he was to have a hope of catching his flight. But first he must speed Zara on her way. He only hoped she wouldn't burst into tears.

Zara showed no inclination to cry. She was sitting up very straight, her eyes bright with determination rather than tears and, as Philip came into the room, she took the initiative.

'Philip, I'm going to tell you something that I've never told anyone,' she said before he had a chance to speak. 'First, I want you to swear you will never – never repeat it.'

'Zara, please don't be so dramatic.'

'And don't be so bloody flippant!'

Philip curbed the angry reply he had been tempted to make. He had known that Zara was worried about Patrick, but he hadn't realized until then how close she was to the brink of losing control. The last thing he wanted at that moment was a scene, a pointless row.

'I'm sorry,' he said. 'And I promise. Whatever the confidence is, I'll respect it.'

'All right.'

Nevertheless, it seemed that Zara found it difficult to begin. Philip was tempted to look at his watch.

At last Zara said, 'Philip, years ago you were in love with me, but I was in love with Peter. Heaven knows who Peter was in love with. Himself, I suspect, but he had lots of girlfriends and I was jealous. I think that's why I let you make love to me that night after my twenty-first party. Remember?'

'I remember, yes.' He remembered too that he had regretted it almost immediately. 'What are you trying to tell me, Zara?'

'Patrick is your son, Philip. Not Peter's.'

'Are you sure?' He knew it was a stupid question, but he couldn't help asking it. They had both been a little drunk or –

'Of course I'm sure. Dear God, do you think I wanted him to be yours? If I had to be stupid enough to get pregnant I'd have wanted it to be by Peter. Though I'd always been very fond of you, Philip, you know perfectly well I never had any desire to marry you. So I tricked Peter. I'm not particularly proud of the fact.'

'But the timing?'

'You and Peter went off to the Continent soon after the party. By the time you came back some weeks later I suspected what had happened, so I threw myself at Peter and then insisted on a rapid wedding. It wasn't hard.'

Philip nodded. He had been under no illusion as to where Zara's affections lay. She had made no secret of them, and he had recognized his own feelings for what they were – an infatuation. He had had plans for the future which hadn't included her and, but for that fateful day at Heathrow, he would have hoped by now to be well on his way to fulfilling them.

'Why have you told me this?' he asked, his voice strained. 'What's the point, when you made me promise never to mention it to a soul?'

'Because you've got to choose between your brother who is most likely dead, and your son whom you can help to a full recovery. It's as simple as that, Philip,' Zara said flatly.

To Philip it was not in the least simple. His love of Peter was deep and long-standing. He had never set eyes on Patrick. What was more, there was the undertaking he had made to Sorel. There were the reactions of Sylvia and Tomas if he didn't turn up at Longchamp. There was his – his fear of going 'home' and meeting his father.

'All right. I'll come with you,' he said finally, and thought that Peter, in his place, would have made the same choice.

FOURTEEN

'Disappeared! Hamish, it's beyond belief. Are you telling me that Philip Janvrin has disappeared – just like his brother?'

'I'm afraid so. More or less like Peter, yes, Greg,' Constant replied miserably.

Sorel swore. Constant didn't blame him. Either losing Philip had been the result of astounding negligence on the part of the minder – or the opposition had been very clever. It had not occurred to Constant that Philip himself might be responsible.

'All right.' Sorel bit off the words. 'Tell me. What happened?'

'Well, it seems that Philip left the flat in reasonable time to catch his plane. He walked to the taxi-rank, which is only about a hundred yards away, and took the first cab. It drove straight to Heathrow, followed by our car. There was a lot of traffic but our man claims he didn't lose sight of the taxi for more than a couple of minutes. However, his view was obscured by other cars and he didn't actually see Philip get out of the taxi at Terminal 4 and go into the airport building.'

'We've got the number of the cab?'

'Yes, and a call's been put out for the driver. He's gone off duty and he's not been located yet, but at least we know that Philip didn't check in for his flight. We've made all the usual inquiries. He wasn't seen at the concourse desk, and he didn't check in at the Executive Lounge.'

'Which suggests he never got as far as Heathrow. It certainly is reminiscent of Peter in Amsterdam.' Sorel shook his head in exasperation. 'Anything else?'

'It may not be relevant, but Philip had a visitor earlier this afternoon – Zara Janvrin, Peter's wife. She was with him quite some while, but she left before he did.'

'Now that just could matter. I wonder – ' Sorel was interested. 'Assuming she was going straight home, she'd be there by now. Get her on the phone, Hamish.'

And five minutes later Sorel was speaking to Zara. He didn't hurry her, and they exchanged pleasantries. She volunteered that she had just driven down from London.

'Did Peter come with you?' Sorel asked.

'Why, no.' Zara, thinking rapidly, sounded surprised.

'But you saw him today?'

'Yes. I went to his flat. How did you know that, Greg?'

Sorel didn't answer her question. 'So Peter's not with you?' he said.

'No. I told you.' She paused and went on, 'Greg, what's this about? I went to see Peter because I wanted him to come home for the weekend. Patrick's had a serious accident and a visit from his father would be a great boost to his morale. But Peter said he had to go to Paris. Surely you know that's where he's gone?'

'I thought he might have changed his mind, and decided not to go till tomorrow,' Sorel lied fluently. 'I'll tell you why, Zara. We sent a man to Heathrow with an urgent message for Peter, but the chap failed to contact him.'

He paused in turn, and then added, in an attempt to appear to dismiss the problem, 'Can't be helped! It wasn't that important. But, my dear, what's this about Patrick having a bad accident? I'm awfully sorry.'

Sorel's sympathy was genuine, and Zara responded. Her mind on her son, she was taken aback when he suddenly asked if she had noticed much change in Peter.

'No – yes.' She hesitated and contradicted herself, thinking quickly. 'I'd not seen him for ages and he's been ill. But you must know that. He seems all right now.' She paused, then, 'Greg, I'm sorry. I can hear the General coming downstairs after his rest. I must go. Goodbye.'

Sorel put down the receiver and paused thoughtfully, without speaking.

Constant couldn't contain his curiosity. 'Well, is Philip there?' he demanded.

'I wouldn't swear either way,' Sorel said slowly.

His secretary came in. The taxi-driver had been located and the man had told a simple story. He had been first on the rank and had been glad to accept a fare to Heathrow. He had dropped his passenger at Terminal 4. He had received a good but not extraordinary tip. It was the only trip to the airport he had made that day, so he remembered it, and had been able to give an adequate description of Philip. He wasn't sure if Philip had gone into the terminal, but thought he had.

'I suppose we'll have to interview the chap,' Sorel said, 'though it doesn't sound exactly promising. Otherwise we'll wait. We can't afford a great hue and cry. Publicity's the last thing we need. It's possible that Philip will surface of his own accord. If he hasn't by tomorrow morning, I think I'll pay Mrs Zara Janvrin a surprise visit in the afternoon. Then we can eliminate that possibility. And maybe the Brig will have a bright idea. It's a hell of a pity he's away this weekend.'

'What about Longchamp?'

Sorel shrugged. 'We'll let the arrangements there stand. Mary O'Donovan can enjoy the races. But unless they're responsible for Philip's absence, presumably Sylvia and her friend Tomas will not be pleased, and they might react. So it would be worth while to keep an extra watch on the flat in case they send some nasties around there. Otherwise, I'm afraid there's not much we can do, Hamish, except wait and see.'

'I suppose not,' said Constant, and nearly added that they seemed to spend a lot of time doing just that. He was genuinely worried for Philip.

Philip had not gone to the airport. Together, he and Zara had had to think quickly and, although the plan they had devised was far from foolproof, it had been the best they could do in the time available. A lot had depended on the willingness of a taxi-driver to co-operate.

In the event, and encouraged by an outrageous bribe, the driver had declared himself willing to do whatever Philip wanted. He had dropped him off in a traffic jam before leaving central London, and Philip had joined Zara in a side street near Hammersmith Broadway. Why such subterfuge was necessary hadn't been altogether clear to her, but Philip had said that if Sorel were told in advance of what was intended he would raise innumerable objections, and might even maintain that the Paris visit was essential.

It was a half-truth. Even if Sorel had agreed, Philip was sure he would have insisted on the minders continuing to follow him, and the followers would have been followed. Philip had no desire to lead such characters, none of whom would be welcome and some of whom might be violent, to his father's house. Nor did he want to involve Zara with them, and thus add to her burden of worry. If his actions annoyed Sorel, he didn't give a damn. And by the time he and Zara had reached their destination he was no longer thinking of Sorel and Constant.

Wytham Court was not a great house. Indeed, for its size its name was pretentious, but it had five acres of land – now mostly rented to neighbouring farmers – stabling and a tennis court; the General had vetoed a swimming-pool. For Philip, whose great-grandfather had bought it in the last century, it was home – the only home he had ever known, full of nostalgic memories. It was the place to which he had returned from boarding school, the place to which he had brought friends from school and from Oxford, the place where he had spent so many happy days, most of them shared with Peter and Zara.

But it was over eight years since he had last been here, and even now his presence was under false pretences. Although it was a warm summer's evening, as he came into the hall the house seemed cold and unwelcoming. The phone was ringing.

'Go on up,' said Zara. 'You'll be in the old blue room. You can put your bag in there. Patrick's in the nursery with his nanny. She won't know you. You'll have to announce who you are. I'll break it to Father that *Peter's* arrived, and I'll join you as soon as I can.'

Philip nodded. His feelings were too chaotic to allow him to speak. He went up the broad shallow stairs, and put his bag in the room that Zara had indicated. It was presumably where Peter now slept on the few occasions he visited the house, and it was pleasant but impersonal, with an adjoining bathroom. There were towels and a new piece of soap by the washhand basin, but no toiletries in the mirror-fronted cabinet. Philip used the lavatory, washed his hands and splashed cold water over his face. He could no longer postpone his visit to Patrick.

He met a young woman in a Norland nurse's uniform on the landing outside the nursery and introduced himself. She greeted him with enthusiasm, her plain face lighting up with pleasure.

'Oh, I'm so glad you've come, Mr Janvrin. Patrick keeps on asking for you and it'll cheer him up no end to see you. It's miserable for him having to rest in bed for so long, and in such lovely weather.'

Philip pulled himself together and smiled at her. 'Small boys shouldn't have accidents with bicycles,' he said.

'No, indeed.' She opened the nursery door. 'Patrick, look who's come to see you.'

'Who?' The slight figure lying on his back in the middle of the bed couldn't have sounded more bored. Then he saw Philip standing in the doorway. He struggled to sit up, his eyes suddenly bright, and held out his arms, 'Dad! Dad!'

Philip didn't hesitate. 'Hello, Patrick,' he said and, going forward, hugged the child tightly.

As Philip released him Patrick sniffed loudly. 'You've got your nice smell on, Dad. What did you say it was called? Guer – something?'

'My aftershave lotion? It's called Guerlain.' Philip blessed Sorel's devotion to detail. 'I'll bring you some as soon as you start shaving.'

From then on it was simple. Patrick did most of the talking and Philip only had to interject the odd comment. It gave him a chance to study the boy. Dark-haired and blue-eyed, there was no doubt that Patrick was a Janvrin, and Philip, glad that he had yielded to Zara's persuasion, warmed to him.

Zara found them laughing together. And as she and Philip started downstairs, leaving Patrick to his supper, she said, 'It's so wonderful to see him like that, happy again and animated. I don't like deceiving him, but I'm sure it was the right thing to do. Philip, I'm grateful to you.'

'Nonsense! Incidentally, don't you think you'd better start calling me "Peter" in the house, just in case someone over-hears?'

'Of course! Listen – Peter. I hope there won't be any unpleasant repercussions for you. That was Sorel on the phone when we arrived.'

She told him briefly of the conversation, but he had no time to think about the call. They were interrupted by a voice that he instantly recognized as his father's, calling from the hall below.

'Is that you, Peter? What are you two whispering about? Come along and have a drink.'

Philip steeled himself but, though the old man peered at him, he showed no sign of suspicion. He asked what 'Peter' had been doing and, while Zara poured drinks, Philip repeated his story of catching a mysterious bug and being hospitalized.

'Surely you could have let us know,' General Janvrin reproached him. 'I'm used to you neglecting us, Peter, and so is your wife, but it's a different matter when it comes to neglecting your son. A child doesn't understand the pressures adults suffer from. I appreciate your work takes you abroad a lot, but – '

'Father, please!' Zara protested.

To Philip's surprise his father didn't protest further. He merely said, 'All right, my dear. All right. But I want a word with you after supper, Peter.'

'Yes, Father,' Philip said, and wondered how many times in his life he had uttered those words.

The evening passed without incident. The meal was simple but well cooked and served; the Janvrins had a working housekeeper who, with Zara and some part-time help in house and garden, managed to run Wytham Court in a manner approximating to that which Philip remembered. He went upstairs to say good-night to Patrick, and returned to find his father alone.

'You pour us a couple of brandies, Peter,' George Janvrin said, 'and then we'll have a talk while Zara's busy with her various arrangements for tomorrow. It's time to be frank. I may not have too many years ahead of me and I'd like – '

'What is it you want, Father?'

Philip had not intended to speak so abruptly, but he need not have worried. George Janvrin's eyes might be failing, but there was nothing wrong with his mind. The retort came stinging back.

'To make you see your duty – a duty you seem unable to discern for yourself.'

Philip was embarrassed. It was not his duty that was under discussion, but Peter's. He was not responsible for it, nor did he wish to hear it being dissected. But short of saying good-night and walking out of the room, he had no choice.

'Very well, Father,' he said. 'Go ahead. I'm listening.'

'First, as I said before supper when Zara shut me up, there's the fact that you neglect your family. You don't care a damn about your wife or your son, and you're in danger of losing them unless you make an effort.'

'Losing them?'

'Zara has what in my day would have been called an admirer. He's a nice young man, a lawyer, and he's admitted to me that he'd like to marry her.'

'But he can't marry her. She's married to Pe – ' Philip stopped just in time, then hurried on. 'If you're thinking of a divorce, Father, it's out of the question. You must know that. We're both Catholics. Zara would never want it, and I – I'd never agree. What about Patrick?'

'What about Patrick indeed! You're concerned for him now, when it suits you – and for Zara. But mostly you don't care, Peter. You're a – a selfish bastard. God knows the last thing I want is for your marriage to break up, but I warn you. Zara's still young and she's attractive, and so is Malcolm Derwent. What's more, he's considerate and he's around. If you treat your wife like a piece of furniture, Peter, don't blame her if she looks elsewhere.'

There was silence. The old man had said all that he intended to say on the subject. Philip had no comment to make. Instinctively, though he knew that most of the accusations were probably justified, he felt that he ought to defend Peter, but –

'The second matter also unfortunately concerns our family,' his father continued. 'It's about your brother Philip.'

'Philip!'

'Yes. One of those charities that takes care of ex-prisoners telephoned me. They had heard that Philip had been released early on some compassionate grounds, and they wanted to know if he was here. I couldn't understand why they were interested.'

'What did you say, Father?'

'I denied it, of course, and all knowledge of him. I said he'd have enough sense not to come where he would be unwelcome. But I wanted to warn you, Peter. He might turn up at your flat. Give him some money if you want, but send him on his way.'

Luckily at that moment Zara returned to the sitting-room,

122

preventing what could have been a bitter outburst from Philip. He got to his feet as she came in.

'I'll take *both* your warnings into consideration, sir,' he said. 'And now I'm going to bed. Good-night to you.' He nodded to Zara. He had decided that in the morning, as soon as was decently possible, he would leave the house, and never set foot in it again.

FIFTEEN

In spite of Philip's determination to leave Wytham Court as soon as was feasible the next morning, it was after eleven before he was able even to broach the subject. He had breakfasted alone, packed his bag in readiness for departure and gone straight up to the nursery with the intention of saying goodbye to Patrick. Instead, with the nanny's permission, he had helped the boy, who wanted to get up, to bathe and dress. Then he had been coerced into playing board games with him until the doctor arrived, when he had gone down to the sitting-room to inquire about the times of trains to London.

There he had found Zara and a man whom he had not previously met. Zara introduced the stranger as Malcolm Derwent and the two men, each wary of the other, shook hands formally. Derwent was in his early thirties, fair and boyish-looking, and Philip could appreciate that women would find him attractive. He and Zara had been laughing together as Philip came into the room, and it was immediately apparent that they enjoyed each other's company.

Philip felt in the way. He had to remind himself that he was supposedly Zara's husband, and was in his own home. He had to behave as Peter would have behaved.

'It's a bit early to offer you a drink,' he said to Derwent, 'but what about coffee?' He turned to his 'wife' authoritatively, 'Zara?'

'Yes, of course.' She stood up.

'And could you possibly find a railway timetable for me? I must get back to London. Or do you know the trains? Perhaps I should phone the station?'

'But surely you're not going today?' She was upset and indignant. 'I assumed you'd stay over at least till Sunday evening. Patrick will be so disappointed if you don't.'

'I'm sorry, Zara, but as you know I shouldn't be here at all. I'm going to have some explaining to do as it is, and the sooner I do it the better.'

'Does an extra day actually make a difference? It's too late for you to get to Paris now anyway.'

If they had been alone Philip would have argued. But in Derwent's presence he knew he was unable to debate the matter with any candour, or refer to the talk with his father the night before. He shrugged. He would have to wait. Without committing himself, he abruptly changed the subject.

'What about that coffee, Zara?'

Zara went, leaving Philip with Malcolm Derwent, who emerged from behind the magazine where he had been tactfully sheltering. Philip hoped that he would leave before too long. No one had mentioned that Derwent had been invited to lunch.

'Do I gather you should be in Paris, Peter?' Derwent said. 'I suppose you go there often – and other places too. You must lead an interesting life.'

'You'd be surprised.' Philip couldn't resist the sarcasm, which however seemed entirely lost on Derwent.

'It can't allow you much time for your family. Hard on Zara, especially with your father's failing eyesight.'

'Yes!' Philip said shortly. He had no intention of discussing his brother's affairs with an outsider, especially one who was apparently eager to take Peter's place. 'But one can't always have everything one wants,' he added pointedly.

Derwent opened his mouth to reply, but made no comment, and Philip let the silence grow until his father came in, closely followed by Zara with the coffee and the doctor. The conversation immediately centred around Patrick. The doctor was pleased with his patient and gave Philip the credit.

'That's great,' Philip said, and added, 'After all, that was the purpose of my visit.'

But at once he was ashamed of himself. It was a true and justified remark, but only Zara could be aware of that. To the others it must have sounded unkind and uncalled for, and it would be remembered against *Peter*, which was unjust. He would really have to watch his tongue more carefully.

To make amends Philip walked around the garden with his father and Malcolm Derwent before lunch, and during the meal played his part – or rather Peter's part – by serving the wine and helping Zara. She seemed to assume that she had won her point and he would be staying until the next day, and he didn't disabuse her. Nevertheless, he still hoped to leave during the afternoon.

But the meal, which had begun late, was protracted, and Philip was growing impatient by the time his father, who had lingered over his coffee, was about to rise. Then the housekeeper came into the dining-room.

'There's a gentleman to see you, Mr Janvrin,' she said to Philip. 'I've put him in the sitting-room.'

It was with a feeling of relief that Philip recognized the slight figure, who had been standing by the window and looking out at the lawn. It was Gregory Sorel. He had feared his visitor might be one of Tomas's henchmen, a man of violence, prepared to use force. But relief was quickly replaced by irritation at the nature of the intrusion.

'Hello, Zara. General Janvrin.' Sorel said, as the others followed Philip into the room. He came forward, hand out-stretched. 'You won't remember me, General, but we've met in London. I'm a colleague of Peter's – Gregory Sorel.' He nodded a greeting to Philip.

'Malcolm Derwent.' Derwent introduced himself as Sorel glanced inquiringly in his direction, and the two men shook hands.

'Come and sit down and tell us what we can do for you.' The General gestured to a chair. 'I don't imagine for a moment that this is a social call.'

'Unfortunately not, sir. There's something of a flap on at the office – I'm afraid I can't go into details – and they want us all back. So, as I was lunching in the neighbourhood, I said I'd pick up Peter.' He gave Zara a bland smile. 'I'm sorry to spoil your weekend.'

'But duty calls,' Derwent remarked.

'Quite!' said Sorel.

For some inexplicable reason Philip felt sorry for Derwent. He hastened to intervene. 'I'll go up and pack my bag,' he said, 'and say goodbye to Patrick.'

No one objected, and he hurried from the room. He hadn't unpacked his bag since the morning, which meant that he could allow an extra five minutes with Patrick. He rather dreaded telling

126

the boy that he was leaving, but somehow the explanation he was able to offer as a result of Sorel's sudden visit made the situation simpler, and Patrick took the news philosophically. It was Philip who wondered sadly if they would ever meet again.

He found Zara and Derwent waiting in the hall with Sorel, and went into the sitting-room to bid farewell – for the last time, he told himself – to his father, who immediately took the opportunity to remind him of their conversation. 'Now you've seen Derwent, you'll appreciate what I mean,' he said. 'Be sensible, Peter.'

His goodbyes to the others were quickly over, though Zara urged him to return as soon as he could. He didn't look back as Sorel drove down the drive. He didn't expect to pay another visit to Wytham Court.

'Don't ever play a trick like that on me again, Philip,' Sorel said venomously as soon as they were alone. 'Or I swear you'll regret it.' He gave an angry hoot at the car ahead of him and obediently it let him pass. 'Explain yourself!'

Philip didn't reply directly. 'How did you know where to find me?' he asked.

'It wasn't hard. You're only a damned amateur, after all. Inquiries at Heathrow – which took up the time and effort of people who could otherwise have been better employed – produced no result. This morning we hauled in the taxi-driver you bribed, and I put the fear of God into him. Once I knew you were responsible for your disappearance, the rest was simple guesswork – in spite of Zara's lies on the phone.'

'Patrick had an accident. He's getting better physically, but he wouldn't make any mental effort and he kept on asking for his father. Zara had recognized me at once and – '

'And she persuaded you to play Daddy,' concluded Sorel sarcastically.

'Yes.' Philip was damned if he would show any remorse. 'What's more, my visit worked. The doctor was delighted with the change in the child. So my impersonation of Peter has produced at least some good.'

Sorel snorted, but seemed to have become reconciled to the situation. In any case he next spoke less intemperately. 'It might

127

have produced more if you'd gone to Longchamp,' he said. 'This wretched woman Sylvia's phoned you several times and her messages are becoming more and more irascible. There were a couple of other callers, but they left no messages.'

'Which reminds me,' Philip said. He explained about the telephone call that his father had received, supposedly from a charity concerned with the welfare of ex-convicts. 'I suppose it could have been genuine, but – '

'Unlikely,' Sorel agreed. Abruptly he changed the subject. 'Who's this man Malcolm Derwent?'

'A - a friend of Zara's.'

'A *close* friend of Zara's from the way he behaves.' Sorel shook his head in disgust. 'Poor old Peter! He seems to have lost his son to you and his wife to this chap.'

Philip made no attempt to contradict him. By now they were on the outskirts of London, traffic was heavy, and Sorel had to concentrate on his driving. Philip, thankful for an end to Sorel's biting comments, tried to relax.

He was lost in memories of Zara's twenty-first birthday party, of the night that Patrick had been conceived, of a happy and carefree Peter. Suddenly he realized that the car had stopped, though they had not arrived at the flat.

'This is lucky,' Sorel said.

A few yards ahead of them a small van had drawn out of a parking space. Expertly Sorel manoeuvred into it. The two men got out, and Sorel fed the meter. Then he led the way into a hotel he clearly knew well, for he went straight to the bar.

'Whisky? Gin and tonic, Philip?'

'Gin and tonic, please.'

Philip refused to give Sorel any satisfaction by asking where they were and what they were doing there. He merely followed Sorel to a table in a corner of the bar and took the seat Sorel indicated.

'I'm going to phone,' Sorel said. 'I won't be a minute.'

He was away scarcely more. Philip had just sampled his gin when Sorel returned to sit opposite him and drink deeply. He looked satisfied.

'Hamish Constant should be here in half an hour,' he said, 'depending on the state of the traffic. He'll see you safely back to the flat and – '

Philip laughed. 'Thanks. But couldn't I have caught a taxi if you weren't prepared to drop me off?'

'Philip, use your wits for a moment. Unlike me, Hamish is known in the district as a friend and colleague of yours so, if someone is on the lookout for you – as they probably are – it'll cause no surprise when you turn up with him. And he's a form of protection for you. By yourself you'd be very vulnerable if they decided to turn nasty and demand answers about your absence. You see, though we do make mistakes, we're not fools and we try to take reasonable precautions.'

'Yes. Sorry. I'm not used to such a – a complicated life.' Philip grinned ruefully, and the two of them sat in a surprisingly companionable silence for a few moments.

Then a thought occurred to Philip. 'Incidentally, what should I tell the persistent Sylvia? She's sure to call again and demand an explanation.'

'I've been considering that. The best answer's the truth, or an approximation to it. You went to see young Patrick, who's been ill and has been demanding a visit from his dad, and you arranged for Constant, who had been lunching nearby, to give you a lift back to London. Sylvia may not believe you. Probably she won't, but that doesn't matter. What you have to do is apologize profusely and stick to your story.'

'I'll do my best.' Philip swilled the ice round in his glass. 'Okay. I'll eat dirt to appease Sylvia. Then what? Do I leave the next move to her?'

'You tell her you're going to Brussels on Wednesday for two or three days, staying at the Excelsior.'

'Brussels?' Philip was at a loss. 'Why not Paris, where I'm meant to be now?'

'Too obvious. Brussels is an hour's drive from Paris. The trip may interest her. We hope it will. Come into the office tomorrow and we'll brief you on what you're to do there.'

'Right.'

Philip savoured his gin and tonic and reluctantly accepted the fact that he had to go to Brussels. Paris he knew, or had known, well; it was a city he loved. Of Brussels he had only the vaguest memories, and those were probably inaccurate. But there was no question of refusing to obey Sorel's orders, especially without a valid reason.

'You also tell Sylvia that you're giving a small drinks party on Sunday evening, and you invite her and Tomas.'

'Will they come?'

Sorel shrugged. 'Who knows? Next you invite the Manheims and Carella. After them, Robert Fauvic. That takes in all our suspects. The Contessa has returned to Italy.'

'That makes six guests – and me as host. That's not much of a party. Are you serious about it?'

'Sure. Even if they refuse at first they may turn up on the night. So you'll give a party. You can ask the Mays, too. Hamish will come with his girlfriend, and we'll provide two or three more couples.'

'And the liquor and the small eats?'

'That will be arranged, Philip. Peter used to give the occasional small party, so it won't seem extraordinary.'

'Fair enough,' said Philip.

'But there's one important point. You must make certain that all your invitees know you'll be in Brussels from Wednesday to Friday.'

'In the hope I'll have an "interesting" time there?'

'That's the idea.' Sorel agreed. He finished his drink and put down his glass as Constant came into the bar. 'Here's Hamish. You go with him, Philip. I'll wait a while.'

As soon as they reached the flat Constant and Philip listened to the messages on the answerphone together. Sylvia's voice had become more and more peremptory as she repeatedly told Philip to call her at once, and a minute after Philip switched off the machine the telephone trilled. It was Sylvia. Philip gestured to the bedroom, where Constant picked up the other phone.

'Where the hell have you been, Peter?' she demanded. 'Why didn't you go to Longchamp as instructed? Tomas is very angry. He's far from sure we can still trust you. You're not reliable these days. You disappeared in Amsterdam.' Her voice rose. 'And now you have the nerve . . . '

Philip waited until her tirade had come to an end, then followed Sorel's suggestion and attempted to placate her by apologizing profusely and explaining about Patrick.

'You could have let us know,' Sylvia said. 'You seem to have forgotten what a telephone's for, Peter.'

'It was difficult once I got home.'

'Okay! Okay!' She was impatient. 'When are you going to Paris next?'

'I don't know.' He told her about the arrangements for his Brussels trip.

'Brussels? Wednesday? That's great!'

Sylvia seemed delighted, and Philip seized the opportunity to ask her and Tomas to his party on Sunday. To his surprise she didn't merely refuse; she treated his invitation with scorn and told him not to be a fool. But she concluded by assuring him that he would be contacted in Brussels and that she herself would be in touch on Saturday morning early after his return.

'What did you make of that?' Philip asked when Constant joined him.

'Not much. Brussels, fine. Party, no. Try the others,' Constant said. 'Meanwhile I'll get us both a drink.'

Philip tapped out the Manheims' number and Andrea answered. She and Bernhardt were going to their cottage for the weekend. If they were back in time, which was doubtful, they would come late to the party, and they would bring Carella who would be with them. She wished him a pleasant trip to Brussels.

As an afterthought, she said, 'Where are you staying, Peter?' And when he told her added, 'I know it. It's a good hotel.'

Next he tried Robert Fauvic, who wouldn't commit himself; he might or might not be in the country. He too asked where Philip would be staying in Brussels and told him to 'have a good time', though the remark appeared to lack sincerity.

The Mays accepted the invitation with alacrity, and didn't comment on Brussels. They did, however, ask if he was feeling really well again, which showed understanding, and made Philip regret involving them.

'This looks like being a pretty pointless party,' Constant said, laughing. 'Half a dozen people we really want to come, and not one of them's accepted outright.'

Philip didn't laugh in answer. He was thinking that there would be no party if he failed to survive his expedition to Brussels.

SIXTEEN

Because of 'technical difficulties' – that umbrella term so favoured by airlines – Philip's flight was delayed. It was early evening when he landed at Brussels National. He took a taxi directly to the hotel, where he was welcomed as a regular guest and offered his regular suite. This, he found, was like the hotel – large and comfortable and impersonal, except for the bowl of fruit on the centre table, a privilege presumably reserved for special guests. He showered, changed and went down to dinner.

The dining-room was more than half empty, but the food was excellent and the service good. Philip treated himself to a bottle of wine and lingered over the meal. Surreptitiously he studied the other diners, first, in case there was anyone he recognized and, secondly, in the hope of remembering any faces that he might see again in different circumstances, his enjoyment of the dinner marred by a mood of apprehension he could not dispel.

He had just finished his second cup of coffee when a waiter came to the table and inquired if he was Monsieur Peter Janvrin.

'Yes,' said Philip. 'What is it?'

'There's a gentleman to see you, sir.' The waiter was Flemish and his accent was thick. 'A Monsieur Anton Deleque.'

Philip didn't get the name. 'Who?' he asked.

'Monsieur Anton Deleque. He is in the foyer, sir.'

'Thank you.'

Philip thought for a moment and took his time before rising from the table. He had never heard of a Monsieur Deleque, and had no idea what he might look like. Nor did he have any idea what, if any, relationship existed between this Deleque and Peter. He was soon to discover.

As he entered the foyer and hesitated beside the reception desk, a man leapt to his feet from a sofa in a corner and came hurrying forward, clutching a briefcase under his arm. 'My dear Peter,' he said in French-accented English, his hand outstretched, 'how delightful to see you. I'm so sorry we missed each other in Paris at the weekend.'

'I'm sorry too, Anton.' Philip picked up his cue; obviously he was meant to know the man. 'Alas, it was unavoidable.'

'Ah!' Deleque smiled. 'You see. I am tactful. I do not ask why.'

They shook hands and Deleque led the way to the sofa that he had appropriated. He was a short man, plump, with a ruddy complexion, and his elegantly tailored suit couldn't completely disguise the rotundity of his stomach. It was evident that Monsieur Deleque liked to dine and wine well.

'Can I offer you a brandy?' Philip asked a little hesitantly as soon as they were seated.

Small brown eyes twinkled back at him. 'Do I ever refuse, Peter?'

Thankful that he had chosen the right opening gambit, Philip summoned a waiter and gave their order – he himself didn't particularly want a brandy, but he saw no means of avoiding one – and, as they waited for the drinks to arrive, he became conscious of Deleque studying him. He was therefore not surprised when Deleque asked him how he was, though by now this had become an easy question to deal with. Deleque was sympathetic.

'We've missed you,' he said.

To that there was no obvious response. Philip couldn't ask why he had been missed, or who Deleque meant by 'we'. The waiter, appearing with the drinks, caused a diversion, but still Philip was compelled to await a lead. Deleque seemed determined not to get to the point of his visit.

However, at last he said,'And how is dear Sylvia?'

'She's fine.' Philip was relieved that he could at least link Anton Deleque with Sylvia.

'But not happy with you, *mon cher Pierre*.' Deleque was amused. 'Be careful. She could be dangerous. She's a cold-blooded bitch. I, as a Frenchman, can tell. And such women are most to be feared. I hate to think what might happen if she believed you were cheating on her.'

'How could I cheat on her, even if I wanted to?'

Deleque shrugged. 'Perhaps you could do a little business on the side, as they say. But I feel I must warn you. It would not be advisable.'

'I wouldn't dream of trying,' Philip said lightly. 'Another brandy, Anton?'

Deleque hesitated. Then, 'No, better not. I have to drive back to Paris this evening and the *flics* are always busy on that stretch of *Autoroute*.'

'I'm most sorry to have made it necessary for you to come to Brussels.'

'No trouble. But next time we meet in Paris, eh?'

'Yes, of course.' Philip agreed at once. 'At Longchamp?' he hazarded.

'Longchamp! Certainly not! I am not a betting man.' Deleque appeared almost insulted. 'I shall come to your hotel as usual, Peter. Surely you can't have forgotten the arrangement. It's been some while, but – '

The Frenchman, Philip realized, was puzzled, and beginning to harbour doubts. However, Deleque shrugged and suddenly became brisk and efficient. He reached for his briefcase, which sat securely between his feet, and extracted a gift-wrapped packet, about nine inches by six inches and two inches deep. He passed it to Philip.

'A present for Sylvia,' he said. 'A box of chocs – from Paris, and very good. Actually it's a tin, but I'm sure she'll be pleased with it.'

'I – I'm sure she will.' Remembering the name of the winner at Sandown Park, Philip overcame his surprise; at one moment Deleque was denying any interest in racing and then almost immediately he – 'Is there a message with them?'

'Tell her – ' Deleque snapped shut his briefcase. 'Tell her the next will be Big Bear.'

'Big Bear,' Philip repeated. He thought of asking when and where the horse – if Big Bear was the name of another horse – would be running, but restrained himself. He had already made one stupid error over Longchamp, and he had no intention of making more. He merely said, 'I'll do that, Anton, but I shan't be returning to London till Friday evening.'

'That will be fine.' Deleque stood up and offered his hand. 'Thanks for the brandy, Peter. I'll hope to return your hospitality in Paris.'

'I'll look forward to it. *Au revoir*, Anton.'

★   ★   ★

Philip abandoned his half-drunk brandy, and went up to his room. He inspected the packet that Deleque had given him with some care, but it told him nothing, though when he tapped it with his nail it did sound like tin, rather than cardboard. He wondered if it could conceivably contain chocolates, as the Frenchman had said.

But that would make no sense. The message about Big Bear could have been telephoned, and it was absurd that Deleque should have been forced to drive three hundred kilometres from Paris merely to deliver some sweets which Philip himself could readily have bought right here in Brussels.

To Philip the problem seemed insoluble. He decided to leave it to Sorel and, mindful of the day when he had handed over to Sylvia the package entrusted to him by Foxy at Sandown without first consulting his lords and masters, he determined not to make the same mistake again. He locked the 'box of chocs' in his bag.

Tomorrow he was due to call on a man at the British Embassy, whom he had been told would be expecting him and would be prepared to help him contact London. Then the problem of what to do about the package would be out of his hands and up to Sorel.

Suddenly Philip had an attack of *déjà vu* – a vivid picture of himself going through the customs 'Green' channel at Heathrow, as he had done on the last occasion all those years ago when he had been stopped and had had his bag searched. It was then that they had found the heroin.

He caught his breath. If he had to face a similar situation on Friday, he was certain some astute customs officer would sense his self-consciousness and his fear and would suspect him. And when he was searched – Philip frowned. After all, the package could contain anything, drugs, uncut diamonds, stolen jewellery, a forger's printing plate. The first thing he must do when he was in touch with Sorel in the morning was insist that some inconspicuous but irregular arrangement be made for his arrival.

Aware that he was letting his imagination run away with him, Philip threw his bag into the bottom of the wardrobe in disgust. It was still early, but there was nothing to do but go to bed. He certainly wasn't going to a nightclub. For a while he studied the

135

literature on Belgium that the hotel provided for its guests. Then he put out the light and tried to compose himself for sleep.

Philip passed a poor night, beset by frightening dreams; he woke frequently, sweating. It was not until an hour before dawn that at last he fell into a deep and dreamless sleep, only to be woken by the telephone.

'Your morning call, Monsieur,' a voice said in English.

'Thank you.'

Philip ordered breakfast. He had washed and shaved, though not yet dressed, when the waiter came in with a tray, and he was feeling reasonably fresh. The waiter arranged breakfast on a table in the window and drew up a chair, saying, '*Bon appétit, Monsieur.*' Philip thanked and tipped him, and was about to stretch out a hand to pour his first cup of coffee when he saw the envelope propped against his glass of orange juice.

It was an expensive envelope, thick and cream-coloured. Presumably it had been delivered to the hotel by hand, for it was unstamped and bore only the name 'M. Janvrin' in typescript, without any address. Philip's first thought was that it must be a communication from the hotel management. He slit it open with the knife provided for his breakfast and extracted the single sheet of matching paper. This had an engraved address, but a handwritten message. There was no date and no personal greeting.

Philip stared at it in disbelief. The handwriting was Peter's. Philip would have sworn to it. He knew of no one else who wrote the letter 's' in such a distinctive and peculiar way; at the beginning or end of a word or if it were doubled within a word it appeared like a small capital, though by itself in the middle of a word it looked quite normal.

But how could Peter have known he would be in Brussels, at this hotel? How could he have sent the message? And the message itself? Philip read it for the second time.

'Meet me at the above address, between seven-thirty and eight-thirty tonight. Ask for Melissa. Please come.'

It was signed 'Peter', and to Philip the bold careless signature looked totally familiar. He did not believe it was a forgery, and, in his days of innocence before his involvement with Sorel and Constant, he would have unhesitatingly accepted the message as genuine. But not now; not in his present circumstances. His brother must have been either tricked or forced into writing a false note – a message to ensnare him.

Absentmindedly Philip drank his glass of orange juice and poured himself a cup of coffee. He started to butter a croissant. This, he thought, could be the breakthrough, the lead to Peter for which Sorel had been hoping, so there was no question but that he must do as the message asked. Nevertheless, there was no need to walk into a trap unprepared. He must get Sorel's advice and, if necessary, assistance.

He felt the thickness of the notepaper between thumb and forefinger, and ran his finger across the sharp engraving of the letterhead; the owner of *La Maison d'Or* – the name suggested a restaurant or a nightclub – was evidently not lacking in money. He got up and fetched the tourist literature from his bedside table. Yes, *La Maison d'Or* was listed as a restaurant with twice-nightly cabaret; booking a table was recommended. To judge from its small but elegant advertisement it was expensive, chic – and probably eminently respectable. The sort of place, Philip thought unhappily, where Peter would be at home. On the surface it didn't sound dangerous.

And Melissa? Wasn't that the Greek for honey? A honey trap? Or yet another of Peter's girlfriends? Why did all their names end in 'a'? Philip wondered illogically. Of course Melissa might turn out to be Andrea or Carella or even the Contessa, under a pseudonym.

But not Sylvia. Whatever else he was, M. Anton Deleque with his hints concerning Box of Chox and Big Bear, was a genuine player in whatever game was in progress, and his call at the hotel the previous evening would have been quite pointless if the intention had been to follow it with this invitation to the proposed meeting at *La Maison d'Or*.

As he returned to his neglected breakfast, Philip realized that the more he learnt – or guessed – about Peter's activities, the more he was beginning to suspect that Sylvia and Tomas had no connection with whatever group was responsible for his brother's disappearance. But if not they, who? The Manheims? There was some evidence, perhaps, but it was vague and inconclusive, to say the least. In any case, involved or not, they were an added complexity he could well do without.

He could only hope that the assignation at *La Maison d'Or* that evening would throw some light on Peter's whereabouts and, he admitted ruefully, that he himself would escape from it unscathed.

SEVENTEEN

At ten o'clock Philip took a taxi to the British Chancery on rue Joseph II, and asked for Sebastian Lisle. All he knew about Lisle was that he was a First Secretary with some nominal consular appointment, and, according to Constant, a close friend of Sorel. Reading between the lines Philip surmised that the 'nominal consular duties' were merely a cover for more secret work. In any case, Sorel had said he would be briefed on Philip's mission and was to be trusted absolutely, if – and this was where Philip supplied his own rider – Gregory Sorel was to be trusted absolutely.

Lisle came down to the reception desk himself, greeted Philip and arranged for his pass before taking him along to a small, comfortably furnished inner office. He waved Philip to a chair.

'Coffee?'

'Please.' Philip was aware that Lisle was studying him closely.

Lisle was something of a surprise. He was about Sorel's age, but otherwise they could not have been more different in appearance. Lisle was big and strong, sandy-haired and red-faced; Philip could imagine him boxing or rowing or playing rugger for his university, but certainly not fencing, as Sorel had done. Even his voice, though quiet, revealed suppressed power.

The coffee came quickly, a whole pot, accompanied by a plate of assorted biscuits. Lisle poured, his hands seeming incongruously large for the task.

'Now,' he said, 'what can I do for you? I know about you and I'm at your service.'

'I imagine it would be possible for me to have a private and secure phone conversation with Gregory Sorel in London,' Philip said tentatively.

'Nothing simpler.' Lisle pointed to one of the instruments on his desk. 'That's my scrambler. I'll put you through, say hello to Greg and leave you to it if you like. All right?'

'Fine. And thanks.'

Minutes later Philip was talking to Sorel. First he told him of the visit from Monsieur Anton Deleque of Paris the previous evening and the package he had promised to deliver to Sylvia.

'You have it with you?' Sorel asked.

'No. I left it locked in my bag at the hotel.'

'Get it and give it to Seb. I'll ask him to send it to me in the diplomatic bag. With any luck we'll be able to examine it, and Hamish Constant will return it to you when he meets your flight on Friday evening. We'll make arrangements with the airport authorities and, in the meantime, we'll make some inquiries into this Deleque character. Anything else?'

'Yes. And this will surprise you. I've had a message purporting to come from Peter.'

'What?' Sorel was delighted when Philip explained. 'Great! We're really getting some action at last. You'll go to this place, of course.'

'Of course!'

'No need to be sarcastic. Have you this message with you, or did you leave that in the hotel too?'

Now who's being sarcastic? Philip thought, but he answered mildly. 'I've got it on me.'

'Good. Give it to Seb for the bag. That all?' Sorel was abrupt.

'That's all – for the moment.'

'Right. Then let me speak to Seb. And – and, Philip, remember. We'll do our best for you and I'm sure you'll do your best for us. Good luck!'

'Thanks,' Philip said, though he guessed from the tone of Sorel's voice that the man was uttering these sentiments merely because he thought it might encourage him to stick it out – and take whatever might be coming to him.

'I'll get Lisle,' he said.

Lisle, who had been sitting on the corner of his secretary's desk, got up as soon as Philip came into the outer office. 'Greg wants a word? I thought he might.' He went into the inner room, shutting the door so as to exclude Philip. It was several minutes before he poked his head out and beckoned to Philip to join him.

'Greg says you've got a note that's almost certainly a fake. May I see it?'

Philip took the note from his wallet and passed it over. 'As I told Sorel, I'd swear to the handwriting. If Peter didn't write it, whoever did must be an expert forger.'

'Maybe. But I've got an idea.' Lisle rummaged in a desk drawer and produced a small square metal object which he unfolded. 'Know what this is?'

'Some kind of magnifying glass?'

'Exactly. In fact, it's what's known as a linen proofer. It's used to count threads to the inch in materials, but in the absence of more sophisticated equipment it's useful for examining documents.' While he spoke Lisle had carefully extracted the single sheet of paper from its envelope and was busy studying it.

After a minute he began to nod with satisfaction. Then he looked up and grinned at Philip. 'Damn it! I'm right! And so are you!'

'You mean Peter wrote it? But that's good, terrific! If he wrote it, he must be alive – and probably somewhere in Brussels.' Philip let his words trail away as his suddenly soaring hopes diminished.

Lisle had started to shake his head. 'I'm afraid it's not as simple as that,' he said. 'I believe your brother wrote it, yes. But that was probably some time ago. Unless I'm mistaken that is a tracing from an original – the care with which each letter's been formed shows up under the glass. And incidentally, as far as I can see, there's only one set of fingerprints on it. They're yours, I assume?'

'Yes. It never occurred to me – ' Philip began to apologize.

'For Heaven's sake, why should it?' Lisle didn't have Sorel's acid tongue. 'Anyway, I'll write Greg a memo with my ideas on the subject. His experts may prove me wrong. They often have in the past. Meanwhile, you'll be away to your hotel to collect this package, and everything can go off in the bag this afternoon. It'll be in London tonight. Okay?'

'Fine.' Philip couldn't hide his disappointment as once more he accepted that the chance of Peter being alive was growing daily less and less probable.

It was noon when Philip returned to his hotel. After claiming his key from the concierge he went up in the lift and opened the door of his room. He had taken two strides before he became aware that he was not alone.

A man was standing by the bed. He was a small, thin, wiry-looking character with a sadly drooping moustache. He wore dark trousers and the kind of white jacket favoured by waiters. But this was no waiter.

The door of the wardrobe was ajar. Philip's bag had been removed and now sat on the bed, its locks obviously forced. The package that Anton Deleque had given to Philip for Sylvia was clutched to the intruder's narrow chest. He had already removed the wrapping paper, and Philip could see that the contents did indeed look like a tin of chocolates.

For a few moments the two men stared at each other, as if frozen. Then the intruder reacted. He looked wildly around as if seeking a means of escape, but there was none except the door by which Philip had entered and in front of which he now stood, blocking the way. The intruder had little choice. He hesitated only fractionally before he charged forward.

Philip waited. He was taller and should be stronger than his opponent, and the time he had spent in combat training at the safe house had given him confidence. But he hadn't reckoned with the little man's cunning. The intruder was within a yard of Philip when he pulled back his arm and hurled the tin at Philip's face. As a missile it was hard and heavy.

It caught Philip at the side of the brow, just missing his eye, and instinctively he shied away. The cover had come off the tin, either as it hit him or because it had already been loosened and, to add to his discomfort, he was showered with chocolates. He stumbled and nearly fell.

Meanwhile the intruder, seizing the opportunity he had created for himself, had slipped past Philip, flung open the door and was dashing down the corridor at speed. Pursuit would have been quite useless. Philip abandoned the idea almost as soon as it crossed his mind.

He kicked the door shut behind him and leant against it. He was breathing hard. Apart from the beating up he had suffered shortly after his arrival at Peter's London flat, there had been only threats of violence. Otherwise he had been physically unharmed – until now. He could feel blood seeping down his cheek and his eye was closing. He wasn't a coward and he hadn't spent seven years in jail without witnessing vicious fights, but he had never been able to accustom himself to them.

With a hand held over his injured eye he looked about him. The carpet was scattered with chocolates, some of them squashed. So Anton Deleque hadn't lied, Philip thought. He bent and picked up the lid, which was plain except for an elegant scroll. 'Mary,' it said, 'Rue Royale, Bruxelles.' But if Deleque had been telling the truth these should have come from Paris. He assumed it wouldn't be difficult to buy them there, but why should the man have bothered if he were coming to Brussels anyway? Like so much else it made no sense.

Philip went into the bathroom and bathed his face in cold water. It was not as bad as he had at first feared. He would have a nasty bruise in a few hours but, though his eye hurt, it appeared undamaged. He sighed with relief. He wouldn't need medical help. But he needed to change his shirt, which had blood on the collar.

Going to the drawer which held the few clothes that he had brought with him, Philip realized that the intruder had searched them. But the man had ignored a small box containing a pair of cuff links which belonged to Peter; they were of no great intrinsic value, but well worth the attention of a casual sneak thief. Moreover, it was surely out of character for an ordinary thief to open a gift wrapped package and then proceed to inspect its contents – which, it seemed to Philip in retrospect – the intruder had been about to do when he was interrupted.

His shirt changed and ready to return to the Chancery, Philip wondered what to do about the chocolates. Even if they had still been complete he wouldn't have been able to arrange them neatly in the tin. The moulded paper cups had been damaged and the tin dented. Deleque's present for Sylvia was in a sorry state. But it might still be useful to Sorel. He only hoped that it could be duplicated in time for the gift to be handed to Sylvia.

Philip did his best to replace in the tin the chocolates that were whole. The broken and squashed ones, which had done the carpet no good, he wrapped in paper tissue. These, with the tin and the fancy wrapping paper, he put in a bag provided by the hotel for dirty laundry. He trusted that Sebastian Lisle would have the means to make a suitable parcel to send to Sorel.

*   *   *

143

'Where the hell have you been?' Lisle demanded as his secretary showed Philip into his office. 'I was about to send out a search party.' He peered at Philip's face. 'Good God, have you been in a fight?'

'Not exactly. It takes two to fight, and I didn't do much. Believe it or not, I was attacked with a tin of Belgian chocolates. Here are the remains – the evidence. Present for Sorel.' Philip handed Lisle the hotel bag and briefly explained what had happened. 'Sorry it's such a mess. I shall need an identical tin, you realize?'

'That's all right. We'll cope. Give me ten, fifteen minutes, then I'll take you off *Au Roi d'Espagne* and buy you a Gueuze – or a Trappiste if you'd rather. Then we can go around the corner to lunch. I know a great little place in the rue des Bouchers.'

'It sounds good. But could you translate?'

Lisle laughed; his laugh, like his voice, was powerful but controlled. 'The old King of Spain is a bistro in Grand'Place, very popular. Gueuze and Trappiste are brands of beer. Gueuze is a bitter, and Trappiste is mild. I always drink Gueuze myself but, come to think of it, Peter drank Trappiste, though he wasn't a great beer drinker. Perhaps you'd better do the same. You never know. We might meet a chum of Peter's – or one of his enemies.'

'Okay.'

On the whole Philip would have preferred to have had a drink and a sandwich in the hotel bar by himself. After the events of the morning he was feeling depressed. It hadn't escaped his notice that Lisle spoke of Peter in the past tense and, with the evening threatening, he could have done without the strain of impersonating Peter throughout lunch.

'Incidentally,' said Lisle, grinning, as he made for his office door with the laundry bag. 'I've made some inquiries about *La Maison d'Or*. It's a top-class restaurant, but rumour has it that upstairs it's a most select cathouse.'

'A brothel?'

'That's right. It gives one food for thought, doesn't it? We'll have to make some careful plans. Melissa could prove dangerous.'

EIGHTEEN

The taxi set Philip down in front of *La Maison d'Or*. It was a house at one end of a majestic terrace – typical of certain areas of Brussels and not far from the Grand'Place. Its main distinguishing feature was the royal-blue canvas canopy extending across the pavement from its doorway, above which the restaurant's name was picked out in discreet golden lettering. A doorman in a royal-blue and gold uniform hurried forward to assist Philip from the cab, and stood by while he paid off the driver.

'*Bonsoir, monsieur.*'

'*Bonsoir.*'

Philip passed under the canopy into a square hall, where a young woman in a royal-blue evening dress sat behind a reception desk. She smiled at Philip, but gave no sign of recognition.

'*Bonsoir, mademoiselle,*' said Philip. '*Je m'appelle Monsieur Janvrin.*'

'*Bonsoir, monsieur. Vous êtes bienvenu.*' As she spoke the receptionist was checking a list of names she had before her. She must have pressed a bell unseen by Philip for a man in a dinner jacket appeared through a curtained alcove to her left, and she murmured, 'Monsieur Janvrin.'

The maître d' greeted Philip and swept back the blue and gold curtain to allow him to enter the restaurant proper. Here the same colour scheme of royal-blue and gold persisted. The room was only of moderate size though curtains at one end obviously concealed a small stage. The tables were well-spaced, offering privacy, and each had a centrepiece of fresh flowers. The lighting was discreet, and to Philip, following the maître d' to a table at one side of the room, the whole place was redolent of opulence, wealth and elegance; he found it difficult to believe that upstairs was a brothel.

The maître d' drew out a chair for Philip at what was clearly a most desirable table, close to the stage and against a wall; it was laid for two. A waiter unfolded a napkin and spread it across Philip's knees. Another offered him a menu. A third, unasked, brought him a bottle of champagne in an ice-bucket. The maître d' hovered until the wine had been poured.

'*On m'a dit que vous attendez quelqu'une, monsieur,*' he said.

'*Oui.*' Philip hesitated, then he added, '*J'attends Mademoiselle Melissa.*'

'*Bien sûr, monsieur.*' The maître d' showed no surprise at the mention of the name. He bowed and retreated.

Philip, who had been a little overwhelmed by all the attention he was receiving, sipped his champagne and pretended to consider the menu while he tried to accustom himself to his surroundings. The time was a little after eight-thirty. Even now the tables were pleasantly occupied, and the place would presumably fill up before the cabaret. There was a buzz of conversation and a general air of conviviality as waiters moved swiftly about their business.

Philip studied the other guests. Mostly they were couples, but there was a party of six who were clearly celebrating some family occasion, and two foursomes. No one, however, looked in the least familiar to him and he again turned his attention to the menu. He supposed that good manners demanded he should wait for Melissa before going through the business of choosing and ordering a meal, which there was a possibility he would have no chance to eat.

Glancing up from the menu, Philip saw that the maître d' was ushering another couple into the restaurant. They were a man and a woman in their thirties, and this woman did look vaguely familiar. The pair were well-dressed but in a quiet and restrained fashion. They seemed pleasant but uninteresting and neither of them was particularly noticeable. Unobtrusive was the word that occurred to Philip.

They were shown to a table on the other side of the room and suddenly Philip identified the woman – she was Sebastian Lisle's secretary. He had paid her almost no attention when they had met in the Chancery and he realized he had no idea of her name. But he found it hard to believe that her presence here this evening was the result of pure chance.

Having seated this couple, the maître d' had returned to the entrance to greet a young and strikingly beautiful girl in a white dress that clung to her tall, slender figure. As she began to walk across the room almost every male present turned to watch her. Many of the faces registered envy when they saw the table to which she was being shown.

Philip leapt to his feet when she came to a halt in front of him. 'Here I am at last,' she said. *'Bonsoir.'*

The waiter drew back a chair for her as Philip said, 'Melissa?'

'Yes, I am Melissa.'

Philip resumed his seat and motioned to the waiter to pour the girl a glass of champagne. Close to, Philip could see that she was even more attractive than she had appeared at first glance, with glorious long corn-coloured hair that to his inexpert eye looked natural, and large grey eyes. She was also much younger than he had thought; he doubted if she was yet in her twenties.

'I cannot eat with you. I do not have the time.' She spoke English with a pretty French accent, and she sounded nervous. 'But you'll join me later, won't you?'

'Of course I will,' Philip responded. 'That's why I'm here, isn't it?' he added enigmatically.

'I shall be waiting.' As she sipped her champagne she let her hair fall forward so as to obscure her face. 'In an hour the early cabaret will start. The lights will dim. If you quietly slip through that door, a little to your left behind the hanging, I shall be there to escort you to your brother.'

She gestured briefly towards a floor to ceiling tapestry. Philip hadn't realized that it concealed a door. He glanced across the room at Lisle's secretary. She and her companion seemed absorbed in each other and were paying no obvious attention to him or the girl with him.

He turned to the girl, aware that she had been watching him through her hair. Now she tossed it back so that he could see her face. To his surprise her eyes were wet with tears.

'I do not know who you are and I do not care. But I do not like to be used for a purpose such as this.'

It was scarcely more than a whisper, and for a moment Philip was not sure that she had spoken. When he had grasped her meaning, he asked at once, 'What purpose do you mean?'

This time it was she who hesitated. Then she appeared to come to a decision. 'It is not true what I said,' she answered haltingly. 'I know nothing of your brother. But I overheard them talking. They want to question you and then – then I

147

think they will kill you, unless perhaps you give the right answers.'

'Who are *they?*'

'The one who is important is called Otto. I don't know his other name. He has a bad leg and walks with difficulty. He doesn't belong here, but he has some form of control over this place. I do not understand.'

'Tell me – '

But there was no time. A waiter was approaching to take their order. The girl drained her glass and pushed back her chair. There was nothing Philip could do to stop her.

'*A bientôt,*' she said.

Philip half rose. '*A bientôt,*' he echoed, but he doubted if she heard him; she was already disappearing behind the wall tapestry.

The waiter showed no surprise at her departure, but merely cleared her *couvert* from the table. Philip gave his order, choosing dishes at random. He had forgotten what they were before the waiter had left the table. The girl – he thought of her as Melissa though probably it was not her name – had shaken him. He couldn't decide whether or not she was genuine. But what would have been the point of staging such a scene? Having taken the trouble to lure him to *La Maison d'Or* they – whoever they were – wouldn't want to frighten him away immediately. He wondered what would happen if he got up now, and simply walked out of the place.

It was unlikely that anyone would try to stop him. They wouldn't dare. This was an élite restaurant with a reputation to maintain. The last thing they would want would be a public brawl. But, Philip reflected, there was no future in such a retreat. He had come to get information about Peter, and so far he had learnt little. He could imagine Sorel sneering at him for running away, calling him a coward.

And perhaps he was a coward. After his lunch with Lisle in the rue des Bouchers, he had walked, regardless of anyone who might be following him, to the Parc de Bruxelles and eventually found his way to the Cathédrale St-Michel, where he had spent more than an hour, thinking about the past, about Peter and Zara and the little boy Patrick. He had been fortunate to find a priest who had been prepared to hear his confession. He was as ready to die now as he would ever be, he thought wryly, but he dreaded the violence that would probably precede his death.

His thoughts were interrupted by the waiter, bringing the Parma ham and melon he had ordered. He was not hungry, but he forced himself to eat. At one point he gave what he hoped was a casual glance at Lisle's secretary. She was laughing merrily at some joke her companion had made, and Philip restrained a sigh. He had little faith in the protection that Sorel, and Lisle, had promised.

The lights dimmed, but still gave enough illumination for the diners to see what they were eating and drinking. The curtains masking the small stage at the end of the room drew back to reveal a tall brunette in a gold lamé dress, standing beside a grand piano which a man in a dinner jacket was playing softly. Philip realized that he had for some time been conscious of music in the background, pleasing and unobtrusive.

Without introduction the girl began to hum, and then to sing. She had a typical nightclub singer's voice with which she sang a typical cabaret number, intimate and husky. The buzz of conversation at the tables subsided, but didn't cease entirely. Clearly this was not the star attraction.

Philip rose slowly to his feet and moved towards the hanging tapestry. The girl whom he thought of as Melissa had not told him to be quick, but she had implied a degree of stealth which he equated with not loitering on the way. Nevertheless, he took his time. He wanted to be sure that he was seen leaving the restaurant by this private door.

Now that the moment which was to bring him face to face with his enemy – Peter's enemy – had arrived, he felt exhilarated rather than apprehensive, and he was determined that whatever happened to him should not be a complete waste. Lisle had pointed out that if 'they' had merely wished to kill him it wouldn't have been difficult, so they too were probably in search of information. Any confrontation could not fail to be interesting.

It was a temptation to glance across the room to the table where Lisle's secretary sat with her companion, but Philip resisted it. He slid behind the tapestry and felt for the handle of the door. It opened inwards and he stepped forwards into a dimly lit

149

passageway. The beautiful girl with the corn-coloured hair was standing at the bottom of a flight of carpeted stairs.

'*Chéri*,' she said, and held out her hand to him.

'Hello, Melissa,' Philip replied, and moved towards her.

But he never reached her. He heard the door behind him click shut. At the same time he was seized, his arms pulled behind his back and his wrists pinioned. Then a hood was dropped over his head. Someone punched him in the small of the back and he fell to his knees, only to be pulled upright immediately. The attack was over very rapidly and he had no opportunity to resist even if he had wished to do so.

'*Allez-vous-en!*'

Philip stumbled to the bottom of the stairs and, urged on, began to climb. He counted the steps. There were twelve before he was turned right, then three more before he was pushed through a doorway and down on to what seemed like a hard kitchen chair. But he sensed that he was in a comfortable room. The carpet felt thick beneath his feet, and he could smell furniture polish, roses and cigar smoke.

'Good-evening, Mr Janvrin.'

It was a rich, deep voice, vaguely familiar to Philip, though he couldn't place it for a moment. Then he realized that it was not the voice but the accented English that was reminiscent. It had reminded him of Bernhardt Manheim. And he wondered if the man addressing him was Otto, and if he were a German.

'Mr Janvrin, shall I call you Peter – or Philip? I think I shall call you Philip.'

'I don't care a damn what you call me. What the hell do you think you're doing, treating me like this?' Philip tried to sound both frightened and angry. 'Are you crazy? You send me a stupid letter – '

Because of the hood over his head Philip had no warning of the blow. Delivered with vicious force, it caught him on the side of the face which was already bruised from the tin of chocolates and, with his hands tied behind him, he could do nothing to save himself. He fell heavily and lay on the carpet, breathing hard. If this was merely the beginning, he thought . . .

Then someone – it must have been a strong man, Philip registered, to lift a dead weight so easily – picked him up and swung him back on to the hard chair.

'Don't be a fool, Philip,' the deep voice said. 'You'll only make things worse for yourself. Let us conduct our business in as civilized a fashion as circumstances permit. In the first place, you are *not* Peter Janvrin. Admit that.'

'What makes you so bloody certain?' It was only an attempt at oral aggression.

'That's irrelevant. We know.'

'How can you be sure?'

There was a harsh, mocking laugh. 'Because Peter's dead. He was picked up on his way to Schiphol several weeks ago and, after a jolly party which I regret to say he was in no position to appreciate, he went for a drive, fell in the sea and was drowned.'

'You murdered him!' Philip said. 'Oh God, why?' He bowed his head as if defeated.

'Not I, personally. I don't perform such tasks. As to why, in our line of business you have to be able to trust your colleagues, and Peter had become untrustworthy. He tried to double-cross us.'

'Your line of business?'

'You ask too many questions, Philip Janvrin. Suppose you answer a few instead. We believed Peter was dead, drowned, but there was a chance – a hundred to one, a thousand to one – that he had been saved, so when you appeared, claiming to be Peter, we wondered and naturally investigated. And as a result of these investigations, as I say, we know you're Philip.'

'Because I haven't lost the tip of my little finger?'

For a moment there was silence. Then that harsh laugh came again. 'Clever boy! So you know that Peter had lost his fingertip. Did you know he lost it while setting a rat trap for a friend he was staying with? Careless of him.'

The Contessa, Philip thought. He was learning a lot. Too much. They clearly had no intention of giving him any opportunity to pass on the information.

'Yes, Philip, you're right. That – among other things – gave you away. But why did you do it? Why did you undertake this ridiculous impersonation of your brother?'

'It just happened – by chance.' Philip had expected the question and had discussed possible answers with Sebastian Lisle. 'You know I spent seven years in prison?'

'Yes – and served only a part of your sentence. Can you explain that?'

'No. I can't. I've wondered myself. But mine not to reason why, I was only too glad to be free. But a couple of weeks after I was released I found I was practically destitute. My money was running out, and no one wants to employ an ex-con.'

'Spare me the sob story, Philip!'

'All right. Well, in the end I went to my brother for help, somewhat reluctantly, I must admit. To my surprise Baker, the porter at Peter's block of flats, mistook me for Peter who, it seemed, had been away for a while. I thought quickly and told him I'd lost my keys and he let me into the flat. I rummaged around and found spare keys and some money in the desk. So I went shopping. Everyone accepted me as Peter. So did Mrs Robyn, Peter's cleaning woman. And after that it was simple. I spread the story that I'd been seriously ill and even Peter's friends didn't doubt me. You don't want me to go into details, surely?'

'*Simple*, Philip? Just happened by chance, Philip? Do you expect me to believe that?' The voice was suddenly savage.

'Why not? It's the truth.' Philip winced as he waited for another blow, but it didn't come. 'There were one or two hiccups, but apart from them – '

'Don't lie to me, you – you – ' A flood of abuse followed. 'The whole thing's been a – a provocation, hasn't it – an operation organized by Peter's office? They arranged everything for you, didn't they?'

'No.' Philip knew that his position was growing weaker.

'Don't be a fool. There was no way you could have done it by yourself. It was a professional job. We're professionals, too, and we appreciate such work.'

'I don't know what you mean.'

'Don't you? Are you seriously telling me that you managed to keep Peter's flat properly sanitized, so that when we turned it over there was nothing whatever to suggest that you were *not* Peter? And even your hotel room here in Brussels! Peter's clothes! Peter's toiletries! Peter's cufflinks! And you expect me to believe you thought of all this yourself? No, it was that damned man Aubyn and his outfit – Peter's old outfit. Wasn't it?'

The voice was beginning to sound less and less controlled, as if its owner was working himself up into a fit of rage, but whether this was a natural reaction or a fabricated performance merely intended to frighten, Philip could only hazard a guess. He wished he could have seen the man's face.

'How did you know Peter was dead, if they didn't tell you? Answer me that, Philip!'

'I didn't know,' Philip replied hastily. 'I was expecting Peter to turn up at any moment. I was sure he wouldn't mind my making use of his flat. I – '

'You lie! You lie! Aubyn told you he was dead. You might have deceived a porter and some silly servant or some shopkeepers, even Peter's acquaintances. But if Aubyn learnt that Peter had reappeared he'd have been on your doorstep in hours. And you'd never have deceived him. He knew who you were, all right. He knew you were Peter's brother. And he knows you're here at this very moment. You took that letter signed Peter straight to the British Embassy this morning, reporting to your masters. Well, it won't do you any good. I am your master now, so you tell me how much Aubyn has discovered about Peter – and about our business.'

'What do you mean?'

'Listen, Philip.' The voice had suddenly become soft and venomous. 'We've brought you here to find out what Aubyn knows or suspects. Otherwise we could have disposed of you days ago, as we disposed of Peter. So, one way or another, you're going to tell me what we need.'

'I don't know what you're talking about,' Philip repeated truthfully. 'Do you mean Peter's involvement with racing – horse-racing?'

'No! I do not! Don't be a fool.'

'What then?'

'Fair enough. You want it the hard way.'

Philip anticipated the blow, but it was worse than last time. It was like an explosion in his head. He fell with the chair on top of him, the room seeming to wheel around him. When he hit the floor he lay there, half-stunned. He clung to the carpet because he thought it was moving. Then he felt excruciating pains in different parts of his body, and realized that someone was methodically kicking him with what felt like metal-capped shoes.

The kicking went on for a long time. Then it stopped, but he knew it would recommence in a minute, and he tried to roll himself into a ball, to make himself as small a target as possible. At that moment he would have told Otto – if this was Otto – anything the man wanted to know. But he couldn't tell him what he didn't know himself. Then he thought of Peter who had suffered this and worse, and was filled with anger.

His hood had become dislodged as he fell and struggled to avoid the blows that were being aimed at him. He tossed his head and the room revolved around him again. He shut his eyes tight. But he had managed to rid himself of the hood and now could hope to see the face of the man who had arranged Peter's death and was doubtless about to arrange his own. He opened his eyes.

He saw bits of a broken chair, a stretch of brown carpet, the front panel of a mahogany desk, and a pair of jeans-covered legs standing over him. He lifted his head slightly, but he still couldn't see the man behind the desk, his interrogator.

The next instant he heard distant shouting and footsteps pounding up the stairs. The door burst open. Smoke seemed to pour into the room.

And a strange voice cried, '*Vite! Vite!* Get out! The place is on fire!'

NINETEEN

The next few minutes were a nightmare of confusion. Later, Philip found it almost impossible to recall exactly what had happened and when.

He was lying on the floor. He was consumed with pain. And the warning cry of 'Fire!' sent an additional spasm of fear through him – a spasm that appeared to accentuate his agony. Nevertheless, with an instinct to escape from the smoke that was beginning to fill his nose and mouth and was making him cough – each cough further anguish – and the flames that he could imagine only too vividly, he began to struggle to his feet. The chair hampered him, as did the fact that his wrists were still tied behind his back. He managed to get on to his knees, only to fall over on his side.

He was aware of someone shouting in German and realized that it was the man who had been interrogating him. But the harsh, arrogant voice had disappeared, to be replaced by a desperate high-pitched appeal for help. Then a large foot trod on his leg, and at the same time an object fell close to his head. Squinting through eyes that were becoming increasingly watery he saw it was a stick with a silver knob.

The smoke was now in his throat and lungs and he was having difficulty in breathing. But hands were disentangling him from the chair. He was lifted into a sitting position and – blessed relief – a wet cloth was tied around his face. The cloth smelt of champagne.

'Can you walk, Philip? Can you walk?'

It was a moment before he understood that the question was addressed to him. 'I'll try,' he croaked and somehow, with help, he rose to his feet.

'Good man! You're okay now. Let's get out of here.'

'And don't worry. There's no fire.'

There were two voices, one of them, Philip registered, a

woman's. But what was she saying? No fire? She must be mad! What about the smoke? No smoke without fire. He was falling again.

'Quick, he's passed out,' someone said.

'No!' Philip insisted. It wasn't true. He hadn't passed out. 'No! I'm all right,' he said.

He remembered little of what happened next. He had a vague impression of half walking, half being carried, out of the room, down stairs, along a passage and through a door into the open. The cloth was removed from his face. He took great gulps of cool night air. He blinked the water from his eyes. Miraculously his wrists were unfettered and free.

He was aware of people, a lot of people, some in uniform – firemen and police – running, shouting instructions, giving orders; and others, sightseers, just standing and watching. He saw police cars, fire-fighting vehicles and an ambulance. But he was being urged down a side street, away from the activity.

'Come on, Philip! Hurry! Seb will be waiting.'

For the first time he took in his three rescuers: a man whom he had never seen before, Lisle's secretary and her dinner companion. 'Thanks,' he said.

'Don't thank us,' the unknown man replied. 'Sorry we were so slow, but the bloody door was locked.'

Philip didn't know what door was meant, but it didn't matter. He was with friends. He was safe. Otto wasn't about to kill him. He wasn't going to die horribly in a fire. Subconsciously he squared his shoulders and, though it cost him considerable pain, managed to walk quickly until they rounded a corner and found Sebastian Lisle waiting for them. Thankfully he climbed into the back of the car.

'Philip, what's the damage? Are you all right?' was Lisle's first question as he drove off.

'Apart from being kicked and beaten and only just beginning to breathe again,' Philip answered, 'I'm all right. And thanks for the rescue,' he repeated.

'We've the Embassy doctor waiting for you,' said Lisle. 'We thought it might be necessary before we start the debriefing. Then, all being well, what you'll need most is a good strong drink, or two, or three. You must have had an exciting time. I trust all's well that ends well.'

Philip settled himself in the corner of the car and shut his eyes. 'Damn you and your cheerfulness, Sebastian Lisle!' he muttered under his breath, but he didn't really mean it. He was too exhausted to feel any animosity, except towards Otto. He wished he could have seen the man's face. He thought sadly about Peter, and drifted into a state of half sleeping, half waking. He was aware of muffled conversation around him, of the car stopping and starting, obviously at traffic lights, and then, as he later learnt, for Lisle's secretary to collect a second car. This last halt was followed by a long, clear run until eventually they reached their destination.

'Here we are,' Lisle said. 'Luckily my wife's away. She's taken our youngest to visit his grandma. So we shall have the place to ourselves.'

Philip was vaguely surprised. The vision of Lisle as a family man seemed slightly unreal. The house was also something of a surprise. He had caught only a glimpse of the exterior as he was helped up the front steps, but his impression had been of a substantial home with a fair-sized garden. The interior was comfortably furnished in the Belgian manner but, apart from some books and toys lying around haphazardly in the sitting-room, the place seemed to lack personality.

'Ah, here's the medical man waiting for you, Philip. You'll be staying here tonight. I'll show you to your room and the doctor can examine you there.'

'But I don't – ' Philip, recovering, began to protest.

'Don't be silly. We've got to take care of you. We can't start pouring whisky into you, or asking you a lot of questions, till you've got a clean bill of health. A beating-up and smoke inhalation! Of course you need a physical.'

Upstairs, in a twin-bedded room, the doctor made him strip and gave him a rapid but thorough examination. 'A lot of bruising, but no bones broken, and no concussion, as far as I can tell. You must have a hard head. But you'll be stiff as hell in the morning,' the doctor concluded. 'Okay, you can get dressed now. I'll leave you some tablets for the pain.'

Downstairs again, Philip was made to lie on the sofa, propped up with cushions. The others were drinking and, after a nod from the doctor, Lisle put a dark glass into his hand before ushering the doctor to the door.

By the time he returned, the others had introduced themselves. Philip gathered that Lisle's secretary was called Valerie White, and her dinner companion, who was both her husband and a colleague of Lisle's, was Simon. The other man, whose name was Michael Lindsay, was a member of Sorel's staff from London and, though older, was not unlike Constant in appearance.

'One of my minders?' Philip asked.

'I do my best.' The man grinned ruefully.

'Everyone's done their best tonight,' Lisle said. 'Philip may have had a rough time, but he's safely here and none of us has been arrested.'

'Arrested?'

Lisle laughed. 'We were responsible for the fire, though it wasn't a real fire,' he said, 'and indirectly for the police raid on the brothel. I'm looking forward to reading the papers tomorrow. There are going to be some juicy stories. But let's get down to business. I've switched on the recorder, and you start, Philip. Everything. Even the smallest detail.'

'All right. I'll begin at the beginning,' Philip said. 'First of all, I was expected at the restaurant, and they knew I'd be meeting someone. Melissa arrived late, and turned out to be only a kid, seventeen or eighteen, I'd guess. She was scared and didn't stay to eat.' He told them about the instructions she had given him, and ended, 'She did try to warn me.'

'She did more than that,' Valerie said.

'She certainly did,' Michael echoed. 'She unlocked the door behind that tapestry for us. I was trying to break it down without much success. And she told us where you were.'

'Incidentally, her name is Colette. We asked our waiter about her earlier, and he was surprisingly forthcoming. He said she was the proprietor's *petite amie*, but Monsieur Lesaux was absent this evening.'

'That would fit,' Philip said.

Dismissing the thought of what might have happened to him if the door had not been unlocked, he explained what the girl had told him about the man called Otto having some kind of interest in, or hold over, *La Maison d'Or*, and went on to relate his own encounter, presumably with this Otto. By now he had their full attention, and no one spoke till he came to an end.

Lisle made the first comment. 'Poor Peter!' he said. 'He must have been trying to nobble Otto and his mob, but they caught on to him before he could report back. What a waste! What a bloody waste!' Suddenly he recollected himself. 'Philip, I'm sorry. Peter was a dear colleague of ours, a friend, but of course he was your brother. And – and you've done splendidly.'

'Thank you.'

There was a general murmur of agreement, but Philip was aware that the sympathy was largely reserved for his brother, not for him. He supposed he couldn't blame them. He was helping them, but he was not one of them – they couldn't forget or forgive his past. Nevertheless, he answered their questions willingly and to the best of his ability.

Finally Sebastian Lisle said, 'That's great. You've given us a lot of leads, Philip. I've a feeling *La Maison d'Or* – apart possibly from Lesaux – will prove a dead end, but this girl Colette and some of the pros from the upper floor may be useful in helping to trace Otto. A pity you didn't actually see his face, but we've got a fair amount to go on. It'll be a busy day tomorrow. Simon, you and Val had better buzz off home now. Michael and Philip will spend the night here.'

As they rose to go Philip protested. The whisky had deadened the worst of his pains and he was curious. He wanted to know how his rescue had been organized.

'That's quite a story,' Simon laughed, 'but Seb will tell you. He planned it.'

'And, praise be, it worked,' Lisle said when Valerie and her husband had gone. 'Timing was the tricky part. As soon as you disappeared behind the arras, as it were, Michael left the restaurant, ostensibly to fetch something from his car, but in fact to warn me. I allowed ten minutes. Then I phoned the fire brigade and the police. I said there was a fire at *La Maison d'Or*, and a gentleman upstairs had had an accident. I guessed that would set the cat among the pigeons, as they say.'

'But the fire – ' Philip began.

'A few smoke bombs,' Michael said, 'but very effective. They created a certain amount of chaos and provided us with a chance to follow you. Val had asked what lay behind the tapestry, so we knew there were offices and store rooms and the proprietor's private suite – presumably there's another way to the other rooms upstairs. It was a blow to find the door locked, but luckily Colette or Melissa or whatever you call her solved that one, and here we all are.'

'Feeling happier, I would surmise, than many people who were in that establishment tonight.' Lisle gave a broad grin. 'So, bed for you two. You know the room and I'll follow as soon as I've made some calls.'

Even had he wished to, Philip was in no position to argue. The strain of the evening, plus several large whiskies and a couple of pain-killers, had done their work well. He was already half asleep and he could imagine nothing more desirable than a warm and comfortable bed.

And ten minutes later that was where he was. He had washed perfunctorily, cleaned his teeth with a new brush provided by Lisle, refused an offer of pyjamas, and managed to adjust his bruised body to the mattress which was firm, but far more yielding than the one he had been accustomed to in prison. He was asleep before Michael Lindsay had got into the twin bed next to him.

Philip woke, instinctively turned over, and was at once conscious that he was one large ache. He gritted his teeth and sat up. He could still smell smoke, and at once memories of the previous night flooded back. He drew a deep experimental breath and released it slowly, wincing.

'Good-morning!' The door had opened, and Michael came in carrying a breakfast tray. 'How do you feel, Philip? You've slept well. It's ten o'clock.'

'I don't feel as happy as you sound, but I'll survive, and that breakfast looks tempting.'

'Dig into it, then. Afterwards I suggest a long hot bath to ease your bruises, but there's no hurry. We'll lunch here and then drive in to the Chancery to get our bags. Mine's already there. I checked out of my hotel yesterday afternoon. Simon will be collecting yours this morning and paying your bill. With luck Seb may have news for us, and anyway he's anxious to have a word with you before you go back to London.'

'Right. Will you be travelling with me?'

'On the same flight, but not with you, and someone else will take over from me when we reach Heathrow. However, I'll be coming to your party on Sunday evening.'

'My party? God! I'd forgotten all about that.'

Michael grinned. 'I'm not surprised, but won't you be interested to see who turns up?'

'Yes, I suppose so. I – ' Philip stopped, a piece of buttered toast halfway to his mouth. 'Not only had I forgotten that party, I'd forgotten Sylvia. What am I going to do? She'll be expecting the present Deleque gave me for her.'

'That tin of chocolates? Incidentally, I'm sorry I didn't afford you any protection against them.'

'It's *not* that funny,' Philip said. 'Sylvia has violent friends, and I don't relish the idea of being beaten up again, not at the moment.'

'Don't worry! I'll phone Seb and remind him you'll need a replacement. Meanwhile, relax.'

Philip recognized that this was good advice, but it wasn't easy to follow. Apart from his physical discomfort he still had to accustom himself to the idea that Peter was dead. Until his enforced meeting with the man he assumed was Otto he had cherished a residual hope that somehow and somewhere his brother was alive. Now he no longer had that hope, and he could foresee the innumerable problems that would arise for his family, especially Zara, because of the manner of Peter's death. It was useless to worry about them, he knew. After all, he had related problems of his own that were more immediate. Nevertheless . . .

He was glad when, after lunch, an Embassy staff car appeared and drove him to the Chancery with Michael. This time he took notice of Mrs Valerie White as, the perfect secretary once more, she showed him into Lisle's office.

'Come in, Philip! Come in!' Lisle welcomed him. 'How are you today?' He sounded tired.

'Battered, but I'll survive – at least until they try again.'

'Yes, we've been giving some thought to that.' Lisle was perfectly serious, but the remark was the reverse of reassuring. 'The consensus of opinion here and in London is that you're relatively safe for the moment. Otto didn't get what he wanted from you, and they'll know you've reported everything you can about last night, so they'll have to do a rethink on the situation.'

'And so I get a temporary reprieve?'

'Probably. But don't count on it. These people – we don't really know who they are yet, but it's clear they're clever, unscrupulous and not slow to act. When the police went round to Monsieur Lesaux's apartment to tell him what had happened at *La Maison d'Or*, they found him in his salon – dead.'

'Dead? Good God!'

'Shot. The girl – the one who helped us – Colette-Melissa, was in the bedroom, also dead. It had been made to look as if he'd shot her and then himself. The police are suspicious, but – ' Lisle shrugged. 'Anyway, there go our two best leads to Otto.'

'I'm sorry.' Philip was thinking of the girl.

Lisle looked at his watch. 'Time you were going, Philip. The staff car will take you to the airport. Val has your bag in the outer office. She's bought a tin of chocolates, and had it gift-wrapped, so that it looks identical to the one Deleque gave you. Michael will be on the flight with you, and Hamish Constant will meet you at Heathrow. We'll keep you posted if there's any more news of Otto. Meanwhile, I'll wish you luck.'

'Thanks,' Philip said drily. 'I think I'll probably need it.'

TWENTY

Philip was sweating when he walked quickly through the 'Green' channel at Heathrow. Every step he took he was conscious of the searching gaze of the customs officers standing behind their long tables, or apparently idling in conversation in his path. One passenger had already been stopped, and the man gave Philip a rueful glance as he started to unpack his suitcase. Hurriedly Philip looked away; he had no wish to be implicated, even to the minimal extent of returning the man's gaze. He held his breath.

Even at the exit to the main arrivals hall, where he was delayed by a woman who was having trouble manoeuvring her trolley through the automatic doors, he half expected to hear a voice call, 'One moment, please, sir.' But nothing happened and he knew he was safe. He also knew that his reactions had been absurd. Even had his bag been searched it would have yielded nothing of interest to the customs officers. But still he could not forget the last time he had made such an inbound journey.

As promised Hamish Constant was waiting at the barrier in the 'meeting and greeting' area. He waved. 'Hello, Peter.' He seized Philip's bag with one hand and with the other gripped his arm. 'Good journey?' he asked loudly, and then murmured. 'Limp as we leave, and try to appear in pain.'

'That won't require much acting ability on my part.' Philip was tart.

Constant grinned. 'I'm glad you've not lost your sense of humour at any rate. Let's go, Philip. Come to think of it, I should have brought you a walking stick to support your poor leg, shouldn't I?' he added, falsely solicitous.

They were weaving their way through a throng of passengers and porters and trolleys laden with luggage when Philip suddenly stopped. He stared at Constant, his mouth slightly open.

'What is it? Are you all right?'

'Yes. I – I – It was your mention of a walking stick. It reminded me of something I'd forgotten. It could prove to be important.'

'Well, leave it for the moment. We can't deal with it now.' Constant was impatient. 'My car's parked illegally and I don't want yet another ticket.'

Holding Philip by the arm Constant led him out of the terminal building. Obediently Philip limped beside him, though he doubted if anyone was interested in his progress. Then he caught sight of a small fair woman whom, for one moment, he mistook for Sylvia, and accepted that he could be wrong.

They reached the car almost simultaneously with a traffic warden but Constant, using all his charm and making much of his 'sick friend', persuaded her to be lenient. Constant threw Philip's bag into the rear seat and they drove off. Philip, glancing back at the woman, noticed another bag beside his own.

'Yours?' he asked.

'That's right. I'm coming to stay with you over the weekend. I'll sleep on the sofa. Mrs Robyn, duly warned, bought us lots of good food this morning. So we can hole up very comfortably.'

'What about this party that Sorel made me organize for Sunday? And Sylvia? She's sure to phone.'

'Everything's laid on for the party. All you have to do is play host. You'll have plenty of support from me and Michael Lindsay and one or two others; let's hope some of our villains turn up, otherwise it will be rather a waste of effort.'

'And Sylvia?' Philip persisted.

Constant didn't answer at once. He was busy concentrating on his driving while he negotiated the roundabout which would take him on to the M4 and into London. The traffic was heavy. Philip didn't press him, and it was several minutes before Constant, doing a steady sixty in the centre lane, spoke again.

'When Sylvia phones, as I agree she will, you tell her you were mugged when leaving a restaurant in Brussels yesterday evening, and you've sprained your ankle, so that you can't possibly meet her anywhere. Try to persuade her to come to the flat.'

'Suppose she refuses?'

'I don't think she will. Presumably she'll want Deleque's present, though that's a bit of an oddity. The chocs from the original tin have been analysed and luckily they and the tin and

164

the wrapping paper are perfectly ordinary. Otherwise, we'd have had to think hard about the substitution.'

'Perfectly normal?' demanded Philip, surprised.

'Perfectly, I assure you,' replied Constant. 'Anyway, Philip, you tell Sylvia you're not leaving the flat whatever the circumstances until Monday when you'll be going into the country on a course for a few days. How long you'll be away depends on your ankle. You'll have to be vague, but you can remark that you'll be having a trip to Paris very soon, and see if she rises to that. We'll go into details later.'

'How much of this is true, Hamish?'

'All of it, apart from your ankle. And cheer up! The course is intended to be a rest cure.'

'Good,' said Philip. 'I only hope you're not proposing to fatten me up for the kill.'

Constant laughed. 'Not yet. We may get a breakthrough out of the blue, but there are a hell of a lot of questions still to be answered. Major questions, many of them – such as what this Otto and his gang are in the business of, and how the Sylvia woman relates to it.'

He glanced at Philip, but Philip was gazing out of the car window and thinking of his brother. By now they had reached the outskirts of London and traffic had slowed to a crawl with occasional brief bursts of acceleration. It didn't make for a comfortable ride, and when Constant braked sharply to avoid a van that had changed lanes in front of him without warning, Philip winced with pain.

'Sorry,' Constant said. 'Luckily it's not much further to the flat, though at our present rate of progress it'll take a while to get there. This traffic is diabolical! In the meantime, Philip, tell me what suddenly hit you at Heathrow. My remark about a stick sparked it off, didn't it?'

'Yes, it did. Hamish, it may not be important, but I forgot to tell Lisle. When I was lying on the floor in that room at *La Maison d'Or* breathing smoke, just as Michael Lindsay and the others burst in, something fell on me. I could just see what it was – a walking stick, black, probably ebony, with a silver knob. Is it fair to assume it was Otto's? He's said to have a bad leg.'

'Probably. Anyway, we'll inform Greg as soon as we get in.' Constant was enthusiastic. 'Who knows? It might well help.'

Then, 'Hold on,' he said urgently. Seizing a chance offered by a gap in the traffic he swung his car to the right into a side street, and less than five minutes later they reached their destination. 'Here we are at last,' he said triumphantly. 'You must have a talk with Sorel.'

Sylvia telephoned at eight o'clock on Saturday morning and demanded that 'Peter' should meet her for lunch *Chez Henri*, a small restaurant not far from the flat. Philip said it was impossible, and explained. Sylvia argued, but Philip, urged on by silent gestures from Constant, was adamant.

'Sylvia, it's absolutely out of the question.'

'Peter, it's important! You met Anton?'

'Of course. I have a present for you from him, and he sends messages. But, Sylvia, I can only walk with the greatest difficulty. I've stiffened up after a night's sleep and, believe me, my ankle's giving me hell.'

'I hope I *can* believe you.'

Philip heard the hesitancy in her voice and pressed home his advantage. 'Sylvia, I've a colleague staying with me at the moment. The office was worried about me being attacked, even though muggings aren't all that unusual in Brussels. But he'll be out shopping if you come in around twelve, and anyway there's no reason a girlfriend shouldn't drop in to see me, is there?'

'No-o. All right.' She had made up her mind. 'But, Peter, if you're trying to play some trick on me you'll regret it.'

'My dear Sylvia – '

Philip put down the receiver and shook his head. Sylvia had cut him off. However, she had agreed to come to the flat.

'You know, Hamish,' he said, 'I find it more and more difficult to accept that Sylvia and Tomas and these racing people are connected with Otto and his mob.'

'Peter must have thought they were.'

'Yes, I suppose that's true. But what I don't understand is why he didn't confide more in Sorel, or at least in Brigadier Aubyn. As far as I can make out, he seems to have been working completely on his own.'

'To be honest, Philip, it was his one failing. He was a brilliant operator in many ways, but he liked to work solo, and as a result he became overly secretive. He hated to give out information until he was absolutely sure of all his facts. It made him extra vulnerable and – '

Constant didn't finish the sentence, but Philip could guess what he might have said. Such behaviour on Peter's part could lead to disaster for others as well as himself.

Sylvia arrived at the flat punctually at noon. Constant had gone to do some unnecessary shopping. Philip, wearing pyjamas and a dressing gown, opened the door to her, supporting himself on the doorframe as he did so.

'Thank you for coming,' he said, limping ahead of her into the sitting-room.

She studied him carefully. The bruise inflicted on his face by the tin of chocolates was a greenish purple, and the studied care with which, having waved her to a chair, he lowered himself on to the sofa, was genuine and required no acting.

'You have been in the wars,' Sylvia said.

'I told you. You never seem to believe me these days.' Philip made himself appear disgruntled. 'Anyhow, there's Anton's present on the table beside you.'

'Thanks.' Sylvia picked up the packet and began to strip off the fancy wrapping paper.

'You're going to open it here?'

'Yes. Why not?' The paper removed, Sylvia held up the tin. 'My box of chocs, Peter. Does anything odd strike you?'

'Only the stupidity of Deleque coming all the way to Brussels to buy chocolates,' Philip said coldly. 'Or am I the one who's being stupid? I assumed your so-called present would be coming from Paris.'

Sylvia smiled slowly. 'Don't be angry, Peter. It was just a small test. Tomas finds it difficult to trust you again, after that disappearing act of yours. You can't blame him. It was very expensive for us.'

'So when *is* he going to start to trust me again?'

'Who knows? Soon, perhaps.'

Philip thought quickly. 'Sylvia,' he said, 'Anton told me that Tomas and you suspected I might be doing a little business on the side. If so, you're quite wrong.'

'I'm glad to hear it. What else did Anton say?'

'He said the next would be Big Bear.'

'Sure, depending on when you go to Paris again.'

'That shouldn't be too long. As I told you on the phone, I've got to go on a course for a few days. It'll be a cross, I hope, between a rest cure and getting me really fit again. After all it's only a short time since I was desperately ill, and since then I haven't always been treated in a friendly fashion – as you can see for yourself.'

Sylvia regarded him doubtfully. 'I'm never quite sure whether you're telling the truth or not,' she said suddenly. Then her head jerked up. 'What's that?'

'Don't panic. It's just the friend who's staying with me.'

Hamish Constant came into the sitting-room. He was carrying a basket full of fruit and vegetables. 'Peter, I've got some lovely asparagus – ' he began, and stopped. 'Hello!' He smiled at Sylvia. 'I didn't know Peter had a visitor. I'm Hamish Constant, and you're Florence Nightingale under a different name. You've even brought him some chocolates, I see.'

It was a small *tour de force* on Constant's part, but Philip knew that Sylvia was shrewd. It was inevitable that she would distrust Constant's ingenuous charm, and she would certainly expect 'Peter' to dominate the conversation.

'Hamish,' Philip said quickly, 'this is Sylvia, a friend of mine. We were going to have a drink. Do put that shopping in the kitchen and come and join us.'

'I'll be right with you.'

'Peter!' Sylvia had stood up as Constant left them.

'You can't go now. He'd think it peculiar,' Philip said urgently. 'Sit down, Sylvia, and I'll get us a drink. What will you have? Cinzano?'

'Yes. Very well,' she agreed reluctantly. 'It's lucky it doesn't matter about the chocolates, isn't it?'

'Oh, we'd have thought of something!'

Philip got up painfully and limped to the side table where drinks were kept. He was rather enjoying the situation. He had not seen Sylvia so lacking in composure before. Purposely he was slow in making the drinks and Constant returned.

'Gin and tonic for me too, Peter, as you're on your feet. There should be plenty of ice. I filled the bucket this morning.' Constant sat down opposite Sylvia and leant towards her. 'It's good for him to move around a little,' he said confidentially. 'Otherwise he gets dreadfully stiff.'

'How uncomfortable.'

Constant ignored her obvious lack of sympathy. 'Incidentally, Peter introduced you just as Sylvia. What's your second name?'

'Smith.' Sylvia hadn't hesitated.

'Mrs or Miss or Ms?'

'Whichever you prefer.'

'In that case I'll just call you Sylvia. Do you live near here?'

'Mr Constant, is this an interrogation?'

'I'm sorry. I didn't mean to seem inquisitive. It's only that I've got my car close by and I hoped you'd let me give you a lift home.'

'Thank you, but I don't need a lift.'

Philip thought it was time he intervened. 'Hamish, you're making a nuisance of yourself,' he said. 'However, you may ask Sylvia if she's coming to my party tomorrow.'

'No, I am not, as I told you before, Peter. And I've changed my mind about that drink. I must get – '

What happened next was an accident, but Philip was to take full advantage of it.

Sylvia, having decided to leave, jumped to her feet, unaware that Philip was almost at her shoulder. He was carrying a small round tray on which there were three glasses and somehow, startled by his proximity, Sylvia managed to knock the tray from underneath. The glasses went flying, distributing their contents largely over Philip, but also spattering Sylvia. She staggered back, twisted her ankle and fell.

Constant was quick to go to her aid, lifting her up, asking if she was hurt, producing a clean white handkerchief to mop the damp patches on her suit, creating an exaggerated and unnecessary commotion which, though Constant was unaware of it at the time, turned out to be a most useful diversion.

Philip bent to pick up the tray. Beside it lay Sylvia's handbag, half open, the provocative pink corner of what was obviously a driving licence sticking out in its little plastic case. And fortunately the side showing personal details was uppermost. It took only a moment for Philip to slide out the case, glance at it and replace it. Then, the bag shut, the tray retrieved, he was standing up.

'I'm sorry, Sylvia. I hope I've not ruined your suit.'

169

'A few spots. It'll clean.' She was abrupt but, seeing her bag on the chair in which she had been sitting, she relaxed. 'You got the worst of it, Peter. No matter, you'll clean too.'

Casually she slung her bag over her shoulder and, after more apologies from Philip, said goodbye. Constant saw her to the lift and Philip went to change his clothes.

'So what did you think of her?' Philip asked.

'Formidable!' Constant gave the word its French pronunciation. 'And expensive. That suit of hers must have cost a packet – several hundred, I'd guess – and her diamond ring was at least a couple of carats.'

The two men were having their delayed pre-luncheon drinks. They had cleaned up the mess to the best of their ability, but there was a nasty stain on the carpet.

'Incidentally,' Constant continued, 'I'm pretty certain that our little Smith woman is a Mrs, rather than a Miss. There was the obvious mark of a ring on the third finger of her left hand.'

'That was observant of you. I never noticed,' Philip admitted. 'However, I did learn something of importance today. Her name's not Smith. It's Sylvia Jean Brelado, and she lives in Hampstead. I didn't see the full address. While you were picking her up and dusting her down I managed to get a glance at her driving licence. It came out of her bag when she fell.'

'Well, I'm damned! That's brilliant. Even if she gives the man we've got outside the slip again today – and she's a slippery lady – we ought to be able to trace her.'

Constant lifted his glass. 'Philip,' he said, 'I drink to you. Brig Aubyn will be offering you a permanent job next.'

'That I doubt,' said Philip, who couldn't imagine himself as one of Gregory Sorel's colleagues.

TWENTY-ONE

The party on Sunday evening was not a success from the point of view of the absent Sorel. It failed to bring about a confrontation between the Manheims on the one hand, and Sylvia and Tomas on the other, as he had hoped. However, on the credit side, most of the guests seemed to enjoy themselves, and there were some interesting if enigmatic moments.

The first guest to arrive was Michael Lindsay, accompanied by a tall, dark vivacious girl whom he introduced as Flora. They were followed almost immediately by Jeannette, an attractive blonde who turned out to be a French Canadian. Constant had explained to Philip in advance that these girls were casual friends, and had no connection with or knowledge of Brigadier Aubyn's establishment. They had merely been invited to provide a normal and credible background for the party.

John and Pam May were the next to ring the front doorbell and, after them, Robert Fauvic, who assured Philip that Carella and the Manheims were hoping to come, if they were not delayed by traffic on the way back from their cottage.

'Lucky people to have a country cottage,' Constant said. 'Where is it? Far from London?'

'In Sussex.'

'My favourite county,' said Pam May. 'Where in Sussex? East or West?'

'Near the Kent border.' Clearly Fauvic didn't intend to elaborate.

There was a pause before anyone else appeared. Philip kept people's glasses full and Mrs Robyn, who was acting as a maid for the evening, passed around plates of canapés, hot sausage rolls and little pastry shells stuffed with mushrooms. Conversation was general and grew louder as everyone drank more. It might have been any small party in central London on a Sunday evening.

'There's your doorbell again,' Robert Fauvic said suddenly.

'So it is. What good hearing you have, Robert,' said Philip, who realized that Fauvic must have been listening for the sound. 'Who do you think it can be? The Manheims, perhaps?'

Indeed, it was Andrea and Bernhardt Manheim, full of apologies for their late arrival. Carella was not with them. They had had a tiring journey from the country, and she had pleaded a headache. She sent her love and excuses.

Marvelling that they could behave so normally when there was at least a strong probability that they were aware of what had happened to him in Brussels, Philip introduced them to his other guests. They knew Robert Fauvic and the Mays, of course, who were most solicitous about Carella, but the others were strangers to them, and Philip would have dearly liked to know what they made of this collection of individuals, and of the actions of Jeannette in particular.

The French Canadian girl, who by this time was very slightly drunk, had opened the tin of Belgian chocolates which had been left on a side table in a prominent place. She offered them to Bernhardt as Philip gave him a glass of champagne.

'Chocs all the way from Belgium,' she said.

'Thank you, no.'

'Actually, I bought them for a friend of mine, but she didn't want them. She said they were too fattening.' Philip was constantly surprised by the ease with which he lied nowadays.

'They're absolutely lovely.' By now Jeannette had eaten two. 'Are you sure you won't try one?'

'Quite sure, thank you.' Bernhardt was excessively polite. 'With champagne, I prefer something more savoury.' He took a smoked oyster from a tray that Mrs Robyn was proffering. 'I'd forgotten you were going to Brussels, Peter. Good trip?'

'Appalling! Some fools let off a smoke bomb in a restaurant where I was dining, and then I was beaten up by a couple of thugs. Look!' He pointed to the bruise above his eye.

'Good heavens! Poor Peter!'

Andrea had replaced Jeannette who, having in happy ignorance brought up the subjects of chocolates and Brussels, had drifted away to talk to Michael and Flora. Andrea's voice was mocking rather than sympathetic.

'You complained to the police, of course, or did your Embassy do that for you? It might carry more weight.' Philip noticed that she said *your* Embassy, rather than *our* or *the*, as if she were purposely dissociating herself from Britain.

Suddenly Philip experienced a surge of anger. These people were probably responsible for Peter's death, at whatever degree they themselves were removed from the actual killing, and responsible too for what he himself had suffered at *La Maison d'Or*. Let them sweat a little, he thought.

'Actually, the authorities were lucky. They've got a good description of the main character and his large side-kick.' Philip looked directly at Bernhardt Manheim and saw his eyes narrow; it was the first time Manheim had shown any emotion during the evening. 'As you can imagine I shall be delighted to be a witness when they're arrested and tried.'

He had scarcely finished speaking when Philip was aware of Constant at his side, and Constant's hand gripping his upper arm. Then the doorbell rang again. This time he heard it without prompting.

'That must be Sylvia,' Constant said. 'I thought you said she and Tomas weren't coming.'

'They didn't think they could make it.' Philip could feel Constant's continuing pressure on his arm, urging him away from the Manheims. 'Excuse me,' he said to them.

Constant followed him out into the hall. 'What the hell do you think you're doing, Philip?' he muttered angrily. 'Do you want them to kill you? Manheim looked as if he would gladly have obliged you right then.'

Philip grinned apologetically as Constant gave him a small push towards the front door. His thoughts had turned to Sylvia and Tomas. Neither of the Manheims had reacted to their names and they would now be warned, but Sylvia, faced with the couple unexpectedly, might show some reaction. He opened the front door. The woman standing there was not Sylvia.

'Hello, Peter. I'm sorry I'm so late.' Reaching up to kiss him on the cheek, she added in a whisper, 'Mary O'Donovan. You remember?'

Philip nodded. He was speechless. The last person he had expected was this woman who had come to his rescue at Sandown Park races when he had so nearly betrayed himself to Sylvia's chum, Foxy Pringle.

'I only flew in from Dublin this morning, Peter,' she was saying as he led her into the sitting-room, her Irish accent becoming very pronounced. She stopped and regarded the other guests. 'There's not a soul here I know,' she said. 'I thought this little gathering would include a few of your racing friends, Peter.'

'Not this evening, Mary.'

'And you weren't at the Curragh yesterday. In fact I've not seen you since you had that big win on Box of Chox at Sandown. What's come over you?'

'I have to earn a living sometimes.'

'You don't buy vintage champagne on your salary, dear boy.'

There was general laughter, and Mary O'Donovan said, 'Now introduce me.'

Somehow Mary, whom Philip had thought of as the prototype of everyone's maiden aunt when they had met at Sandown, had made herself the centre of attention. Perhaps it was because she was so different from the other women there. Middle-aged, with a trim figure but without make-up, her greying hair cut short in an indeterminate style, she lacked any kind of glamour. But equally it was clear that she didn't care a damn if the hemline of her velvet skirt dipped, or her nails were clipped square and remained unvarnished. She refused to compete.

Introductions completed, she turned to Philip. 'You'll be going to Longchamp for the *Prix d'Excellence*, Peter, won't you?' she asked him.

Philip had never heard of the *Prix d'Excellence*, but he assumed it was the name of a race. By now he was beginning to understand the workings of Sorel's devious mind, and he understood that Mary O'Donovan was not giving him instructions, which could easily have been relayed by Constant, but was making sure that the information was available to the Manheims.

'If I can arrange it, yes. I've got to go on a short course, but I'm due for a trip to Paris soon after that, so if the dates fit – '

'I'm sure you'll manage to wangle it, dear boy.' Mary looked around her. 'Or am I giving you away to your colleagues?'

'Not to worry,' Constant said. 'The FCO doesn't strictly approve, but we all know how addicted Peter is to racing. Anyway, this isn't an office party – just friends.'

'Good!' Mary's smile was wide with innocence. 'Though I must admit I was hoping to get one or two good tips for Longchamp this evening.'

There was more laughter. Then Michael Lindsay said that he and Flora must go, and Jeannette asked for a lift. The party had started to break up. The Manheims left soon after, followed by John and Pam May, who made Philip promise to come to dinner when he returned from Paris. But Robert Fauvic, who had been drinking steadily, showed no inclination to leave until Mrs Robyn started to clear away plates and glasses.

'Suppose I should go,' he said reluctantly.

'I'll come with you.' Mary O'Donovan was brisk, waving away Philip's objection to her departure. 'Do you know anything about racing, Mr Fauvic?'

'Not me. I think that betting's a fool's game.' His voice sounded thick.

'Then I won't advise you to put your money on Big Bear in the *Prix d' Excellence*.'

'Big Bear?' Philip queried before he could stop himself.

'To place.' She smiled at him, and included Constant. 'Goodbye for now, Peter. See you at Longchamp.'

Philip smiled in return. He wished he could have felt as pleasurably optimistic about his visit to Paris as Mary O'Donovan sounded.

The dishwasher, loaded by Mrs Robyn before she left, was churning away in the kitchen. Philip and Constant had discussed the party over a cold supper. Constant had accused Philip of being too aggressive to the Manheims. In the circumstances Philip considered this a poor joke, but Constant had insisted.

'It wasn't wise to show your hand so openly,' he said.

'Why not? Will it make any difference in Paris? Sorel's set me up nicely, hasn't he? Mary O'Donovan made it clear when I should be there and where I could be found.'

'Philip, you did agree – '

'Sure, but I'm only human, Hamish. Brussels was not a picnic, and it's perfectly obvious the situation is hotting up and becoming more dangerous. And now I know that Peter is dead – '

'You've no proof of that,' Constant intervened quickly. 'Otto could have been lying to you.'

'Perhaps, but I don't think so.' Philip shrugged. 'I suppose you don't know when this *Prix d'Excellence* is run, do you?'

175

'No, but we'll discover tomorrow.' Constant looked at him anxiously. 'You're tired, Philip. As you said, Brussels was no picnic, and I'm afraid we tend to forget that for so many years you – you haven't been living a normal life.'

'What is a normal life? Do you lead a normal life, Hamish? And Sorel and Michael Lindsay and Mary O'Donovan and – '

'Okay!' For once Constant was annoyed. 'But *we* chose it! I don't imagine you *chose* to go to prison!' There was a silence. Then he said, 'Sorry, Philip. I suppose I'm a bit fraught too. Look, I'll finish clearing up. You go to bed and get some sleep.'

'All right. Good-night, Hamish.'

And indeed Philip was quickly asleep, only to be woken an hour later by his bedside telephone. His first reaction was that it would be more threats of violence, though it was a while since he had received any, and he was fully prepared to slam down the receiver. Then he thought of Sylvia, and lastly of Sorel. Zara never crossed his mind, but he recognized her voice at once.

'Is something wrong?' he asked.

'Not more than usual, but it's not easy to stay down here and not worry, to go on pretending to Dad and Patrick. You might have phoned and let me know what was happening.'

'I've been abroad.'

'I've heard that excuse before.'

'And I've no news for you. I'm sorry, Zara.'

'They haven't given up trying to find – '

Philip interrupted her before she could utter the name over an open line. 'No,' he said.

'That's all you can tell me?'

'Yes, unfortunately. How's Patrick?'

'Much better. Your visit worked wonders. I suppose you couldn't come – '

'No!' Philip said again, before she could complete the sentence; he was never going near Wytham Court again.

'Well, you might at least send Patrick a postcard. It wouldn't be much bother for you and it would mean a lot to him, especially if it came from abroad.'

'Right. I'll do that. I'll be going to France soon.'

'Thank you.'

He waited, but she had nothing more to say except goodbye and good luck, and once more Philip composed himself for sleep, but now sleep was slow to come. The hours passed, until finally he drifted off, thinking that Hamish Constant had been right. The simple life he had led for so long in prison had ill fitted him for the complications of the world outside, the supposedly real world, even the so-called normal world of Zara and his father.

TWENTY-TWO

Sylvia – Sylvia Jean Brelado, as he now knew her to be – phoned Philip early in the morning of the next day, Monday. As far as he could make out, she was anxious about only one thing: the dates of his next trip to Paris. As Philip had as yet had no chance to find out when the *Prix d'Excellence* would be run, all he could do was temporize by telling Sylvia that he would be there in time to take in that race.

'That's next Sunday,' she replied immediately. 'Fine! You'll be contacted as usual.' She hung up.

Philip reported the conversation to Constant, and by about noon they were driving through the wrought-iron gates and up the short tree-lined drive to the 'safe house.' Philip, getting out of Constant's car, regarded it with something that approached affection. He found it difficult to believe that it was such a relatively short time since, on the edge of desperation after his release from prison, he had been brought here. So much had happened in the meantime.

The front door was opened by Ada, the housekeeper, who welcomed him as an old friend. 'Nice to see you again, sir. I've put you in the same room as before. I thought you'd like it.'

'Thank you,' Philip said. 'That'll be fine.'

He followed Constant, who insisted on carrying his bags, across the marble-tiled hall and up the wide staircase. The room was just as he remembered it, even to the bowl of fresh fruit and the selection of magazines. In a way, it was like coming home.

He went to the long windows, opened them and stepped out on to the balcony. In the distance, where the lawn ended in a wood, he could see a gardener busy at work, and he could smell the scent of new-mown grass. It was a quiet, peaceful scene – for the time being a true 'safe house' – a safe haven from the violence and obscure ambiguities which had dogged recent events.

Constant interrupted his ruminations. 'There'll be drinks in the sitting-room when you're ready, Philip,' he said. 'Lunch at one.'

'Thanks, Hamish.'

Alone, Philip unpacked the clothes he had brought with him. Then he went into the bathroom and washed his face and hands. His face in the mirror was pale, the bruise over his eye still livid, and he looked more decrepit than he felt. He gave himself a wry smile and went downstairs.

Constant was already in the sitting-room. 'A lazy day for you today, Philip, a free day. Tomorrow Dr John wants to take a good look at you and, depending on what he says, Gervase will give you some gentle exercise and start to get you in shape again. Now we know the *Prix d'Excellence* is being run next Sunday, we've less time than we imagined. However, Sorel's coming down later tomorrow, possibly with the Brig, and we'll have a conference. With luck there'll be some news. Now, what would you like to do today?'

'What would you suggest?'

'What about a rest after lunch, then a walk or a swim? And later a quiet evening to yourself? You must have had enough of my company recently.'

'Sounds great. Nothing too energetic.'

'I promise you that.' Constant laughed. 'Let's start with a drink.'

The rest of the day passed as pleasantly as they had anticipated. Philip, appreciating Constant's tact, particularly enjoyed the evening. Ada brought him up a simple meal on a tray, and he sat in the window, watching the light fade and thinking, with sorrow but no bitterness, of what might have been if he'd not been caught importing heroin into the country.

Brigadier Aubyn and Gregory Sorel arrived the following afternoon, earlier than expected. Constant had had to climb rapidly out of the swimming-pool, fling on some clothes and obey their summons. Philip, whose presence had not been demanded, continued to swim idly up and down the pool, enjoying the caress of the water on his body.

Dr John, who had given him a rigorous examination that morning, had tut-tutted over his many bruises and insisted that he should have another easy day, but had given him a reasonably clean bill of health. So he had been gently massaged and been put through some mild exercises. Then he had walked and rested, and now he was swimming. Above all, he had taken the opportunity to compose his mind.

It was not until six o'clock that Constant knocked on Philip's bedroom door and asked him to come down to the sitting-room.

'There's news, Philip, bags of news!'

'Of Peter?'

Philip, looking up from the book he was reading, saw Constant's face change. It was as if all his enthusiasm had drained from him, leaving him devoid of expression other than a vague exasperation. He might have been a schoolmaster pestered by a boy who insisted on asking the same stupid question over and over again. Nevertheless, Constant made an effort to respond.

'No, Philip, not directly, but the news is – fascinating, and we hope it's getting us nearer our goal.'

Philip didn't bother to inquire what that goal was. He was fairly sure that it differed from his own. By now he was all but convinced that Peter was dead, but he had no real desire for revenge and, though he would be glad to put an end to Otto's game, this was not his main aim. What he wanted above everything else was proof of Peter's death, so that Zara could marry Malcolm Derwent, Patrick could have a father and he himself could be free.

He followed Constant downstairs. He was feeling much better, relaxed both physically and mentally, and ready to face the others – even Sorel.

'Come in and sit down, Philip. How are you?' Brigadier Aubyn was friendly.

'I'm all right, sir. Thank you.'

'Dr John's still slightly worried about you.'

'John fusses too much,' Sorel said.

Aubyn paid no attention to this remark. 'We want you fit for Paris next weekend, Philip.'

'I guessed you would.'

'Of course. You'll go straight from here on Saturday morning. As I gather you know, the *Prix d'Excellence* is on Sunday. The French, more sensible than we are, have no inhibitions about Sunday race-meetings; nor do they have betting other than on the Pari Mutuel system – very much like our Tote.'

'I know,' said Philip. 'I've managed to learn a little about racing.'

'Good. Now, in France you'll have such support as we can give you, though it won't be much as we don't wish to involve the French authorities. But with luck we'll get a genuine breakthrough. You've done well so far, Philip. Thanks to you we've already made some headway, and we believe we're on the verge of solving this mystery, or rather one half of it – unfortunately what may turn out to be the less important half. Greg will explain what I mean.'

With that, Aubyn heaved himself out of his chair. 'I have to get back to London now, but I wanted to see you, however briefly, before I went, just to say keep up the good work. Remember, even if Otto was telling the truth and poor Peter is dead, we need to know how he died and why, for everyone's sake. You appreciate that?'

'Yes, sir.' There was no other possible reply, but when Aubyn and Sorel, who was escorting the Brigadier to his car, had left the room, Philip turned to Constant. 'When I was at school, Hamish,' he said, 'that would have been called a fairly meaningless pep talk. It's a long time since I've been on the receiving end of one. What do you think?'

Constant laughed. 'Maybe you're right. But the Brig really is pleased. We do seem to be making progress. Wait till you hear what Greg has to say.'

The first remark made by Sorel on his return was, 'We know you're familiar with drugs for people, Philip. Are you equally familiar with dope for horses?' It was not an auspicious beginning. Constant murmured a protest, which Sorel ignored. He regarded Philip sardonically.

'The answer to your question is no,' Philip said.

'Then you're about to learn. However, I must make one thing clear to start with. We've traced Sylvia and Tomas – '

'Thanks to Philip's quick wits,' Constant interjected. 'Our man lost Sylvia again on Saturday when she left the flat – in Harrods of all places.'

'If you've finished, Hamish?' The words, like particles of ice, made Constant flush. 'As I was saying,' Sorel continued, 'we can find no connection between Sylvia and Tomas Brelado – who, incidentally, is Sylvia's husband – and the Manheim lot. The Manheims may go to Ascot. It's a social event. But they're not enthusiastic racegoers, they don't own horses and have no interest in the beasts. They're happy to drink champagne in one of the hospitality suites when the occasion demands, but no more than that.'

'I see,' said Philip. 'You've made your point. You confirm what I've thought for some time. But is it any help?'

'Yes, because it's important to know your enemy – or enemies. I'll give you a run down. First, Sylvia and Tomas, Mr and Mrs Brelado, are both British citizens. She was born thirty-one years ago in the East End of London. Her parents ran a market stall, but she was a clever girl and won herself an education. She married Brelado ten years ago, and hasn't looked back since. He owns half a dozen betting shops. They have a large house in Hampstead and a villa in Spain and they live high on the hog.' He paused. 'So much for facts. When Hamish has poured us some drinks I'll get on to suppositions.'

This gave Philip a minute to think. He was impressed by the investigative effort that must have been needed to produce so much information so quickly, and doubtless there would be more to come. But Sorel's earlier introductory remarks about dope still disturbed him.

'This is where we begin to create our own scenario,' Sorel continued. 'I'll sketch out what I believe, and I want either of you to offer objections or support if you can. We'll hope to get further that way – call it "brain-storming" if you like. Now, I would imagine that Peter, who was a keen racegoer, met Sylvia at a meeting, found her attractive and cultivated her. And when she discovered that he often went abroad she encouraged him.'

Sorel glanced questioningly at Philip, who shook his head. He didn't understand the implications of what Sorel was saying. He accepted that there might be some kind of illicit betting ring in which Peter had got himself involved, but he saw no necessary connection with Peter's trips abroad.

'You may not know this,' continued Sorel, 'but Mary O'Donovan, among her other talents, is by way of being an expert on the racing world. She's produced an interesting theory which seems to me to fit. I'll keep it brief, but you need some background.

'Most horses that win a race in Britain are tested for dope, and sometimes the Stewards order a test if a horse has run inexplicably badly. If any banned substance is found the horse is usually disqualified, even if it was administered innocently, for example in accidentally contaminated foodstuff. I'm told that the techniques for discovering if a horse has been doped are very sophisticated and constantly improving, but – and this is relevant to the theory – drug manufacturing can often be one step ahead of forensic science.'

Sorel paused to sample his drink before going on. 'Mary tells me that she's heard rumours of a new drug – still possibly in the experimental stage – that doesn't show up with current testing methods. Apparently, it can come in the form of a lump of sugar or a sweet and therefore can easily be administered. It might not be illegal to import the stuff into the UK – I just don't know – but anyone who intended to use it would want to keep his possession of it very quiet indeed, and certainly would be wary about bringing it in himself – or herself. Mary believes that Sylvia may have used Peter to – '

'Are you suggesting that Peter would – '

'No, Philip, I'm not suggesting that Peter was like his brother, and prepared to smuggle drugs – human or animal. But it would have been typical of him, if he'd suspected that some racket was going on, to try to find concrete proof before informing the proper authorities – which is what he should have done at once, I admit.'

'Philip, it does fit,' Constant said quickly, seeing Philip's doubtful expression. 'Think! Peter goes to Amsterdam on duty. Some of this dope is supposed to be delivered to him then but, possibly because he's attacked, he never hands it over to Sylvia – and that costs Tomas money, a loss you remember he complained about. When Peter reappears, as they think, they no longer trust him. The box of chocs, as Sylvia said, was a kind of test.'

'Wasn't Peter taking an awful risk?' Philip asked. 'After all, it must have been Tomas's thugs who beat me up at the flat.'

'Peter was used to risks. They come with our job. But it is no part of our job to expose racing rackets. There are special security people for that.' Sorel was positive. 'This operation, it would seem, was a bit of private enterprise on Peter's part.'

'So where does all this lead? What happens about it now?' Philip had good reason to ask. 'What am I to do at Longchamp next weekend? Back Big Bear? Each way?'

'You'll have to play it by ear, as you did at Sandown Park. Mary O'Donovan will be around to advise you and, as the Brig said, you'll have some support. Anyway, Philip, in spite of that beating up you got, Tomas and company are not the real menace.'

Philip nodded a reluctant agreement. He couldn't pinpoint the flaw, but he sensed that there was something wrong with the analysis that Sorel had just outlined and the scenario he had described. Peter could be rash, he knew, but –

'What have you learnt about the "real menace", then?' he inquired.

'Not much, I regret to say. The Brussels police have got precisely nowhere in their investigation of the deaths of Lesaux, the nominal owner of *La Maison d'Or*, and the girl Melissa. But we've got a fair description of Otto, and the silver knob of the walking stick left in that upstairs room at the restaurant was engraved with the initials OVH, so there's hope of tracing him. At the moment, however, his link with the Manheims is purely circumstantial, though personally I'm prepared to accept it.'

'He knew how Peter lost the tip of his finger,' Constant said. 'He must have some connection with the Contessa.'

'Monique Scribini, yes.' Sorel was thoughtful. 'I'm quite aware that she must fit in somewhere.'

'Have you got any idea what these people are after or why they wanted Peter dead?' Philip persisted. 'You've never told me what he was doing in Amsterdam. You said he'd successfully completed his mission, whatever it was, but – '

'So he had, and it's not relevant, I assure you. However – ' Sorel appeared to hesitate. 'There's no reason why you shouldn't know something. Before he left for Schiphol he phoned us to say he'd come across something really hot. Unfortunately he never had the chance to tell us what it was.'

'And you haven't a clue?'

'No!'

Immediately Philip thought that Sorel was telling him a direct lie, and a glance at Constant confirmed his feeling. Hamish Constant was shifting in his chair, a sign that he was embarrassed. Philip said, 'At least you must have some clue as to what Otto – assuming Otto is the big white chief – will arrange for me next.'

Sorel shrugged. 'It's quite clear that he's got unfinished business with you, so we assume he'll take the initiative. He might arrange for you to be kidnapped in order to complete the business. Alternatively – '

'Alternatively he'll decide it's a waste of effort and will have me disposed of too?'

'That could be right.'

Philip gave a humourless laugh. 'You might try to sound a little regretful, Sorel. After all, in spite of everything, we are meant to be on the same side.'

'Sometimes one has no choice of one's allies, Janvrin,' Sorel replied coldly. 'However, I'm sure you know the saying that to sup with the devil you need a long spoon.'

In the silence that followed this remark there was a tap on the door, and Sorel was summoned to the phone. Philip didn't see him again before he left for London the next day.

TWENTY-THREE

'We are commencing our descent to Charles de Gaulle airport and will be landing shortly,' announced the very English voice of the British Airways captain in charge of the Saturday afternoon flight. 'The weather in Paris is good – hot and sunny. There is a risk of thunder later today or tomorrow, but it won't inconvenience us. I hope you have enjoyed your short flight with British Airways.'

As his voice ceased with a crackle over the speaker, and the cabin crew took up the familiar litany of the landing routine, Philip stared out of the window of the aircraft. He could see nothing but huge white billowing clouds. He was remembering the last time he had been in Paris, with Peter. Involuntarily he sighed.

'Cheer up!' Michael Lindsay, who was in the seat beside him, grinned encouragement. 'By the time we get into Paris and to our hotel, it won't be long before we can have a pre-dinner apéritif. And with any luck we'll be on our way home on Monday.'

'And if we don't have any luck?'

'Then we won't have achieved anything, which would be disappointing. But the consensus of opinion is that at worst we'll gain some information – and every little helps.'

'Regardless of the price paid for it?'

'Philip, I scent a certain *je ne sais quoi* about that question. Something's bugging you?'

Philip glanced sideways at Michael Lindsay. He liked the man, as he liked Hamish Constant and Mary O'Donovan, because all three treated him as a human being. Okay, he didn't expect them to ask an ex-con – especially one with his kind of record – to meet their friends and families, but he couldn't understand the hatred that he so obviously aroused in Gregory Sorel.

Suddenly he said, 'Michael, do you know why Sorel's dislike of me is so – so intense? I hardly expect to be loved in my circumstances, but Sorel really seems to hate my guts. It's as much as he can do to be civil to me, but I've never done him any personal harm.'

'He believes you might have, indirectly.' Lindsay gave an embarrassed smile.

'What?'

'Hasn't Hamish told you?'

'No! I asked him. He just said that Sorel had a short fuse, which may be true, but doesn't account for his attitude to me. For heaven's sake, Michael, what *is* the trouble? It makes life even more difficult than it needs to be, when Sorel doesn't trust me, and I can't trust him.'

'Yes, I can see that. It doesn't make it easy for any of us.' Lindsay hesitated, then plunged ahead. 'Philip, Greg Sorel has a particular reason – a good one – to hate anyone concerned with drugs. About the time you were on trial it was discovered that his twin sister, whose name was Caroline, had become a heroin addict. Not long afterwards she took her own life.'

'Oh God!' Philip was horrified. 'Poor Greg! Thank you for telling me. I had no idea.'

Lindsay looked at him curiously. He said, 'Of course it's not fair to blame you directly for Caroline's death, but – ' He shook his head. 'Perhaps you should have been told before, Philip. It might have helped.'

Philip didn't see how. He might have had more sympathy for Sorel, but his sympathy was the last thing Sorel would want. He was glad when they came out of the clouds, and not long afterwards the bump and the noise of the reverse thrust indicated that the plane had landed. At least this prevented further conversation. He hoped that Lindsay wouldn't revert to the subject again.

They took the airport bus to the terminal at Porte Maillot, and from there a taxi to the hotel which Peter had always favoured when he visited Paris. It was a comparatively small establishment, but its location in Neuilly had several advantages. It was within walking distance of the Métro and a direct line to the Place de la Concorde in the heart of the city. It was close to the Bois de Boulogne and, a fact not to be disregarded, thus fairly close to Longchamp racecourse. It was also very comfortable and, surprisingly for a French hotel of its size, possessed its own restaurant.

They were welcomed by the proprietor, a Madame Duclos, who said how good it was to see Monsieur Janvrin again. Clearly he was in for a busy weekend, she added. There had already been two telephone calls for him. The messages were in his room.

A porter carried their bags upstairs and showed them to adjoining rooms that overlooked a charming small courtyard, where some guests were sitting, already enjoying their apéritifs. As soon as the porter had gone, Lindsay joined Philip.

'Your phone messages?' he queried.

'One from Sylvia's friend, Monsieur Deleque, with a request to call him. Number provided, luckily. The other from a Monsieur Colombe, of whom I've never heard. No number left, but he'll call tomorrow.'

'Interesting. I'd guess you won't hear from this Monsieur Colombe again. I suspect that, whoever Monsieur Colombe is, he was just making sure you were expected here. They haven't wasted much time, have they?'

'Neither lot, it would seem.' Philip had been thinking how pleasant it would have been if, never having heard of Sylvia or Otto or Sorel, he could have stayed in this hotel by himself – or with Peter. 'Shall I phone Deleque now?'

'Why not?'

It was clear that the number he had been given was that of Deleque's home. A woman answered the phone. He heard her shout, *'Anton! Un coup de téléphone,'* and a child crying in the distance. When Deleque came to the phone he sounded hurried and nervous. As soon as Philip identified himself, Deleque spoke in English with an abrupt question.

'When do you leave Paris?'

'Monday.'

'I cannot come on Monday. Tomorrow evening I will come. You'll be there at the hotel.'

Philip was not sure if the last sentence was an order or a question, but he agreed that he would stay in the hotel the following evening. 'After the race-meeting,' he added, though this remark elicited no comment from Deleque.

Instead, Deleque said, 'This is a big one, Peter. Remember that. This is important. No tricks.'

'Of course not, Anton. Don't worry,' Philip said, but he felt a spasm of doubt. He wished there had not been this complication of horse-doping to add to potentially more pressing problems. Why had Peter let himself become involved with it, he wondered irritably. He said, 'See you tomorrow. Goodbye for now.'

He repeated the conversation to Lindsay, and they considered its implications together, though there was little to be learnt from it. They had to await developments. So much would depend on what happened between now and the races, as Lindsay pointed out.

'Do we stay in the hotel until it's time to go to Longchamp tomorrow afternoon?' Philip asked.

'No. I thought we might have a drink and some dinner here, and then take a walk in the Bois to get some exercise. And in the morning I wondered if you'd like to go to Mass?'

Philip was touched. 'I would indeed. Thanks, Michael.'

Lindsay grinned ruefully. 'Don't thank me, Philip. Orders. Don't forget you're the red rag Sorel wants to wave at the bull.'

Philip slept badly. The dinner had been excellent and the walk afterwards around a little lake called La Mare St James enjoyable – and without incident. As he tossed and turned he blamed the too-hard bed and the curious French bolster, but in fact it was his over-active mind that was keeping him awake. He couldn't rid himself of thoughts of Sorel and his twin sister.

He had never himself taken drugs, in spite of their availability; certainly he had had no personal experience of the devastating effect of hard drugs on anyone close to him. He wondered how he would have felt if it had been *his* sister who had become an addict and committed suicide. It was on this thought that eventually he fell into a fitful sleep.

He was woken from the nightmare – an inexplicable nightmare. He had a gun and he had to shoot either Peter or Sorel. He didn't know why, but there was no other option. He wanted to save Peter. He didn't even like Sorel. But he knew it was Peter he must kill and Gregory Sorel he must save. As he pulled the trigger, his gun aimed at Peter, he woke, the sound of the shot confused with banging on his door.

'For heaven's sake, Philip,' Lindsay said, 'I was seriously thinking of getting the pass key from Madame Duclos. I was afraid something had happened to you.'

'Sorry, I was fast asleep.'

'You must have been.' Lindsay came into the room followed by a waiter carrying a tray on which was breakfast for two. 'I thought we might break our fast together. There's no hurry. The nearest church is a ten-minute walk from here in the Place de Bagatelle, and the Mass isn't till eleven.'

'Breakfast in bed,' said Philip. 'This is a treat. You know this part of Paris well, Michael?' he added when the waiter had gone and Lindsay was pouring their coffee.

'I should. I lived in an apartment on the Avenue Maurice Barres when I was first married.'

'You're married?' Philip was surprised.

'Divorced. Marriage and our job don't usually flourish together. Inevitably we neglect one or the other. It takes a very understanding woman to cope. Mine wasn't.'

Philip was reminded of Peter and Zara. 'I'm sorry.' It was the conventional reply.

'No need. Two good things came out of it. I have a twelve-year-old daughter and she lives with my parents, and I became a Catholic.' Lindsay paused. 'More coffee?'

'Please.'

Philip realized that the casual question had put an end to Lindsay's confidences. He thought of Sorel and his dead sister again, of Michael Lindsay and his marriage, of Constant, Lisle, Mary O'Donovan, even Brigadier Aubyn. He was intimately connected with all these people, but he knew so little about them and their private lives.

It was a beautiful Sunday morning, with blue sky and sunshine and no hint of the thunderstorm that the British Airways captain had threatened the previous day. The church was full without being packed, the singing good, the sermon short, the atmosphere devotional. Philip came away feeling relaxed and content.

The two men started to stroll back to their hotel in companionable silence. They reached the junction with the rue de

Longchamp and turned right. It was a pleasant walk, without much traffic. And Michael Lindsay was caught off guard.

The car came from behind them at a moderate speed. Then, without warning it accelerated, mounted the pavement and drove straight at them. Though he was taken by surprise, Lindsay's reactions were swift. Alerted at the last moment by the sudden increase in engine noise, he used his shoulder as a battering ram and heaved Philip, who was walking on the inside, through an open gateway in front of a small apartment block. While Philip sprawled on the gravel Lindsay had no chance to save himself.

The car hit him, picked him up, threw him on to its bonnet and carried him twenty-five yards before tossing him into the road like a sack of garbage. He lay still. With a screech of tyres the car drove on, gathering speed as it went. By the time Philip had staggered to his feet it was a distant dark shape that might or might not have been a Mercedes.

Philip ran to where Michael Lindsay lay spreadeagled on the ground and knelt by him. A Renault drew up beside them and two men got out. Concierges hurried from the neighbouring apartment blocks and a young couple stopped and got off their bicycles. Michael Lindsay groaned.

'Thank God! He's alive! Please, someone, get an ambulance quickly.' Without thinking Philip spoke in English, but it didn't matter.

'Allow me. I'm a doctor,' said the older man who had emerged from the Renault.

His younger companion helped Philip to stand and the doctor took his place beside Lindsay. Philip was whey-faced and shaking; he knew that Michael Lindsay had saved his life, but at what cost? One of the concierges had hurried to telephone. Philip sat on a nearby wall and waited. Other people gathered.

The *gendarmerie* were the first of the authorities to arrive, closely followed by an ambulance. The doctor and his companion gave their version of the incident. Philip answered questions, produced his passport, explained that Lindsay and himself were English visitors having a short break in Paris. It was only a few minutes before Michael Lindsay was lifted carefully into the ambulance which, the doctor directed, should take him to the American Hospital in Neuilly. Philip was allowed to go with him.

The ambulance drove fast, and fortunately the hospital was

close. The driver pulled up in front of the emergency entrance within minutes. The para-medic who had been sitting in the rear with Philip opened the doors of the ambulance and stepped down. Philip, who by now was in control of his emotions, glanced at Lindsay before getting out.

Michael Lindsay's eyes were open. His lips moved. Philip bent over him. It wasn't more than a whisper, but Philip caught the words.

'Phone Sorel! Phone Sorel! Quickly!'

'Yes, Michael. All right. As soon as I can,' Philip said, but he doubted if Lindsay had heard; his eyes had closed again and his face was grey.

Philip was relieved but not surprised to catch Sorel in his office. He explained briefly what had happened, treating the matter as if it had been an ordinary hit-and-run accident. The hospital had given him the privacy of a small room with a phone, but he was conscious of speaking through a switchboard on an open line, and there was no need to be explicit with Sorel.

'How is Michael?' was Sorel's first question.

'Badly hurt. I don't know how badly yet, but it could be very serious.'

'All right.' There was a pause, during which Philip imagined Sorel weighing the alternatives, making his choice, deciding which pawns to move. Then Sorel continued, 'You are not to worry about Michael, Janvrin. As soon as we've finished this call I'll get on to the Embassy and they will look after him. As far as you're concerned, you must keep your appointment – or at least go to Longchamp – this afternoon. Tell Mary the story. Tell her I'd like you both to return tonight.'

'I can't make it tonight.'

'Why not? You're too vulnerable without Michael, and there's nothing to be gained by taking further risks after this episode.'

'It's simple. Deleque left me a message to phone him, and we've arranged for him to come to the hotel this evening.'

'I see. Okay, then. If you can get a late enough flight, do. If not, early tomorrow. You'll be met. And, Janvrin, take care! It's useless to acquire information if you can't pass it on. You understand?'

'Yes, I understand,' Philip said. He was speaking to no one. Sorel had already cut the connection without even bothering to say goodbye. As for wishing him luck, Philip reflected, that sort of amiable hope was out of the question.

TWENTY-FOUR

It was nearer three o'clock than two when Philip set off for Longchamp. In spite of Sorel's instructions, he had delayed his departure from the hospital until an official from the Embassy, who introduced himself as Charles Stafford, had arrived.

Stafford was middle-aged, with greying hair and, to judge from his appearance and behaviour, more senior than Philip had expected. He was also reassuring, seeming to accept the situation as fairly routine. He volunteered that Sorel had spoken to him; he would take care of Michael and deal with all the formalities. All Philip needed to do was pay Michael's hotel bill and pack his bag to be collected later. There was no reason for Philip to wait at the hospital, for by then Lindsay was in the operating theatre. It was pointless for him to stay. If he wanted to he could phone later and inquire about Michael's condition.

Sunday afternoon was a time for relations and friends to visit their sick. A couple, laden with flowers and fruit, descended from a taxi as Philip came out of the main door. He waited impatiently while they paid the driver, and finally allowed him to grab the cab. He gave directions, not to the hotel – paying Michael's bill and packing his bag could wait – but to Longchamp.

'Someone died and left you a nice little fortune to squander on the gee-gees, guv'nor?' asked the driver.

'No!'

'People don't usually go straight from the hospital to the races.'

'I suppose not.' Philip's mind had been on Michael Lindsay, and it was with a slight shock that he realized the cab-driver was speaking English, albeit with an American accent. At once he suspected a trap of some kind.

'Are you English?' he demanded.

'French Canadian. From Montreal. My wife's French.' The man replied laconically. 'You know Paris well, guv'nor?'

'I've not been here for some years.'

194

'Then you'll see a lot of changes.'

Philip relaxed. The driver was clearly harmless, but he liked to talk. He kept up a running commentary until they reached Longchamp. Even when Philip was paying him, he said, 'Remember that old windmill over there at the north end of the racecourse, guv'nor? It's all that remains of a thirteenth-century monastery, or so they say. A great landmark, that is.'

'I remember it.' But now he was at Longchamp he was in no mood to inspect landmarks, ancient or otherwise. He had no time to waste.

'Keep the change,' he said hurriedly, over-tipping in his haste to get away.

'Gee, thanks, guv'nor. Good luck with picking the winners,' the man called after him.

Philip waved in acknowledgement, as he went through the gates and on to the course, buying a racecard on the way. He was wondering where he was most likely to find Mary O'Donovan, and he noted that a race – a sprint – was due to start shortly. Therefore he decided that the parade ring would be his best chance. But he couldn't see her. There were too many people around the flower-bordered, tree-encircled ring, watching intently as the horses walked slowly past, waiting for their jockeys to mount before cantering down to the start. Then he felt a hand on his elbow. He whipped round.

'My, but you're jumpy today, Peter. Been burning the candle at both ends?'

'Oh, it's you!'

With relief Philip recognized the foxy face of Frank Pringle, whom he had last seen at Sandown Park. Foxy was grinning broadly. He was displaying none of Deleque's nervousness, and seemed completely at ease. The logical assumption was that he was not involved in the latest import deal to which Deleque had referred.

It was taking a risk, he knew, but Philip asked, 'You've got a present for Mrs Brelado?'

'Who?' Foxy's face was blank.

'Mrs Brelado – a close friend of Sylvia's.'

'Never heard of her.' Foxy peered at him suspiciously. 'Look, what is this, Peter? I do my job and you do yours. It doesn't pay to be curious, old son. Just take what the gods give, that's my motto and, if you want my advice, you'll adopt it too.'

'Don't worry. I'm not a fool.' Philip spoke lightly.

'It's all very well for the likes of you. You'd get away with things I never would.' It appeared from this apparently inconsequential remark that Foxy was not altogether appeased.

'Tough luck!' was the only reply that occurred to Philip.

Foxy glared. 'Here, take this.' He thrust a packet into Philip's hand. 'Five thou – Francs, of course – on Big Bear to place in the *Excellence* – that's the race after next. All proceeds go to Sylvia, unless you've squared with her. I've made my bet, so I'm okay and I'll say bye-bye till next time, Peter.'

'Goodbye.'

Philip absorbed Foxy's orders, hoping there would be no next time. Then he heard someone calling his name. 'Hi, Janvrin! Peter Janvrin!' A young man was pushing his way through the crowd of racegoers towards him.

'Hello, Peter,' he said on reaching Philip. 'You remember me? Colin O'Donovan, Mary's nephew.'

He was in his middle twenties, of medium height and powerfully built. His grin was infectious, but his eyes never remained still, as if he were bored with his present company and seeking someone more interesting. He didn't inspire Philip with trust, though Philip guessed that what he might well be doing was searching for anyone taking an untoward interest in them.

'Remember you?' Philip said hesitantly. 'Frankly no – er – Colin. Where's Mary?'

'Up there.' He pointed to the six-tiered grandstand. 'And we'd better get a move on if we don't want to miss the next race. But what about Michael? Isn't he with you?'

'I'll tell you when we've found Mary.' Philip was partially reassured by the reference to Michael Lindsay. 'You lead the way, Colin.'

The glance that Colin O'Donovan gave Philip was shrewd and amused, but he did as he was asked. As he had said, they found Mary in one of the grandstands, focusing her field glasses on the *Pelouse*, the cheap public enclosure the other side of the race track, where for a nominal entry fee racegoers and their families could lounge on the grass and picnic if they wished.

Mary kissed Philip on both cheeks. 'You're late,' she said. 'I was starting to worry. Where's Michael?'

There was no hope of being tactful. 'In the American Hospital in Neuilly. We were involved in a hit-and-run.'

'Oh, God! Is he bad?'

'Not good. They're operating. He saved me.' Philip told them the full story of events since his arrival in Paris, including the instructions he had received from Sorel and the fact that he was expecting a visit from Deleque later in the day.

He had scarcely finished speaking when there came the thud of hooves, and a dozen horses thundered past, accompanied by a roar from the crowd. The favourite had won, apparently. The grandstand emptied quickly as people went to the bar to console themselves, to celebrate after collecting their winnings or to place their bets on the next race, the big one, the *Prix d'Excellence*.

Mary, who had absorbed Philip's tale in silence, suddenly took charge. She said, 'I'll go and phone British Airways and get us on the last flight to London this evening. Philip, you stay here with Colin.'

'I have to put this bet on Big Bear. I've not had a chance to do it yet.'

'All right. Then we'll meet before the race either here or at the parade ring.'

Mary went off to phone, and Colin escorted Philip to the Pari Mutuel building. There were queues at all the *guichets*.

'What's the bet?' Colin asked.

'Five thousand francs. To place. I've no idea whether Big Bear's a favourite or an outsider.'

Colin laughed. 'You can't be much of a gambler.' He glanced at the newspaper he was carrying. 'According to this Big Bear's not got much of a chance, so the pay-out could be good. And an each-way bet might not be much of a risk. Shall I put a hundred of my own on him?'

'Providing you don't hold me responsible if you lose it,' Philip said. His distrust of O'Donovan had evaporated, and he was beginning to enjoy the man's company.

From the Pari Mutuel they went to the parade ring. Big Bear was certainly not impressive. He was a large bay gelding with an ungainly walk. His jockey was an apprentice. Philip realized that the circumstances were not unlike those that had surrounded Box of Chox at Sandown, though this was a vastly more

197

important race – so important that it was preceded by a fanfare of trumpets and a lengthy parade on the course.

In the end, by stretching out his neck, Big Bear managed to place third, a long way behind the front runners. Colin was pleased. He went to collect their winnings.

By the time he returned to join them Mary had decided there was no reason for staying any longer at Longchamp. She had managed to obtain three seats on the nine-forty flight to London, and had arranged that they should be met at Heathrow. Now she wanted to organize their departure.

The skies were darkening, the promised thunderstorm becoming more likely every minute, and they were lucky to find a taxi just outside the racecourse. It dropped Philip off at his hotel with Colin, and took Mary on to the hotel close to Porte Maillot where she and Colin were staying. She would bring Colin's bag with her and would join the men in Philip's room. The concierge would be warned that Philip was expecting a visitor, and Philip could meet Deleque in the lounge.

They agreed that provided Deleque arrived before eight they would be able to get to the airport in time to catch their flight. But it all depended on Deleque. If he failed to arrive until later, they would have to make new plans.

The phone rang once while they were waiting, and Philip hastened to answer it. But it was merely another call from the mysterious Monsieur Colombe who, when Philip answered as 'Monsieur Janvrin', cut the connection without speaking.

'I would guess that gentleman's got a name that doesn't suit him,' Colin remarked.

'You think he could be the chap who ran Michael and me down this morning? There was nothing dove-like about that one, certainly.'

'I wouldn't be surprised. He might well have realized he'd got the wrong man. You'd better be careful how you cross the road when you get back to London, though probably they won't try the same ploy twice.'

Colin O'Donovan spoke with such impersonal candour that Philip had to grin. But it was no joke. Michael Lindsay was witness to that. He wondered what they would try next, for there was no doubt there would be a next time. These people obviously didn't hesitate to kill. In comparison Sylvia and Tomas and their horse-doping were almost virtuous.

Philip made one call himself – to the American hospital. The news was encouraging: the operation had been successful and Michael Lindsay had regained consciousness. The three of them breathed a sigh of relief.

At seven o'clock, when Deleque had still not put in an appearance, they decided that at least they could go down for an early supper. On Sunday evenings the hotel served only a cold buffet, and this proved perfectly adequate.

But, as a social occasion, the meal was hardly a success. They were much too tense. The question mark over Deleque's arrival meant that the approach of every waiter, who might be bringing the hoped-for summons to the reception desk, became a moment fraught with anxiety.

At last Mary O'Donovan put their thoughts into words. 'Where on earth is this Deleque man? It's seven-thirty. If he doesn't come soon we'll have to abandon our flight.'

Ten more minutes passed before a message was brought to their table. Anton Deleque was in the lounge. Philip found him sitting on a settee, mopping his brow with a silk handkerchief. Propped up beside him was a large stuffed cuddly toy – a big bear. Philip stared at it in disbelief as Deleque jumped to his feet to offer a clammy hand.

The bear, encased in plastic, was about eighteen inches high. It wore a bright blue suit with a stiff white collar and a red bow tie. Its expression was amiable. Any small child would have loved it.

'Is that for Sylvia?' Philip asked.

'Yes. Big Bear.' Deleque pointed to a label that hung round its neck. 'It's a pity he's not a horse. It would be more appropriate but – ' He laughed nervously.

'But I can't take that,' Philip protested. 'It's too big to go into my bag.'

'You don't want to hide him in your bag. Tuck him under your arm. Make it look casual. Lots of travellers take home big stuffed toys as gifts for their kids. It's not unusual.'

Deleque was right, Philip thought. He remembered seeing a

woman carrying a large rabbit on the flight from Brussels. Nevertheless, he balked at the idea.

'You must, my dear Peter. You've no option.' Deleque was leaning towards him so that Philip could smell the garlic on his breath and see the sweat on his upper lip. 'This damned animal squares my account. So, no more for me. Not unless my wife gets pregnant again, and it won't be by me if she does. I've seen to that.'

Philip saw no point in trying to persuade Deleque to elucidate these seemingly senseless comments. But, though he realized it was a stupid question, he did ask, 'You mean you've been doing this for the money?'

'What else?' said Deleque. 'You don't imagine I'd take such risks for fun, do you? But tell Sylvia this is the last. She'll have to find someone else.'

'She won't be pleased.'

'No. That woman's a bitch, but I don't think she can touch me. Anyway, I'm not getting in any deeper. It's a mug's game. If you've got any sense you'll get out too. But you like playing with fire, don't you, Peter?'

Philip hesitated. 'Sometimes it's unavoidable,' he said at length.

Inevitably the irony was lost on Deleque. Philip glanced at his watch, wondering if he had time to offer the man a cognac. He felt rather sorry for the Frenchman. But Deleque was already on his feet, eager to get away. He refused the drink, though with some reluctance, explaining that his young son was ill and he needed to get home. It reminded Philip of Patrick, and his promise to Zara to send the boy a postcard from wherever he was abroad. He reproached himself for having forgotten, and wondered if the concierge or Madame Duclos could help.

'Here, take Big Bear,' said Deleque, picking up the toy. 'Guard him well. He's precious.'

Philip, surprised by the weight, nearly dropped the animal. 'It's heavy,' he said without thinking.

'*Mon Dieu*, what do you expect?' Deleque shook his head. 'Peter, sometimes you behave as if you're crazy, especially since your illness.' His small brown eyes peered into Peter's face. 'You will be careful, won't you? This is no time to take foolish risks.'

Philip hastened to reassure him. 'You bet I'll be careful, Anton,' he said.

'What flight will you be on tomorrow? I have to let Sylvia know. She'll meet you at the airport.'

'She will?' Philip was taken aback. He thought fast; he must allow Sorel a reasonable opportunity to examine the bear. 'I'll be on the British Airways flight that gets in around noon,' he said, trusting there was one. 'I'll look out for her.'

'Right.'

They walked together to the hotel entrance. A couple of women, coming in, smiled with amusement at the man with the big bear under his arm. Sheepishly, Philip returned their smiles.

Deleque stopped in the doorway and held out his hand. 'Goodbye, Peter. I won't say *au revoir* because I don't expect we shall meet again, but I wish you *bonne chance*.'

'Goodbye, Anton, *et bonne chance*.'

And, as Peter returned to collect the O'Donovans he thought that Deleque was probably going to need good luck if he were to escape scot free from his involvement with the Brelados.

TWENTY-FIVE

The storm that had been threatening since the afternoon finally broke as Philip and the two O'Donovans set off for Charles de Gaulle airport. In the typical fashion of the Paris basin, thunder, like a fierce animal, growled deep, shocking with an occasional roar. The skies over the city were rent with jagged cracks of forked lightning. Then the rain came.

It descended in a deluge, and was partly hail. It rattled on the roof of the taxi and rendered the windscreen wipers useless, so that the driver was forced to slow to a crawl. When it eased and the visibility improved he increased his speed, but the road was awash with water, each vehicle throwing up spray on the one that was following it. To drive fast was an impossibility.

Mary was constantly glancing at her watch. 'We should just make it,' she said as they neared the airport.

'Unless Philip's bear causes a delay,' said Colin.

'It's not *my* bear.' Philip was firm.

Colin laughed. But he had his mind on his job. He had the money ready for the taxi-driver the moment they reached the terminal, and he shepherded them swiftly and efficiently through the formalities. The final call for their flight had come over the public address system some minutes earlier, but the aircraft had not yet been closed up. With only hand baggage they were allowed through and Mary was proved right; they just made it.

Big Bear had been safely stowed away in the locker above Philip's head, and as the aircraft took off he leant back in his seat and closed his eyes. He had had no lunch and very little dinner. He was tired and hungry. While they were waiting for their taxi to arrive at the hotel he had scribbled a brief message to Patrick on a postcard provided by Madame Duclos, who had promised to mail it for him. Suddenly he remembered that in his haste he had forgotten to copy Peter's distinctive handwriting. He could only hope that Zara would think of some credible explanation. It was too late for him to do anything about it now.

The flight was bumpy, but after a while Philip must have drifted into sleep, for the next thing he knew was being shaken violently. In fact the plane was bucking as it descended through the turbulent thunder clouds towards Heathrow. They landed soon afterwards, and found that here too the rain was pouring down. It suited Philip's mood. He found it difficult to respond when, as they were gathering up their belongings before leaving the aircraft, Colin murmured, 'Don't leave Big Bear behind, whatever you do, Philip.'

'Would you like to carry the wretched animal yourself?' Philip's smile was wan.

'Don't worry!' Colin O'Donovan had realized that his facetiousness was unwelcome. 'It's okay. Everything's under control.'

And indeed it was. At the end of the airbridge Hamish Constant, accompanied by a British Airways official, was waiting to greet them. Constant took Philip's bag, but let him retain the bear, and a few curious glances from less privileged fellow-passengers were cast at the small party as it disappeared through a door marked 'Private. Staff Only'.

They walked in almost total silence through what seemed to Philip an extraordinarily long series of green-painted corridors, from behind which came the clatter of computer printers and the murmur of voices. Circumventing both immigration and customs controls they emerged into the rain-sodden open air. A limousine was waiting at the kerb, another smaller car behind it.

'Au revoir, Philip,' Mary said; it was the first time she had called him by his real name.

Colin merely nodded, but he was holding out his arms for the bear, which Philip relinquished gratefully. Then the O'Donovans were running for the humbler vehicle and Philip was being urged by Constant across the pavement into the limousine. The chauffeur drove off immediately.

Constant explained. 'Mary and Colin are going to the office to report to Greg and hand over the bear.'

'Doesn't Sorel ever sleep?'

Constant grinned. 'Not much. He's wedded to his work as it were. And there's the time element to consider. If that bear's got to be taken apart and put together again for you to hand over to

Sylvia around noon tomorrow, some quick work's going to be necessary. Mind you, I don't know if that's what Greg will want you to do. It may not be physically possible to repair the animal. In which case he'll have to come up with some bright idea to deal with the situation.'

Philip grunted. Although he had no desire to be beaten up by the Brelados' thugs again, Sylvia was the lesser of his worries. He would have preferred Sorel to come up with some bright idea about Otto's crowd, who were obviously far more dangerous. It seemed to him a pity to waste too much effort over a racing racket, however illegal or immoral, when the same effort might be deployed to better effect in tracking down cold-blooded killers. However, it wasn't his business to question Sorel's judgement; he had to accept that the man knew what he was doing.

On reaching central London, they were driven not to Peter's apartment – which Philip now considered to be his 'home', in as much as he had one – but to a small house in Chelsea. There was a light above the front door, but otherwise the place was in darkness.

'This house belongs to a woman whose husband was in the army with the Brig and she helps us from time to time,' Constant explained. 'She's well-trained. She doesn't ask questions. Greg thought it best that you shouldn't go to the flat tonight, but I've collected some clean clothes for you. I'll go straight to the office in the morning to get Big Bear, and Sorel may decide to come back here with me before we go to the airport; otherwise I'll bring any necessary instructions.'

Philip nodded his acquiescence. He was wondering if there was any hope of getting something to eat before they went to bed. To judge from the darkness of the house he thought it unlikely. But he was wrong.

Almost the first thing Mrs Grainger asked them was what they would like. 'There's soup and sandwiches,' she said. 'Cheese, fruit and whatever you care to drink.'

'That'll be wonderful,' Philip said quickly, before Constant could refuse.

Mrs Grainger smiled at him. She was a striking woman in her fifties, tall and big-boned, with a particularly serene and amiable expression. She was also a good cook. The soup was home-made, and Philip was glad of a second helping. He ate his full share of the sandwiches too, and felt compelled to explain that he had had little to eat all day. But Mrs Grainger merely smiled again, showing no curiosity.

'I'm off to bed now,' she said as she cleared away the last of their supper. 'Your room's the first on the left at the top of the stairs, but do help yourself to a nightcap before you go up. You remember where the liquor's kept, Hamish?'

'Thank you, yes, Mrs Grainger. There's only one thing – breakfast. Will eight be okay?'

'Of course. Good-night to you. I hope you both sleep well.'

Curiously it was Philip who fell asleep at once, exhausted by the events of the day, while Constant, listening to Philip's steady breathing in the bed next to him, lay awake. With Michael Lindsay out of action, Sorel had given Constant primary responsibility for Philip and this worried him. In the short time he had known Philip Janvrin, he had grown to like him in spite of his past record, but he had no doubt that Sorel considered the ex-convict to be expendable.

Gregory Sorel sat at his desk. He was red-eyed from lack of sleep and he needed a shave. His tie was loosened, the top button of his shirt undone and his usually immaculate persona was scarcely recognizable. In front of him, propped up in a sitting position by a pile of books, was Big Bear.

The technicians had done their work carefully, but at the moment Big Bear was in an equal state of disarray. All his clothes had been removed, and lay in a neat pile to one side of him. On the other side was his head, which had been unscrewed from his fur-covered fibre-glass body. Somehow, as a result of this indignity, his expression had changed so that his brown button eyes stared reproachfully at Sorel.

The time was six-thirty. In half an hour Brigadier Aubyn would be delivered to the office by his chauffeur. Sorel, as requested, had phoned him earlier, as soon as the bear and his clothing had been thoroughly examined, and the contents of his inside analysed. The Brigadier's reaction had been unprintable.

Now Sorel went to the cloakroom to have a wash and tidy his

clothes. As he returned through his assistant's office to his own room, he plugged in the kettle. By the time his electric razor had given him a smooth skin, the kettle was singing.

Although there was a machine at the end of the corridor that dispensed a variety of drinks, Sorel refused to use it. With reluctance he accepted instant coffee, but mostly in the office he drank tea, China tea bought by himself, and he drank it from a Spode cup, which he replaced whenever it became chipped. This careful routine greatly amused Brigadier Aubyn, though he didn't show his feelings; he had a sincere respect for Greg Sorel and his dedication to his job.

The Brigadier went straight to Sorel's office. He settled his heavy frame into the visitor's chair, but his presence dominated the room. 'So that's the animal,' he said, poking a finger in the direction of Big Bear. 'Quite a turn-up for the book. Isn't that what your racing fraternity would say?'

'It's a pity we can't ask Peter,' Sorel remarked sadly.

'Yes, indeed. But you must accept that it's he who let us in for all this. It's really none of our business, Greg, and it's complicated what we ought to be doing.'

'It wasn't Peter's fault that he got clobbered by Otto's crowd before he could get evidence against the Brelados.'

'True, but surely he could damn well have told us about his suspicions.'

'Then you'd have told him it was none of our business, sir.'

'So I would, and I'd have been right. Incidentally, can that bear be put together again?'

'Oh yes, sir. There's no problem.'

Aubyn sighed. It was useless to argue with Sorel on the subject of drugs; he was fanatical about the stuff, any form of it. It was this fact that had drawn Sorel close to Peter Janvrin during the latter's distress at Philip being arrested and jailed for drug-running. And now between them the Janvrins had landed him, Dermot Aubyn, with the problem of explaining to the head of the Drug Squad at the Met how he just happened to know that at around noon today . . . He would have to do a lot of telephoning before then.

'You'll brief Philip, Greg, or get Constant to do so. He'll need to know what's going to happen.'

'I'd rather he didn't, sir. I think it might affect his behaviour and cause the Brelado woman to be suspicious. After all, we don't want her to run off and leave him to be caught with the goods – not this time.'

'Very well, Greg.' Brigadier Aubyn heaved his great bulk from his chair. 'But I must insist that he's given full cover. We won't gain anything if one of Otto's minions skewers him with a knife or shoots him in the back while he's handing over that wretched bear to Sylvia Brelado. It would merely complicate the situation for us. Incidentally, I shall make sure the Drug Squad square arrangements with customs, so that Philip Janvrin's not stopped by accident – and I'll also do my best to make sure they take no action until Sylvia Brelado's well away from Philip.'

'Yes, sir,' Sorel said.

On reaching Heathrow Philip and Constant almost exactly reversed their path of the previous night from air-side to limousine. Escorted by a British Airways official they marched down the same green-painted corridors until they came to a small VIP lounge. Here they waited until the official was warned that the flight from Paris had arrived. He then led them through further passages into the crowded baggage hall, where they were struck by the usual barely-concealed hysteria as passengers searched for the right carousels and the right luggage. He pointed to one trickle of passengers, who having passed through immigration, were hoping to claim their luggage as quickly as possible. 'That's the first of the Paris crowd,' he said. 'Our timing's spot on.' He sounded pleased with himself. Constant pushed Philip gently forward.

'Good luck! And don't worry! It's all arranged. See you later.'

Philip nodded. He fell in behind a couple of businessmen with bulging briefcases and walked fast, carrying his overnight bag in his right hand and Big Bear under the other arm. His instructions, relayed by Constant when he returned to the house with Big Bear, had been minimal, to behave as if he had just come off the flight, meet Sylvia and hand over the bear. No one paid him any attention. Nevertheless he was unpleasantly aware of the stuffed toy he was carrying. After what Michael Lindsay had told him about Sorel's sister he had more understanding of Sorel and his personal feelings, but he didn't place any greater trust in him.

His apprehension was reinforced when on entering the 'Green' channel he found himself behind a middle-aged woman and a small girl. The wretched child had spotted Big Bear, and couldn't take her eyes off him.

'Look, Gran! Look! Isn't he beautiful?'

Big Bear had certainly recaptured his pristine appearance. He was once more fully dressed and, with his head screwed on again, his benign expression had returned. Even in his plastic covering he was irresistible.

The little girl put out a hand to touch him. 'Could I hold him for a minute?' she asked.

'No!' Philip said sharply, too sharply, drawing back. The last thing he wanted was a piping voice to draw attention to the bear by telling everyone around how terribly heavy the animal was.

The woman, who had been about to smile at Philip, changed her mind at Philip's tone and pulled the child back close to her. 'You mustn't talk to strangers, dear,' she said loudly. 'You never know what sort of person they might be.'

Philip winced. But fortunately the crowd had thinned and he was able to move forward rapidly. Minutes later he had completed his passage through the 'Green' channel, and had come out into the arrivals hall.

The place was moderately busy. He caught a glimpse of Colin O'Donovan, but he had been warned not to recognize anyone who might be a minder. Then he saw Sylvia Brelado. She was wearing a light-blue suit, beautifully cut to do justice to her neat, petite figure and, as always, her fair hair was perfectly groomed. She looked like a successful businesswoman, capable and self-assured.

She removed her oversized glasses as Philip pushed his way towards her. 'Hello, Peter,' she greeted him, but her eyes, like those of the little girl, were on Big Bear. She replaced her glasses. 'Had a good trip?'

'Highly successful,' Philip said. 'As you can see I've brought you this delightful present from Anton. Incidentally, he told me to tell you he intends to retire.'

'Retire? What rubbish! Of course he can't retire.'

'All I can tell you is that's what he said. He's not happy in his work, it seems.'

208

'Too bad,' Sylvia replied viciously.

'And we were lucky at Longchamp. We made a nice little packet. Let me give you your winnings, Sylvia. Here, you take Big Bear!'

Philip put his bag on the ground, passed Sylvia the bear and reached into his jacket pocket for his wallet. While they had been talking he had been aware of a man standing nearby and taking an undue interest in them. He was a big bruiser of a fellow who suddenly reminded Philip of one of the thugs who had beaten him up shortly after his arrival in Peter's flat. Sylvia's minder, perhaps.

The possibility that Sylvia might have some protection because of the value of Big Bear had not occurred to Sorel, nor to the Drugs Squad officers. This was to have unfortunate consequences. Sylvia put the money in her handbag and then clutched the bear to her before saying goodbye to Philip and moving away from him in the direction of the exit opposite the short-term car park.

Philip watched her go. She was about twelve feet away when two quiet men in grey suits approached her. Philip moved closer to overhear the conversation.

'Mrs Brelado?'

'Yes?'

'I'm arresting you on a charge of importing forbidden substances into the United Kingdom, and of being in possession of such substances. You are not compelled to say anything, but anything you do say . . .'

For a moment the tableau seemed frozen. Then Sylvia's eyes widened as she looked for a means of escape. One of the men, sensing this, made a movement to stop her. Simultaneously the bruiser took two steps forward and brought the edge of his hand in a chopping motion across the back of the officer's neck. The man collapsed.

Sylvia started to run, pursued by the other drugs squad officer, who was in turn followed by her minder. The people around scattered to let her pass, all except Gregory Sorel who, piqued by the Brigadier's order that Philip should be given full cover, had decided to come to Heathrow himself. Determined that Sylvia shouldn't escape with the incriminating bear he ran towards her, and Sylvia, who didn't recognize him as an enemy, made no effort to avoid him.

But her minder, the bruiser, had seen the danger. He was not a thinking man, or he might have hesitated before drawing a firearm in the arrivals hall at Heathrow. And he might have realized that the man he knew as Peter Janvrin, whom he had once been sent to beat up, was close behind him.

Everything had happened very quickly and Philip, taken by surprise, not least at the sight of Sorel, was unaware afterwards of any conscious action on his part. In fact, having automatically picked up his bag, he had followed Sylvia and now, as he saw the thug stop and level a small automatic at Sorel, he brought the bag down hard on the man's arm.

The result was startling. The gun went off. The bruiser uttered a roar of anger mixed with pain and surprise. Then he collapsed, moaning, on the ground. He had shot himself in the foot. Somewhere in the hall a woman, not Sylvia, started to scream.

A shot in the arrivals hall of a major international airport at a time when terrorism was rife! The result could easily have been foreseen. There was general disorder, but no actual panic as the hall filled very rapidly with armed uniformed and plain-clothes Metropolitan Police officers and Airport Police. Walkie-talkies crackled as the routine swung into action and the area was sealed off. The sirens of ambulances and fire engines could be heard approaching.

Any possibility of the quiet arrest for which Brigadier Aubyn had been hoping had vanished. A couple of pssengers from the Paris flight had taken photographs, including one of an 'unknown man' struggling with Sylvia. An even more enterprising character had obtained a videotape of part of the incident. A freelance journalist, at Heathrow on the chance of getting a story, rapidly reported a brief version over the phone. Given a poor day for news, radio and television commentators made the most of the affair that evening, and next day the tabloids were full of it.

Perhaps the best headline read, 'Heroin Haul at Heathrow'.

TWENTY-SIX

'Publicity is the last thing that this department seeks or wants. We may just manage to avoid it on this occasion, but if we do it will be the result of luck rather than judgement. That affair at Heathrow yesterday was a shambles, and I hate to think what the repercussions could be.'

Brigadier Aubyn spoke softly, very softly, and to anyone who knew him this was a sign that he was very angry. Sorel shifted uncomfortably in his chair; his groin, where Sylvia had kneed him, ached, and the hand she had bitten was extremely painful. He too was not in the best of tempers.

He said, 'Sir, none of this would have happened if those damned Drugs Squad men hadn't made their arrest so openly in the airport arrivals hall. Surely it's their usual practice to tail drugs traffickers and see where the product finishes up. I can't think what possessed them yesterday.'

'You've got a point, I suppose,' said the Brigadier, 'but you know as well as I do that one's never clear what these stupid bastards think they're up to.' Aubyn's temper showed in his language. 'They've got other sources, and they play their cards close to their damned plain-clothes chests. Nevertheless, that doesn't excuse our part in the shambles.'

'It could have been worse, sir,' Colin O'Donovan said placatingly.

But the Brigadier was not to be placated. 'Of course it could have been worse,' he replied sharply. 'Greg could be dead or seriously wounded. And so could Philip Janvrin, whom you were supposed to be minding, Colin.'

'And between us we could have let Sylvia get away,' Constant volunteered.

The cold stare that the Brigadier directed at him silenced any further contribution from Constant. 'We!' he said. 'That's the trouble. That's been the trouble all along since Peter got himself involved in this matter. *We* are not responsible for catching heroin dealers or any other kind of dope merchants – especially racing crooks, if that's what Peter really thought they were. This kind of operation's not *our* job. If we happen on oddities that give rise to suspicion we report them to the proper authorities. Once we were reasonably certain that these Brelados had nothing to do with the crew we were after – Otto and his mob – *we* should have left them strictly alone.'

There was silence. Sorel gritted his teeth; he yearned to point out that Aubyn had agreed to their part in the operation, had agreed to permit Philip – his man, if only temporarily – to pass the wretched bear to Sylvia, and then let the Drugs Squad take over. He therefore shared the responsibility for what had happened. Constant was thinking that Philip had had no choice but to continue his brother's relationship with Sylvia Brelado, and it was not his fault that he had failed to appreciate the circumstances. O'Donovan, the least personally concerned with Peter or Philip Janvrin and so the most objective of those present, was annoyed by the Brigadier's criticism that he should have kept a closer watch on Philip at the airport; if he had, Sorel might have been dead by now.

Finally Brigadier Aubyn sighed. 'Well, let's forget the past. This is meant to be a damage assessment exercise. Now consider the damage. None of the photographs of Greg reproduced in the media are recognizable, and he was quick enough to give a false name and pretend he was merely an innocent bystander at Heathrow to meet a friend; luckily that seems to have been accepted. Philip wasn't so fortunate, thanks to the bloody Brelado woman. What exactly did she scream at him, Greg?'

'As I remember, sir, it was, "You'll be sorry for this, Peter Janvrin! No one shops me and gets away with it!" At least it proves the Brelados had no idea that they've been dealing with Philip and not Peter.'

'It also means the media have got hold of Peter's name, which they've attached to a not bad photograph of Philip,' said Aubyn grimly. 'Of course they've been careful about what they've printed or said, but one rotten tabloid has pointed out that Philip Janvrin was Peter's brother, and that old story has been resuscitated. I suppose it was inevitable. If Mary had been right and the Brelados had been importing some kind of horse dope it might have been different, but heroin – '

'Sir,' O'Donovan said tentatively, 'don't you think there's still a possibility Philip could claim that he was just a passenger on the flight who had met Sylvia casually on the racecourse, and that he had no idea why she accused him of shopping her?'

'No, Colin, I do not. It's much too late now for such a story, even if it was ever credible.' The Brigadier glanced at Sorel, who nodded his agreement.

Sorel said, 'In my opinion it would be best if a senior Home Office official issued a statement that Mr Janvrin of the Foreign and Commonwealth Office had been acting on behalf of the Drugs Squad, and they are very grateful for his undercover assistance. It won't stop all speculation, but it should help. Perhaps the FCO could endorse the statement.'

'Perhaps,' said Aubyn, thinking that neither the Home Secretary, who was ultimately responsible for the men from the Met who had bungled the Brelado woman's arrest, nor the Foreign Secretary, who with some justice would object to becoming involved, was likely to view the suggestion with pleasure. 'I'll see what I can do on those lines. Meanwhile, what about Philip?'

'At the moment he's in the flat, sir,' Constant said. 'I told him he wasn't to answer the door or the phone. I thought it would be better if he stayed incommunicado until you'd decided what he should do. The answerphone's switched on. Luckily Peter's number is unlisted, though the people we're concerned with know it. But with luck the media won't get on to him very quickly, even to leave messages.'

'Isn't the main question how Otto's people will react to his involvement with this Brelado affair?' Sorel asked.

'I imagine that either they'll react quickly,' said Aubyn, 'or they'll be scared off for a while. On the whole I fancy the latter, but we'll have to see. In the interval – '

Constant returned to the flat with an armful of newspapers. 'Read all about it,' he said.

'I'm not sure I want to. It's bound to be specious and inaccurate.' Philip was tense.

'It's certainly confused. You – or rather you as Peter – have come out of it rather well, but I'm sorry to say that some of the newshounds have raked up your old trouble with drugs, Philip, though naturally they regard it as Peter's brother's trouble, if you see what I mean.'

'I was afraid of that.' Philip thought of his father and Zara. They were unlikely to see the more lurid tabloids, but there would be at least phone calls from reporters and curious friends, and the media men could go so far as to camp on the doorstep. And there would be more publicity when the case came up for trial. 'Tell me what else has happened,' he said. 'Anything new on Michael?'

'No. He's said to be comfortable and his condition satisfactory.' Constant shook his head. 'Philip, you mustn't blame yourself. He was doing his job.'

'He saved me.'

'Sure. And you saved Sorel, but you won't get much gratitude from our dear Greg.'

Philip was silent, and after a minute Constant continued with the rest of the news. Tomas Brelado had been arrested and, like his wife Sylvia, was being interrogated. Frank Pringle, known as Foxy, and the bookmaker, Blinkers, were also being questioned, as was the Frenchman, Deleque, in Paris – and doubtless there were others who might or might not be named later.

'Poor Anton,' remarked Philip ruefully. 'I can't help feeling sorry for him. He wanted out, you know, Hamish. He told me this was his last time.'

'I find if difficult to be sympathetic towards anyone who – Sorry. I didn't mean – ' Constant stopped, embarrassed by what he had been about to say, and started again. 'Perhaps he didn't know he was dealing with heroin.'

'Oh, I think he did. When he handed Big Bear over to me he made some crack about how the bear ought to be a horse, but I never associated "horse" with "Big H" – Heroin. Unsurprisingly in the circumstances, I conceived of it in racing terms and nothing else.' Philip shook his head in self-reproach. 'I suppose I shall have to give evidence against these people.'

'I don't know. With any luck a written statement or an affidavit of some kind will be adequate.'

'What – in a court, in a trial? With no cross-examination – ?' Philip gave Constant a long look. 'I imagine that by luck, Hamish, you mean that Brigadier Aubyn and all concerned will pull the right strings?'

'You've guessed it, I'm pretty certain.' Constant was unabashed. He grinned at Philip. 'But first things first. The next step is to deal with the characters who've been leaving you messages on the answerphone.'

There had been several callers, though not all had left messages. They included Andrea Manheim who said she had an invitation for him, and her sister Carella who asked for the call to be returned at the art gallery where she worked. The Mays wanted him to dine on Saturday in two weeks' time. Robert Fauvic needed to speak to him urgently, and so did Zara. Altogether they were an interesting bunch.

'What a popular guy you are,' said Constant.

Philip grunted. None of the calls was welcome, least of all Zara's. He could imagine what she would say, the questions she would ask, the explanations she would demand. In the event the conversation was worse than he had expected.

'Father's dreadfully upset. That old business dragged up once more. The phone hardly stops ringing. Of course he doesn't realize it was you and not Peter at Heathrow. For God's sake, Philip, what were you doing? Surely you weren't – not again?'

'I was obeying Gregory Sorel's instructions.'

'I see, or rather I don't. It doesn't make sense. Nothing makes sense. Is there any news of Peter?'

'No. I'm sorry.'

'What's the use of being sorry? What am I to tell Father – and Patrick? Patrick keeps on asking about Daddy and Uncle Philip. Unfortunately he overheard some talk he shouldn't have. And there's another thing – '

'What?'

'Malcolm. Malcolm Derwent. You remember meeting him? He – he wants me to marry him.'

'Well, you can't, can you? There's no proof that Peter's dead, and you're a Catholic.'

'I know. I know. But – I can't go on like this much longer, Philip, telling lies to Father and Patrick and – and Malcolm, pretending you're Peter when Peter could be anywhere. Everything's so damned complicated, and all this Heathrow business has done is make it worse.'

Zara's voice broke and Philip, who had begun to feel irritated, was ashamed of his lack of sympathy. He did his best to reassure

215

her but his words were hollow. Nevertheless, he thought that what she had said was true; none of them could go on like this much longer. The affair at Heathrow, culminating in the arrest of the Brelados, even though it was not actually connected with Otto and his gang, must make them react. To judge from some of the phone calls, they were already doing so.

He said goodbye to Zara with relief, promising to keep in touch, and tapped out the Mays' number. He would get rid of the simple call first. Pam answered and repeated the invitation to dinner. He accepted it because it was easier than refusing. He could only hope for their sake that he would be able to keep the date; the Mays were pleasant people. He thanked Pam again, and was about to put down the receiver when she stopped him.

'Don't hang up, Peter. I want to ask you something. I'd like to invite Carella too, but would you mind? You were so close, you and Carella, and now – Peter dear, I don't intend to interfere, but I know she loves you very much and she's been looking terribly ill recently. Why aren't you kinder to her?'

Philip gritted his teeth. He yearned to say, 'Because I'm not Peter, because Carella and her friends have killed my brother, because they're trying to kill me.' Instead, he merely said coldly, 'There's something you seem to have forgotten, Pam. I've got a wife and son.'

'Yes, of course, Peter. I'm sorry.' She was flustered. 'It's none of my business. But you will come to dinner, won't you?'

'Of course.' Philip relented. 'And do ask Carella if you want to, Pam.'

When Pam May cut the connection almost five minutes later, having told Philip how she and John had read about his bravery at Heathrow, Philip threw a mock desperate glance at Constant. 'Why,' he asked, 'do women talk so much?'

Constant laughed. 'You've two more to go, but why don't you try Robert Fauvic first, while I get us a pre-lunch drink? And I'll see what Mrs Robyn may have left in the fridge, too.'

If Constant had imagined that the conversation with Fauvic would be simple and present no problems, he was wrong. Fauvic was obviously in a highly nervous state. He talked very fast, but said little. He'd read about the affair at Heathrow, but hadn't understood it. He thought it was unwise of Peter to have drawn so much attention to himself. Anyway, it was essential that he and Peter meet without delay.

And after some argument, which seemed to arise from the fact that Fauvic appeared to be torn between his dislike of coming to the flat and his pressing need to see Peter, he finally agreed to come round for a drink at six the following evening. He had given Philip no idea what he wanted.

Interestingly, when Philip phoned Carella Rindini she too wished to see him urgently. She too refused to say why. She didn't trust telephones. But she emphasized that it was important he come to the gallery as soon as possible. He was to make it appear a casual visit, as if he were in search of a small gift, say, and he must not mention it to anyone. She stressed *anyone* – anyone at all. Luckily Andrea would not be there next week.

'You are a popular guy,' repeated Constant when he returned with their drinks, and Philip told him of the calls. 'What do you bet Andrea also needs an urgent consultation?'

He was half right. Andrea suggested that Peter should come down to the Manheims' cottage for the weekend. She didn't stress that it was urgent or important, but when he hesitated she pressed him.

'You must, Peter. Please! Come early Friday afternoon, before the traffic gets too bad, and stay till Monday. I'm hoping you'll bring Robert. He doesn't have a car at the moment, and he'll help you drive if you're thinking it would be too much of an effort. The trains are abysmal, but it's not a bad journey by road.'

'All right, Andrea, and many thanks.' Philip had been wondering how he could find out where the cottage was, but if Robert was to be with him that problem would solve itself. 'Until Friday then.'

'Yes. Friday. Goodbye, Peter.'

Philip put down the receiver slowly. Either he had imagined it, or Andrea's last few words had not been altogether casual. Perhaps they intended that he should have an 'accident' at the cottage. It wouldn't be hard to arrange. The thought was chilling, but Friday was days away.

TWENTY-SEVEN

It had been agreed that Philip, having accepted all the invitations he had received, should go ahead and keep the dates unless or until some unexpected problem arose. So, on Tuesday morning, Constant and Philip took a taxi to Bond Street. Constant paid off the driver, and they walked the last hundred yards to the gallery where Carella Rindini worked.

The day was reasonably fair and dry, though the sky was a sullen grey with a few peeps of blue sky. The traffic, as usual, was heavy and proceeded at a crawl. The pavements were thronged both with hurrying pedestrians, some of whom had abandoned their slow-moving transport and decided that progress was faster on foot, and with dawdlers who had come to shop or window-gaze. In fact, it was a normal, busy London street scene, and not one to suggest violence in any form. Yet it was only a week since a stolen lorry had been deliberately reversed into a famous-name jewellers, and in the course of the raid a passer-by had been killed and a shop assistant badly wounded.

The *Galerie Lamoye* was the antithesis of such a world. The single bronze that occupied the entire velvet-lined window spoke of moneyed elegance. But security had not been forgotten; as with so many such establishments, entry to the interior could only be gained if someone pressed a button in answer to the bell and released the door. Inside, the gallery, with its deep carpet, its display of obviously expensive canvases by a painter of whom Philip had never heard, and its *objets d'art* – all minus prices but again clearly not cheap – succeeded in creating an ambience which it was hoped would tempt an eclectic buyer.

Carella Rindini fitted into this setting perfectly. She wore a simple violet-coloured dress with a heavy silver necklace and bracelet. Like her background, at first sight she looked luscious and expensive. She came forward immediately to greet Philip, her hand outstretched.

'Peter, how nice to see you here. You're quite a stranger to the gallery.'

Philip smiled. Close to Carella he could understand why Pam May was worried about her. She was much too thin, her cheeks hollow, her eyes huge and frightened. She let her hand stay in his for only a second before she withdrew it and half turned away.

'Are you in search of anything in particular?' she asked.

'A small present,' Philip said, 'to take to Andrea, who's to be my hostess next weekend. Perhaps you'd help me choose.'

'Oh no!'

The words were almost whispered, so that Philip was not sure of them. At the same time a man in his fifties with grizzled hair had come out of what was presumably an office at the rear of the shop. He was carrying a large rectangular object – presumably a picture of some kind – carefully wrapped.

He nodded pleasantly to Philip, and spoke to the girl. 'I'll be back in a couple of hours, Carella, though you never know with his lordship. He likes to talk.'

'All right, Boris. Good luck.'

As he watched Boris leave, Philip saw Constant staring in the window as if enthralled by the bronze. They had agreed that he would follow Philip into the gallery after fifteen minutes unless Philip reappeared first. Carella had never met Constant, so that he could easily play the part of a casual visitor.

'Is Boris the owner of the gallery?' Philip asked.

'Part-owner. Bernhardt has money in it and – and other people.' Carella was vague. 'Let's go into the office. We'll hear the bell if anyone wants to come in.'

The office was small and cramped, but surprisingly tidy. There was a desk with a couple of chairs, and pictures were stacked against the walls. Carella gestured to Philip to sit down, but then seemed at a loss as to what she should say or do next.

Philip, mindful that Constant might interrupt them before he had learnt what Carella had on her mind, said, 'Carella, dearest, I haven't got all day. Why did you want to see me so urgently?'

'Stop it!' To Philip's surprise, Carella brought her fist down on the desk in a sudden burst of anger. 'Stop pretending! You're not Peter Janvrin. You're awfully like him, but you're not Peter. You're his brother, Philip.'

219

There seemed no point in attempting to deny it at this stage. 'Yes. I'm Philip,' he admitted.

'And Peter's dead. They killed him.'

'Who's "they"?'

Carella ignored the question. 'I loved Peter,' she said. 'I loved him very much, more than he loved me, I think, but that didn't matter.'

'Why was he killed, Carella?'

'He tried to double-cross them. I don't know exactly how, but Otto was furious about it. Now he says you've got to die too. First you tricked him. He thought you really were Peter or you might be. Then you escaped him in Brussels, and he hates to be thwarted. Besides, he believes you're being used by Peter's colleagues.'

'Carella, who's this Otto?'

'He calls himself Otto Schmidt, but I doubt if that's his real name. He's rich and powerful. He's got several houses in different countries. Bernhardt, my brother-in-law, works for him.'

'But what does Otto do?' Philip was growing impatient.

'I don't know much, but as I understand it he deals in what I gather is nowadays a most valuable commodity – information. For example, he buys photocopies of documents stolen from governments or big businesses, and sells them to the highest bidder. I suppose you'd call it espionage – primarily industrial espionage. As I say, I'm not sure how it works in detail, but I know it's extremely profitable.'

'So?'

'Philip, what I wanted to do was warn you – for Peter's sake, because I loved him so much and I know how fond he was of you – in spite of – in spite of – '

Carella left the sentence unfinished. From the gallery came the ring of someone at the door. Philip guessed that it was Constant, and swore silently at the interruption, though on reflection he was confident that he had learnt all he could from Carella.

'A customer, probably,' Carella said. 'I must go.' She stood up and laid a hand on Philip's arm. 'Philip, be careful, *very* careful. Don't go down to that cottage this weekend. It's dreadful to say it of my family, but Bernhardt will do whatever Otto wants, and Otto is a very dangerous character.'

'I'll be careful, Carella, and thank you for the warning.'

'I did it for Peter,' she said with a wan smile, and led the way into the gallery to let Constant in. He said good-morning politely, and started to admire a small ceramic figurine.

They lunched in a pub off Piccadilly. Constant reasoned that there could scarcely be a safer place for Philip in London in the middle of the day than a West End pub, full as it would be of civil servants, office workers and shoppers up from the country. Afterwards they took a taxi to the Belgravia office. As Constant remarked, one advantage of minding Philip was that he could afford taxis whenever it suited him.

They had lunched well and were, in the circumstances, reasonably relaxed. But as soon as they entered the house, they realized that something had happened. When they showed their passes they were asked to wait a moment, which in itself was unusual. The guard behind the reception desk muttered into the telephone and minutes later Colin O'Donovan appeared, looking subdued.

'The Brig wants to see you at once, Hamish.' He turned to Philip with an unfathomable expression. 'Philip, he wants you to wait in Peter's office for a few minutes.'

'What's up?' Constant could not resist asking as they all got into the lift.

O'Donovan shook his head. 'The Brig will explain.'

'It's not Michael Lindsay?' Philip said. 'He's not – '

'No!' O'Donovan's answer was definite. Then he seemed to relent, and expanded on his reply. 'No, Mike's improving, Philip. It'll take time, but he should be okay.'

'Good.' Philip hesitated, but he had sensed a certain sympathy in O'Donovan's voice and his thoughts immediately turned to Peter. 'Colin, is it my brother? Have you more news? Is it confirmed that Peter – Peter's dead?'

'There's no news of Peter's death.'

The phrasing of this remark struck Philip as odd, but he didn't comment. He was getting used to the linguistic ambiguities that Aubyn's people employed, and it was obvious that no information was to be gleaned from O'Donovan until it suited him. Constant went off to see the Brigadier, and O'Donovan accompanied Philip to Peter's office. He smiled apologetically as

221

he said, 'Won't keep you long. Is there anything you'd like –
some coffee, perhaps.'

'No, thanks. We've just finished lunch. I'll be all right.'

Philip watched the door shut behind Colin O'Donovan. He
was in a familiar room but he felt that the office had turned into
a doctor's or dentist's waiting room; he had the appropriate
sensation – a sensation of apprehension. He steeled himself to
receive bad news, though after O'Donovan's denials he couldn't
imagine its content, and he vaguely wondered if he were taking
part in some kind of psychological test that Sorel had devised.

He had to wait for no more than a few minutes before
O'Donovan returned to take him to Sorel's office. Sorel stood
up as they came in, thanked O'Donovan dismissively and
waved Philip to a chair, staring at him with an odd diffidence
that Philip found hard to interpret. What was more, Philip
thought he looked ill. There were dark circles under his eyes,
his skin was mottled and when he spoke his voice was slightly
hoarse and hesitant.

'Philip, I've received a report on the Brelados and their
drug-trafficking operation. I don't mind admitting that it was –
shattering. Sylvia made a full confession; to the best of her
ability she tried to lay the blame on her husband but, more
importantly, she named a whole raft of names – enough to keep
the authorities busy for weeks, both here in the UK and
abroad. Tomas has also made a statement, which tallies approximately with hers. The way they worked it was this.

'They would let a punter get badly into debt with one of their
bookmaking firms, then suggest that the debt would be written
off if, with no questions asked, a package – a present for Sylvia
– was brought back from a holiday or business trip. Often the
couriers would only be used once, but some became regulars,
especially if they were willing and had suitable qualifications
such as a valid reason for frequent foreign travel.

'These regulars, of course, didn't do it for love. They
expected to be paid and paid well. But if people suddenly
become affluent questions are apt to be asked. The Brelados
had an answer for this. They were, of course, in the centre of
racing circles, and it wasn't difficult for them to arrange that
certain people should be "lucky", as it were. I'm over-simplify-
ing, but you get the idea?'

'Yes.' Philip wasn't sure how else to reply. He couldn't understand why Sorel was going to so much trouble to explain all this to him. 'It was – ingenious.'

'It was a thriving business, damn them to hell! God knows how much money they made at the expense of – of the unfortunates who became addicted.' Sorel's voice suddenly shook with anger. 'Well, now they'll pay for some of the misery they've caused. The tragedy is that others will take their place and the whole rotten racket will continue in a different form.'

For a minute he was silent, then he said, 'I *hate* those who deal in drugs. If you'd ever been forced to see someone you loved, someone young and beautiful, turn into a hideous degenerate who'd do anything, anything for a fix – ' Unable to continue, Sorel buried his face in his hands. It was the first time Philip had known him to show such emotion.

'Your sister,' Philip said softly.

'Yes, my twin sister,' Sorel said at last. He didn't ask how Philip knew about her, but looked him in the eye. 'She killed herself not very long before you were caught smuggling heroin into the country.'

Sorel paused. 'I find it hard to tell you the rest of the story, but you should know that Peter was dreadfully upset when you were arrested. At first he swore you were innocent, but the evidence was incontrovertible and eventually he seemed to accept it. Oddly perhaps, though I had always liked Peter, the whole episode served to form a special bond between us.'

Sorel stopped again, and Philip said, 'Your mutual hatred of drugs and drug-dealing, you mean? All right, I understand that. But why tell me all this now? You've never pretended to like *me*. You've always treated me as a means – an expendable means, I might add – to an end that to some extent we both sought.'

Again Sorel hesitated. Then he said reluctantly, 'I'm telling you because the Brelados have named Peter Janvrin as one of their regular couriers.'

It was Philip's turn to hesitate. Then he said, 'So what? If he'd been investigating a horse-doping racket on his own – '

Sorel opened his mouth to interrupt but closed it again and Philip went on, 'As I said, if Peter had been investigating a horse-doping racket on his own initiative, it would explain why Sylvia threatened me – Peter, as she thought – at Heathrow. I don't recall her exact words, but she screamed something like, "I'll make you pay for this, Peter Janvrin. You won't shop me and get away with it." The accusation was fair enough. I had shopped her, though I didn't know we were dealing with heroin.'

He stopped and this time there was a longer pause. 'Or are you telling me you believe that Peter knew he was investigating heroin smuggling, but didn't explain the situation to the authorities because – because of my earlier connection with the stuff? Is that the idea?'

'No, not exactly, I'm afraid. That was my first reaction, I admit. But I was wrong. We were all wrong. Peter has been bringing heroin and other drugs into the country for the Brelados for the last nine or ten *years*, not just weeks. He really was a long-established Brelado regular.'

Philip stared at Sorel. 'But that would mean that when I was arrested – No! I don't believe it. You're lying, Sorel, for some damned clever reason of your own. Or the bloody Brelados are lying to get back at me – at Peter as they think – for shopping them.'

'Philip, I wish to God you were right on either count, but it's not so. The Brelados were interviewed separately, and made separate statements. Anton Deleque, who clearly bears Peter no grudge, also confirms their story, and there are others who say the same. The Brig will let you listen to tapes of the interrogations, if you wish.'

Philip looked down at his hands, clenched between his knees. He told himself that he still couldn't believe it, that it was absurd to imagine that Peter would – Sorel was deceiving him. He had never trusted Sorel. He had never trusted any of them, not completely. They had got him out of prison for their own purposes. They had used him. And now –

Philip tried to ignore the doubts crawling at the back of his mind, but he remembered Sylvia's attitude to him, a remark of Deleque's that of course he would know how much the French-man enjoyed brandy – little pointers that implied not necessarily a close personal relationship, but a relationship of some duration with the Peter Janvrin they had known. Reluctantly he came to face the fact that Sorel could be telling the truth, and he felt physically sick.

'There's one bit of consolation I can offer you, Philip,' Sorel said at length. 'The heroin found in your bag at Heathrow that time should have been put in Peter's bag. Peter wasn't deliberately letting you take the risk for him. Why should he? He had a diplomatic passport. Even if he had been stopped by chance at the customs, as you were, his bag wouldn't have been searched. It was an accident, a mistake. I honestly believe he was horrified at what happened and he was sure until the last moment that you would be found innocent.'

'But at the end of the day he let me go to prison,' Philip said miserably, for immediately he had forced himself to put the thought into words he knew that it was true. 'Seven years! And it should have been longer.' He recalled what might have been. He thought of his father, the anger and the remorse that he would feel if he ever found out that it was his elder son who had been the drug trafficker, while his younger son was innocent; it would kill the old man. He thought of Zara, who wanted to marry Malcolm Derwent, and of Patrick, who would always be known as Peter Janvrin's son.

'What happens now?' Philip asked bleakly.

'That will be up to you, Philip,' said Sorel. 'You owe us nothing. On the contrary, we owe you a great deal, and you must decide what you want to do. Whatever your decision you'll be given every possible help. This has been a blow, a shattering blow to you, but it's been a blow to all of us too. Peter was a trusted, respected colleague. I would have called him a friend. So we realize it's not easy for you to think straight and make an immediate decision. You'll need to consider the matter carefully, but the choice is yours. No one will blame you if you choose to pull out, to forget Otto and the Manheims and – '

'No!' Philip interrupted. 'I'll see it through. For the sake of my family and for my own satisfaction I have to know exactly what – what happened to Peter.'

'All right. You know the risk you're taking.' Sorel gave Philip a long and searching look. 'The Department won't be ungrateful, as I've said, materially and otherwise. As you must have gathered Brigadier Aubyn can pull a lot of strings and in the changed circumstances he'll not only do what he can, but more than he can.'

'And that, I assume, without being unduly cynical, will include a cover-up of Peter's illegal activities.'

Sorel nodded. 'If Peter were around it might be different but, as it is, yes. We'll cover for him, first because he's served the Department well in the past, and secondly because it's best for us – and we hope you'll agree it's best for you and your family. I imagine that's what you'd want.'

'Oh yes. I realize it would be best for everyone concerned, and whatever he's done I don't think I could ever hate Peter enough to wish him what he deserves.' Philip grinned ruefully at Sorel.

To his relief Gregory Sorel grinned back at him. 'I'm not sure that even I do now, Philip. I once said to you that you could never pay the debt you owed. I was wrong, of course. You owed no debt. But you've paid Peter's debt for him – and overpaid as far as I'm concerned.' He paused. 'There's one thing I want to add. You may wonder why Brigadier Aubyn isn't breaking this news to you himself. He wanted to, but I insisted it was my job; it was the least I could do after the way I've treated you. Anyway, we're going to see the Brig together now.'

This was the nearest Sorel was to get to an apology or an expression of gratitude, but it satisfied Philip.

It was after five when Philip and Constant returned to the flat. Robert Fauvic was due at six. Philip could conceive of few people whom he wanted to see less, and was determined to get rid of the man as soon as possible. They agreed that Constant should stay in the study when Fauvic arrived, but interrupt them after at most an hour. Then he could pressure Fauvic to leave by saying they were going out to dinner.

Fauvic was late arriving, so that Philip began to hope that he wouldn't come at all, but at a quarter to seven the doorbell rang. Fauvic wasn't drunk, but he was not completely sober. He drank the first gin and tonic Philip gave him quickly, and asked for a second. He still had made no attempt to explain the reason for this so-called important visit.

Impatient, Philip at last asked, 'Robert, why did you insist on seeing me so urgently?'

There was a pause. Then, 'Because I'm scared.' Once started the words poured forth from Fauvic. 'They blame me for assuring them you were Peter, but you're not, are you? You're Philip and they're planning to kill you. I overheard Bernhardt talking. I

226

shouldn't have listened, but I did. He said you were due for a nasty accident. Peter – Philip, whoever you are, you mustn't go to the Manheims' cottage next weekend.'

'Oh, yes, Robert. I shall go and you'll come with me,' said Philip calmly.

'No! I won't. Don't you understand?' Fauvic sounded desperate. 'I've done some pretty rotten things in my life, but I've never been involved with – with murder before, and I'm not going to start now.'

'Would you like me to tell Bernhardt Manheim what you've just told me?' Philip asked.

'Oh, no! You wouldn't? God knows what they'd do to me.'

'I expect you'd have a nasty accident, too.'

To Philip's dismay, for he was not a natural bully and took no pleasure in the pressure he was exerting, Fauvic began to sob. Philip took his empty glass and poured him another gin.

'Listen, Robert, either I have a talk with Manheim or you'll meet me here on Friday afternoon and we'll drive down to the cottage together. In addition, right now you'll tell me a few things that I'd like to know.'

Fauvic nodded miserably. He was prepared to co-operate, his resistance to Philip's demands broken by a combination of fear and drink. But it soon became clear that he knew less than Carella Rindini. He had got into debt, the Manheims had bailed him out and since then he had done 'odd jobs' for them. He guessed that Bernhardt acted on the fringe of illegality, but otherwise he was vague. He had never heard of Otto Schmidt and, as far as he knew, Peter Janvrin's relationship with the Manheims could have been purely social.

All this was unsatisfactory from Philip's point of view, but he had to accept the situation. He said goodbye to a half-drunk Fauvic, reminded him again of their date and hoped that the pathetic fool, rogue though he doubtless was, wouldn't walk under a bus before Friday.

TWENTY-EIGHT

'Fauvic's late, Philip. Is he usually a punctual type?'

'I really don't know, Hamish. He wasn't punctual the other night when he came for drinks, and then he was half tight. Let's hope he doesn't arrive drunk today.'

'Let's hope he arrives.'

'I'll give him another twenty minutes, then I'll go.'

'I don't like it.'

'Hamish, you're more nervous than I am. Fauvic could easily have missed a bus or failed to get a taxi; even if he got one, it could have been held up in the traffic. Anyway, now that Greg's discovered where the Manheims' cottage is, I don't need Fauvic's help to find the place.'

It was Friday afternoon. Philip, his bag packed and ready in the hall, was chatting with Constant while they waited for Robert Fauvic. In spite of the warnings from both Carella and Fauvic himself, he was determined to go to the Manheims' cottage for the weekend. Sorel had agreed that if they intended to do him any harm, as seemed more than likely, they would want it to look like an accident, so that there was some chance that if he remained on his guard and took certain precautions, he might avoid trouble.

'I'm going to phone Fauvic,' Constant said at last. 'See if he's left.'

'All right.'

Philip wandered over to the window and looked down at the busy scene below. So far the day was fine, but there was a hint of rain in the air and the prudent were carrying umbrellas. From above, everyone seemed to be in a hurry, rather like a 'fast-forward' replay on a video recorder. Pedestrians walked rapidly or ran to catch a taxi or a bus or to cross the road before the lights changed. Cars went by at seemingly alarming speeds, as if positively inviting accidents. Two double-decker buses, lumbering along, added colour. It was, in fact, a normal Friday afternoon, and yet –

Philip found it hard to believe that he had been equipped for his mission so carefully. Sorel had explained that it would be unwise for an amateur to carry a weapon of any kind – the possession of a pistol, for example, would be convincing evidence that he was more than a routine weekend visitor. However, he had been provided with a leather belt, which he could readily wear with country clothes. It contained within its double sides a miniature radio transmitter, with the antenna leading round the waist. It was activated by pressure on the buckle and would transmit a pulse which would be picked up by a receiver in a van, parked nearby, holding Sorel himself and a group of his men. If they heard the pulse it would signal that Philip desperately needed help, and they would raid the Manheims' cottage immediately. A suspected drugs party could serve as an excuse.

Philip remembered how he had laughed when Sorel had outlined this arrangement, saying that it sounded like part of a script for a spy movie, but Sorel had been adamant, arguing that it had worked in the past, when there had been no opportunity to use a walkie-talkie. And now – Philip glanced at his watch – whether or not Fauvic turned up he would soon be on his way to what many would consider an ideal weekend – a weekend away from the city, spent as a guest in a presumably comfortable cottage in the English countryside. The reality of the situation was so different, so absurd, that Philip suspected few of the people hurrying in the street below would find it credible.

'There's no answer to Fauvic's phone,' Constant said, interrupting Philip's ruminations. 'He must have left.'

'I'll give him five more minutes,' Philip said.

But almost at once the flat's buzzer sounded. Philip went to the intercom and a voice said, 'Robert Fauvic here. Sorry I'm late.' To Philip's relief he sounded sober. 'Shall I come up?'

'No, don't bother, Robert. I'm ready. I'll be right down.' Philip looked at Hamish Constant and gave a wry grin. 'Well, here I go. Let's hope after all this build-up it doesn't turn out to be an ordinary couple of days.'

Constant shook his head. 'I don't think that's very likely. Good luck, Philip.'

'Thanks.'

Leaving Constant to lock up before going off to his own flat, Philip went down to the hall where Fauvic was waiting for him. Robert Fauvic was pale and tense, and it was obvious from his appearance that he had been sleeping badly, but he seemed in control of himself. He greeted Philip wanly.

'The traffic's diabolical today. My cab took ages. It'll take us a long time to get out of London.'

'Then we'd better hurry. My Rover's in a garage in a mews just around the corner, only a few minutes away.'

Philip set off rapidly, but had to adjust his long stride to suit the short legs of his heavy, rotund companion. They walked in silence, making no further attempt at conversation until they entered the mews. Fauvic was panting a little as they reached the garage. Philip put down his bag to get out his keys and realized that in his haste he had left the present for his hostess on the hall table in the flat.

'Damn!' he said.

'What's the matter?'

'I've forgotten the present I bought for Andrea.'

That he had bought Andrea a present was not exactly true. It was Constant who had been charmed by Carella into buying the small ceramic figurine that had attracted him in the gallery and, not really wanting it, had decided it would make a suitable gift for Philip to give to Andrea. 'If Carella comments, you'll have to say you bought it somewhere else,' Constant had said, and he had added ingenuously, 'This way I can put it on my expense account.'

'I'll have to go back for it, Robert,' said Philip. 'No need for you to come. I'll sprint. I shan't be long.' He tossed Fauvic the keys. 'Get the car out, if you will, and meet me at the entrance to the mews. It'll save time.'

'Okay. Be as quick as you can.'

Glancing over his shoulder as he reached the end of the mews, Philip saw that Robert already had the garage doors open, had picked up the two bags and was putting them into the boot of the car. Then Philip turned into the street and slowed to a fast walk. He had gone about twenty yards when he heard the dull boom of an explosion. He stopped so abruptly that a woman with a pram whom he had just overtaken ran into him.

230

'Oh, I am sorry,' she said. 'I hope I didn't hurt you.'

Philip stared at her, but he might have been blind. His mind didn't register her presence. He opened his mouth, but he didn't speak. The child in the pram, sensing some oddity, began to scream loudly. The woman was frightened, but prepared to deal with this strange man.

'It was an accident,' she repeated firmly. 'I'm awfully sorry, but – '

'No. It wasn't an accident,' Philip said. 'It was meant for me.'

Before she could expostulate he had side-stepped the pram and was running back the way he had come. She looked after him, shaking her head in bewilderment. She had heard the boom, but to her it was merely one of the odd noises that were constant accompaniments to city life.

Philip was breathing fast as he reached the mews, partly from exertion but mainly from emotion. He had already pictured in his mind the scene that would meet his eyes, and the reality was much as he had imagined it.

The explosion had taken place in what had been Peter's garage. Both of the doors had been torn off and lay on the cobbles. Black smoke belched from the opening. A few people were hurrying out of the flats and maisonettes above the other garages, taking care to avoid the broken glass from the windows around that had been shattered by the blast. A couple of chimney pots leaned at crazy angles. At first glance, nobody appeared hurt.

As always on such occasions, someone had made it his business to take charge, and was doing his best to order the small crowd that was gathering to stand back. Philip ignored him, but the man seized him by the arm.

'You can't go in there! Can't you see there's a fire? The petrol tank – '

Philip shook off the restraining hand. 'Forget it! There's a man in there!'

'Well, you can't do anything for him. Wait for the brigade!'

'I can try.'

Philip thrust the man aside. He heard the murmur of surprise from the growing number of spectators as he started into the garage. Then the smoke enveloped him. His eyes smarted and tears ran down his cheeks. He could feel the heat and smell petrol and what he feared was the sickly-sweet scent of charred flesh. It

231

was becoming difficult to breathe and he knew he must be quick, or he would collapse and become an additional liability.

He felt his way along the right-hand side of the tangled wreck of what had once been a respectable Rover. He could guess what had happened. Robert Fauvic had got into the driving seat, turned the ignition key and thus set off whatever device had been located under the vehicle. So Fauvic, or what was left of him, should be behind the wheel.

Philip found the car's door handle and burnt his hands badly on it before he realized that the door had buckled and was already ajar. In the confined space of the garage it was impossible to open it wide, but he could reach inside. And by now the smoke was clearing a little so that, by slitting his streaming eyes, he could see the shape of Fauvic's body.

He touched it tentatively and instantly recoiled. What should have been Fauvic's face was bone and blood and pus and torn skin. Regardless of his burns Philip wiped his hands hard on his jacket. He felt physically sick. Then, turning, he staggered from the garage. The officious man had been right; there was nothing to be done for Robert Fauvic except pray for him.

'Are you all right, sir?'

Two police cars had arrived. An ambulance was just turning into the mews, closely followed by a fire engine. The air seemed to be full of the sound of sirens. A police officer was moving the curious further away from the incident. They went reluctantly, especially the officious man.

'I told him it was useless to go in there,' he kept saying, pointing accusingly at Philip.

'But it was brave of him,' a woman said.

'Yes.' There was a chorus of agreement.

Philip was embarrassed. The last thing he wanted was to become a minor hero for the second time in a week. He let a uniformed police officer lead him to one side and sit him on the ground against a wall. The officer waited with him until he began to breathe more easily and became more or less capable of speech.

'Will you wait for the inspector, sir, or shall I help you to the ambulance? They'll take you to hospital and he can see you there.'

But Philip was breathing steadily now, and he had no intention of going to hospital. 'No. I don't want any fuss,' he managed to croak.

The officer hesitated, but almost at once he was joined by a man in plain clothes. 'Inspector Foster, sir,' he announced. 'Can you tell me your name?'

With difficulty, because of the state of his hands, Philip reached for his wallet and extracted the identity card in Peter's name that Sorel had provided for him. The inspector's eyes widened as he looked at it, and from it to Philip; obviously he appreciated the significance of the card and recognized the name of Janvrin.

At that moment the inspector was drawn aside by a man in fireman's uniform, who murmured into his ear.

'Mr Janvrin,' said the inspector, 'I'm told there's a body in the car, and I gather you tried to rescue the victim. Was it your car and can you identify him?'

'It was my car and his name was Robert Fauvic,' Philip said. 'That's all I'm prepared to tell you at the moment, Inspector. But I must ask that you don't release any details – especially Fauvic's name and mine – until you or your superiors have spoken to Brigadier Aubyn. His number's on the back of the ID card. Look, I'm not feeling too well. I don't want to go to hospital, but I live just around the corner. Could you take me there, and come and get a statement later?'

'Very good, sir. Come along then.'

He helped Philip to a police car, and within minutes the uniformed driver drew up outside the apartment block. The porter, Baker, was standing on the pavement, looking up at the sky as if to gauge the weather. He stared at Philip in horror, then hurried forward.

'Mr Janvrin! What's happened? You've had an accident?'

Before Philip could reply Hamish Constant, bag in hand, came out of the building. He had been about to leave when fortunately he had been delayed by a telephone call from his office. Now he took charge of the situation. He thanked the police driver, repeated that Mr Janvrin would be available to make a statement or answer questions in a short while, when he had recovered a little, gave his bag to Baker and led Philip into the hall.

They went up in the lift in silence. Philip was beginning to shiver. At the door of the flat Constant retrieved his bag from Baker and ushered Philip inside.

'What happened?' he demanded the moment they were alone.

233

It didn't take Philip more than half a dozen sentences to tell him. Constant's reaction was to curse the Manheims, which at least relieved his feelings. Then he became practical.

'You did the right thing with the police, Philip. Now you go and have a hot shower and get rid of that smell of smoke. Chuck out your top clothes. They're not wearable any more. I'll dispose of them. And I'll check that the belt still functions. Do you think you can manage?' he added as Philip looked doubtful.

Philip nodded, though his hands were hurting. 'Sure. Meanwhile, could you make me some tea?'

'Of course. I'll put the kettle on. It can boil while I'm phoning the Brig and getting instructions.'

It was forty minutes before Inspector Foster arrived, accompanied by a uniformed sergeant. Philip, in pyjamas and dressing-gown, was holding his tea cup with difficulty in hands which Constant had insisted on treating and bandaging. The Inspector refused tea.

'I've been in touch with your Brigadier Aubyn, Mr Janvrin, but I must still ask you some questions.'

'Of course. But you've not released Fauvic's name, or mine?'

'No, sir. We've taken great care about the information we've given out to the media.' He settled in his chair. 'Now, perhaps you'd tell us what happened.'

At first Philip told the exact truth. He said he hadn't taken his car out of the garage since he had returned from the Sandown Park races several weeks ago, the traffic and parking problems in central London being such that it was simpler to take cabs or use public transport. He admitted that there were no special locks on the garage door, and it would have been easy for an intruder to break in. He agreed that the booby trap on the Rover had almost certainly been intended for him, and it was by pure chance that Robert Fauvic had been killed in his place.

'Do you have any enemies, Mr Janvrin?' the inspector asked.

Philip shrugged. 'None who would want to dispose of me so violently.' It was the only direct lie he had told. 'Unless – '

'Unless?' the inspector prompted as expected.

'I was wondering,' Philip said, obeying Brigadier Aubyn's suggestion, 'if it could have been an attempt at revenge by members of the drugs syndicate – some of whom, as you probably know, I helped to identify earlier in the week.'

'It's certainly a possibility. We'll look into it, sir.' The inspector stood up. 'We won't bother you any more at present. Thank you for your help.'

Constant went to see the police out, and Philip tried to relax but found it impossible. He couldn't stop thinking of Robert Fauvic. He hadn't much liked the man, but he wouldn't have wished that kind of death on anyone. And there was Fauvic's family, if he had any, to consider. Fauvic wasn't married, but he might have had a girlfriend and presumably he had parents, perhaps brothers, sisters, people who loved him.

'Now,' Constant said on his return, 'we shall have a stiff drink. It's early, but no matter. I think we both need one. Then I'll tell you what the Brig would like you to do next, if you feel up to it.'

TWENTY-NINE

As Constant drove him out of London towards the Manheims'
cottage that evening Philip wondered if he weren't crazy to risk
his life again. He could have refused Brigadier Aubyn's request,
for it had been no more than a request, and no one would have
blamed him for refusing. But pride and a conviction that it was
his duty to expose Otto Schmidt and his works prevented him.
There was also another related factor. The hurt of Peter's
betrayal was still raw, though he tried to keep thoughts of it at
the back of his mind, and he had a curious impression that if he
could complete the job for Sorel, the process would exorcise this
residual feeling.

He knew that it would be a worthwhile achievement if he
could force a showdown with the Manheims and, with luck, put
an end to the whole obscure and sorry affair. Then, with that
done, there might be a future to look forward to since his own
innocence was at last established. It was true that he didn't know
how or when this innocence could be proclaimed publicly, but
hope had begun to stir in him – hope he could not suppress. If
once he hadn't cared much whether he lived or died, he certainly
cared now.

'Penny for your thoughts,' Constant said.

'I was thinking about what I would do when all this is over,'
Philip replied, almost ashamed to admit his selfishness.

'Get a nice quiet job and find a nice quiet girl? Marry her, have
children, and live happily ever after?' Constant suggested.

Philip laughed. 'No thanks. I'm sure that's not for me. It's not
what I've ever really wanted.'

Constant glanced at him curiously, but Philip did not elaborate, and Constant was too diffident to persist in personal
questions. After a while he slipped a cassette into place and
Beethoven's Fifth Symphony filled the car and obviated the need
for further conversation. He drove fast, because for once the

traffic was not aggressively heavy, and they made good time. It was shortly after seven when they reached their appointed rendezvous on the outskirts of a village, half a mile from the Manheims' cottage.

Constant drew up behind a large grey unmarked van that was parked on the grass verge. 'Here we are,' he said unnecessarily. He sounded the horn twice. The van's doors opened and Sorel emerged.

Constant touched Philip lightly on the shoulder as he got out of the car. 'Good luck,' he said.

'Thanks!'

Philip slid across behind the wheel as Sorel took the passenger seat. It was a rapid and smooth operation, and Philip's doubts about his ability to drive evaporated as soon as they moved forward. His hands were painful, but holding the steering wheel was perfectly possible.

'Straight on, Philip. I'll tell you when to turn,' said Sorel without a preliminary greeting. 'Fortunately, the layout's excellent for our purposes. There's good cover for the van that will follow us in a few minutes, and I shall be able to get close up to the cottage. Incidentally, it's quite some cottage. Five bedrooms at least, and a double garage.'

'You've checked it out?'

'Of course. That's why I'm here to guide you, instead of Hamish.' Sorel was amused. 'Now, turn right after fifty yards, Philip, then right again and stop after another twenty for me to get out. The so-called cottage will be on your left.'

Obeying instructions, Philip said, 'What happens if the Manheims behave perfectly normally, give me drinks, dinner and see me off to bed?'

'In that case those of us in the van are going to have an uncomfortable night. But somehow I doubt it.'

Philip grinned, but once Sorel had left the car and he was alone, he realized that he would rather have joined him – however uncomfortable the circumstances – than go to the Manheims by himself. The choice, however, was no longer his. He said a silent prayer and drove on to the cottage.

There were lights in several of the downstairs rooms. Philip collected his overnight bag and walked as quietly as the gravel allowed to the front door. He rang the bell. He counted to a hundred before the door was opened to him.

'Hello, Andrea.'

'Phil – Phil – Peter!' Andrea gasped.

She took a step backwards and stared at him, her eyes wide and her face white. He could see the movement in her long, delicate throat as she swallowed convulsively. She seemed incapable of saying anything more. If Philip had hoped to surprise her he had certainly succeeded.

'May I come in?' he said. 'I'm not a ghost, you know.'

She stood to one side to let him pass into the hall. Philip put down his bag and smiled at her, but she didn't respond, and when a voice he recognized as Bernhardt's called out from a room on the left, asking who it was, he ignored her and followed the sound of the voice. His appearance was once again greeted with involuntary surprise by the two occupants of the room, though they were better at suppressing their feelings than Andrea had been.

And on this occasion the surprise was mutual. Philip stopped on the threshold and in his turn stared, not at Bernhardt Manheim, but at his companion, who sat in an armchair, an ebony stick with a silver knob on the carpet beside him. Though Philip had never actually seen the man before, he recognized him immediately. It was Otto Schmidt, and it was he who was the first to regain his composure.

'Come in, Mr Janvrin. Come in. This is a surprise, though not, I must admit, an altogether pleasant one.'

The deep, self-satisfied, autocratic voice made Philip want to shiver, reminding him of the way he had been beaten up and maltreated at the *Maison d'Or* in Brussels. But, determined not to show his emotion, he forced himself to regard Otto with as much contempt as he could muster.

Otto's physique contradicted his voice. He was a small man with an over-large head, a long body and one leg obviously shorter than the other. If these characteristics had in some way contributed to his evil genius, Philip could feel no sympathy. He advanced into the room slowly. Momentarily he had forgotten the Manheims.

Bernhardt's intervention startled him. 'You've met Otto – Otto – '

'Count von Hauler,' Otto said. 'There's no reason why he shouldn't know my real name, Bernhardt.'

'No.' Clearly Manheim was uncertain how to deal with the unexpected situation in which he found himself. Then he seemed to reach the conclusion that he must treat Philip's arrival as a normal social event. He came forward, holding out his hand.

Philip ignored the gesture, for as soon as he had recognized Otto, he had realized that the time for subterfuge had passed.

'We met in Brussels,' he said, 'the Count and I. But it was not a happy meeting – either for me or for him. Don't you know what happened at the *Maison d'Or*, Bernhardt? You just obey the great man's orders and don't ask questions? Is that it?'

A shutter seemed to come down over Bernhardt Manheim's handsome chiselled features, and the glare he gave Philip was chilling – so much so that Philip almost regretted his remark. However unpleasant the orders that Otto might choose to give, Manheim wouldn't hesitate to obey them.

'Sit down, Janvrin. In that chair opposite me. Search him for weapons, Bernhardt.' Otto gestured with a small black automatic that had suddenly appeared in his grasp. Philip held his breath while Manheim made sure that he was unarmed, but the belt and buckle passed without comment. 'Now,' Otto said when Manheim had assured him that Philip was clean, 'I need to know some facts. First, how did you get here?'

'I borrowed a friend's car. It's outside in the drive. My own, as you probably know, is a complete wreck. Luckily I wasn't in it when it blew up. There's not much left of poor Robert Fauvic, who was backing it out of the garage.'

Behind him Philip heard Andrea catch her breath. She was disturbed by what he had said. She didn't want to face the more gruesome results of her machinations. But she wouldn't help him. He wondered who else was in the house.

'So you're alone?' Otto continued.

'Yes.' Philip glanced about him. 'I see you're all drinking. I suppose I couldn't have a whisky and soda?'

'Why not? Fix him a drink, Bernhardt, and you, Andrea, go and tell Carl to look around the garden and make sure there's no one lurking in the bushes. Tell him to be quick and careful. I don't altogether trust Mr Janvrin here.'

Andrea went on her errand without comment, and Bernhardt poured Philip's whisky, and more drinks for Otto and himself. Apart from the gun which Otto kept pointed steadily at Philip's chest it was superficially a friendly scene. Philip heard the front door slam shut, and prayed that when it opened Carl would not be dragging in an unconscious Sorel. The minutes hung heavy, but Otto seemed content to wait and study Philip in silence.

At last there were sounds of Carl returning, and a muted conversation in the hall. Andrea came into the sitting-room. 'Carl says there's no one around,' she said, and Philip had to make an effort not to show his relief.

Otto shook his large head at Philip in mock reproof. 'Your poor father,' he said. 'Two sons. You a fool and – '

Philip interrupted him. 'Not such a fool. Until I found you here I hadn't realized that Bernhardt and Andrea were involved with you,' he lied. 'Nevertheless, several people know I was going to spend the weekend with them and – '

It was Otto's turn to interrupt. 'Of course! Of course, my dear boy. Naturally there will be questions, but by the time they're asked I'll be far away and you will have disappeared, just like your brother. You've been living a charmed life recently, but it can't continue.'

'You mean you'll kill me as you killed Peter?'

'Not exactly. You've been an extraordinary nuisance to me, Philip Janvrin, and I shall give myself the pleasure of killing you personally, as opposed merely to ordering your demise, as I did with Peter. That was purely business. Your brother was a knave and a rogue. All he wanted was money. I paid him well over the years, but that wasn't enough. He tried to trick me – me, Otto von Hauler!' Otto spat the words.

'What did he do for you that you paid him so well – over the years?' Philip inquired.

Somehow the fact that Peter had been in Otto's employ was not an overwhelming surprise to Philip. He knew that he had been half expecting it, though he wouldn't have admitted it, even to himself. But if Peter had been prepared to work for the Brelados, why not for Otto also? There was nothing dirtier than dealing in drugs.

'I suppose there's no harm in telling you,' Otto said. 'You're not going to have a chance to pass it on. And that reminds me – the car you came in. Is it locked?'

'No, and the key's in the ignition.' Philip could see no reason to lie.

'Good! Then you drive it, Bernhardt, and dump it in the quarry. You'll have to walk back, I regret to say. I'll need Carl in here. Send him. But it shouldn't take you more than half an hour if you cut across the fields.' Otto turned to Philip. 'We have a very convenient deep quarry, which is lucky for us and lucky for you. It will give you approximately thirty minutes to live.'

Philip thought of Sorel and the others in the van; he knew that Otto's possession of the gun had changed the situation considerably. There was now no easy way in which he could summon help; at the first sign of a raid Otto would shoot him – and probably as many more of Sorel's men as he could manage. He could only clutch at his belt buckle if he were able to create some kind of distraction. He must seize any opportunity that offered, though at the moment suitable opportunities looked like being few and far between.

'I don't go into the quarry with the car, then?' he said casually.

'No. I shall shoot you, and Carl and Bernhardt, when he returns, will carry you out into the garden and drop you down the nice deep well the Manheims have here. Meanwhile, I'll tell you how your brother helped me before he decided to play silly buggers.'

The schoolboy slang struck Philip as typical of the man, but he merely said, 'All right.'

He wanted to keep Otto talking while he assessed the situation. He had heard Manheim start Constant's car and drive off, but Carl had come into the sitting-room. Carl was the man, Philip suspected, who had at Otto's bidding beaten him up at the *Maison d'Or*. This evening he was wearing a pullover and very tight jeans, so it was fairly clear that he was unarmed, but he was extremely big and powerful-looking, and Philip had to accept that in a hand-to-hand encounter he wouldn't stand much chance against him. Andrea he thought could be ignored. She was sitting to one side of him and he doubted if she would play any part in a showdown.

'I was going to tell you how your brother Peter served me, wasn't I?' Otto said conversationally. 'His big advantage was that he was in a privileged position because of his job with Brigadier

Aubyn's little lot. He had access to Top Secret documents. If he chose, he could meet important people at home and abroad. He could travel freely on a diplomatic passport; in fact, his job involved a great deal of travelling and meeting useful contacts. As a result, under my guidance, he was able to garner a great deal of information, which was eminently saleable if one knew the right buyers. For example, a country such as Iraq – and many others – will pay highly to learn up-to-date details of weapons technology – modern cost-effective methods of creating weapons-grade uranium, for example, testing and calibration equipment, the latest developments in chemical and biological research and so on. Peter, though he might not have access to such material himself, could be extremely useful by suggesting channels that Bernhardt and others of my flock might pursue. Quite apart from such technical matters, information – not necessarily secret information – is the life-blood of modern society, and a spider at the centre of an information network, which is how you might regard me, has need of flies to keep the network busy.

'I assure you it's a profitable occupation, and it was a great pity that Peter grew greedy. I've regretted the necessity for his death. I shall miss him. But I shan't miss you, Philip Janvrin. As soon as Bernhardt returns – ' Otto looked at his watch.

And in that split second when his captor's attention was distracted Philip acted. He had been aware for some time that the only weapon within his reach was the heavy glass tumbler still a third full of the whisky that Manheim had poured him. He threw it straight and hard at Otto's face. Simultaneously he flung himself sideways to get the protection of an armchair.

He registered without realizing it at the time that the gun had fired two rounds. Andrea was screaming, a dreadful high-pitched keening sound.

Philip clutched at his belt buckle. And he knew that now all he had to do was stay alive until Sorel and his reinforcements came – if they came.

It was not going to be easy. Carl, who had been slow to appreciate what had happened, was lunging towards him. Philip grabbed an occasional table which had fallen over beside him and drove it, legs foremost, into Carl's face. By chance one of the legs penetrated an eye, and Carl let out a howl of agony and covered his face with his hands.

Seizing his opportunity, Philip staggered to his feet, eager to put as much distance as possible between himself and Carl. Momentarily he had forgotten Otto. The third bullet caught him in the shoulder and spun him round. He felt the fourth whip past his head, but it missed him.

Then suddenly the room seemed to fill with people. He was lying on the carpet and Sorel was bending over him. The screaming had stopped. A voice – he though it was Colin O'Donovan's – said, 'The woman's dead, shot. We'll have him for murder, at the very least.'

'Otto?' Philip muttered.

'It's okay. We've got him and the big guy,' Sorel said. 'We caught Manheim earlier in Hamish's car, which is why we were so near when you transmitted.'

'Good,' Philip said before he lost consciousness.

THIRTY

It was ten days later. A great deal had happened in that time, but Philip had taken no active part in the events. This was because Brigadier Aubyn wished to keep Philip away from all publicity, until an acceptable scenario could be created for 'Peter' and his supposed activities. Philip had not objected. On the contrary, the decision to keep him out of the limelight had helped to give him a sense of release. He felt that he had kept his side of the bargain with Sorel and had, to the best of his ability, atoned for Peter's actions. There was no more he could do.

He was fortunate to be alive and in reasonably good health. Constant had driven him from the Manheims' cottage straight to the 'safe house' that he now knew well. It had been an uncomfortable journey, but luckily not a long one and, immediately he got there, Dr John had extracted the bullet from his shoulder, treated the wound and redressed his burnt hands. Given a sedative, he had slept for ten hours.

Since then, once he had given a full account of events at the Manheims' cottage, he had been cared for and cosseted and allowed to do as he pleased. The only restriction was that he must not leave the house and its grounds, but that did not mean that he had been kept in complete ignorance of what was happening. He was able to watch television and read newspapers, and Sorel was in constant touch on the telephone. As far as he could judge all was going as Brigadier Aubyn wished, though he expected to learn more when Sorel came to lunch that day.

He breakfasted late. Ada, the housekeeper, brought up his tray and he sat in front of the long windows looking out across the lawns to the distant wood. It was a view with which he had, not unsurprisingly, grown to feel at home. He remembered the first time he had seen it when, after those dreadful, pitiful days following his release from prison, he had been brought to this same 'safe house'.

Finishing his breakfast, he turned from the window. He was glad that Sorel was coming. Like a man recovering from illness, though he scarcely realized it, he was beginning to grow impatient with inaction, and anxious about the future.

Sorel arrived, with Constant, shortly before noon. They both looked tired, but seemed reasonably cheerful. Constant presented Philip with a large suitcase.

'New clothes for you. We thought you needed some. You've certainly been destroying your own wardrobe rather quickly of late – all in the course of duty, we appreciate.'

Philip grinned. 'You're right about that. Any damage wasn't my fault, certainly. And thanks. I hope I'll have a chance to keep these unharmed.'

'We've been doing our best to ensure that,' said Sorel, leading the way into the small sitting-room. 'Hamish, pour us drinks while I brief Philip on the state of the game. But first a piece of really good news. Mary O'Donovan and Colin have gone to Paris to bring Michael home. He'll be coming here to recuperate, so you'll have company from tomorrow.'

'That's great!' Philip was genuinely pleased; he had grown fond of Michael Lindsay.

'Now, as regards our collection of villains. First, the Brelados. They've been charged and they're awaiting trial. It'll be some time before the case against them and their connections is complete, but they've been refused bail, and there's no doubt they'll both get long sentences. And if the sentences are longer because of a suspicion – which as you know has been hinted at in the press – that the bombing of Peter's Rover was an attempt by one of the drugs syndicate at revenge – well, my heart won't bleed for them.'

'It was a bright idea of the Brig's to start that hare,' Constant said, 'and to make it known that Peter had lent his car to Fauvic while he was abroad. Of course we were lucky the people who lived above the garage and rented it to Peter were away and so couldn't mistake Philip for Peter. Otherwise they would never have accepted that Peter was abroad.'

'Apart from that Inspector Foster and a police officer no one in the mews really took a good look at me,' Philip said, 'but don't forget Baker; he saw me when I got back to the flat.'

'The police will keep their mouths shut,' Constant said ominously, putting Philip's drink on the table beside him, 'and so will Baker. I had a quiet word with him.'

'You understand that we consider it of great importance to avoid giving any indication that Peter was in any way linked with the Manheims and von Hauler,' Sorel said, and added, 'It's ironical but fortunate that the only connection between the Brelados and von Hauler's lot was Peter himself.'

'Yes, I appreciate that, but – ' Philip sighed. He could say that he was impressed with their efficiency, but found their approach cold-blooded. 'I feel sorry about Fauvic. After all, he did try to warn me.'

'Better him than you.' Constant was blunt. He gave Sorel his drink and came and sat down. 'Console yourself with the fact that he had no close relations, except for a sister who doesn't seem particularly grieved.'

'What's more, his involvement with von Hauler's set-up was far greater than he pretended,' Sorel said. 'When his flat was searched some very revealing material was found; there was more discovered in Manheim's flat and office, though none in the cottage. When all the people mentioned have been interrogated there are going to be a lot of red faces and not a few resignations among those in high places – politicians, industrialists, civil servants – both in the UK and abroad. It means an enormous amount of painstaking investigation. Seb Lisle, for one, is extremely busy in Brussels. But it'll be worth it if we can stop von Hauler's game and put the man behind bars for life. At the moment he's charged with the manslaughter of Andrea Manheim, with further charges to follow.'

'What about Bernhardt? He's not been given bail, has he?' Philip asked. 'And Carella?'

'Carella's been questioned and forced to surrender her passport, but she's all right. At present she's staying with Pam and John May, who are a kind couple. I very much doubt if she'll be charged with anything.'

Sorel hesitated, then continued. 'As for Bernhardt Manheim, he wasn't granted bail, but he's no longer a problem. This morning he was found dead in his cell in the remand prison. Somehow he managed to hang himself with his trousers. No

246

one appears very surprised. It seems he's been depressed and morose since he heard of his wife's death.'

There was little sympathy in Sorel's voice. 'I think that's the state of play at the moment.'

'The Contessa?' Constant prompted.

'Oh yes, Monique Scribini. She's disappeared. The Italian police and security forces are all looking for her. But she's not considered important. It's known she let her name and title be used in return for money, and she lent her palazzo in Venice and her apartment in Rome for private rendezvous, but probably she did no more than that.' Sorel made a contemptuous gesture.

'Now about the future, Philip.' He smiled doubtfully.

There was a tap at the door and Ada came in. 'Lunch is ready, gentlemen.'

'Good heavens! Time flies, as they say.' Sorel hurriedly finished his drink and stood up. 'Shall I lead the way? We mustn't keep Ada waiting.'

It seemed to Philip that Sorel and Constant welcomed the interruption. Constant too quickly rose to his feet. Maybe they were thankful to postpone discussion of the future. Neither of them referred to the subject during lunch. While they talked of politics and sport, Philip wondered at their apparent reluctance.

They had returned to the sitting-room and Ada had brought them coffee before Sorel said, surprisingly tentatively, 'Philip, there's something we have to tell you, which I'm afraid may make you rather angry.'

Philip regarded him steadily. 'All right. Tell me.'

'It concerns Peter. I shall have to be blunt. He's dead.'

'You've got definite proof?'

Sorel nodded. He seemed to find it hard to continue and Constant, who appeared to be studying one of his shoes with undue concentration, was no help. Philip was puzzled. After Otto von Hauler's repeated assertions that Peter was dead, the fact of his death was no great surprise, and that proof now existed solved a lot of problems.

His father would suffer most, Philip knew. He would grieve, but he would be spared the knowledge of his elder son's true character and behaviour, and young Patrick, though he would be saddened, would suffer no future shame because of Peter. Zara would be able to marry Malcolm Derwent, and all the obvious legal and financial difficulties would be resolved. Philip didn't shrink from admitting that in many ways Peter's death was for the best. Then he recalled what Sorel had said.

'Why should what you've told me make me angry?' he demanded.

'Because Peter died only last Sunday in a private nursing home in south London.'

'What?'

Once Sorel had made this startling announcement he hurried on. 'It's true. Let me try to explain. On the day Peter was due to leave Amsterdam, he took a taxi to Schiphol. It's unlikely he ever reached the airport. Some days later he was pulled out of the North Sea at Scheveningen – that's near The Hague, some miles south of Amsterdam. God knows how he got there, but he can't have been in the water long. Maybe the fact that in the interval he'd been so brutally assaulted that he was unconscious saved him. In any case, he was alive enough to be resuscitated, but he remained in a coma. He was identified quite quickly because, as you know, we'd been searching for him. We had him flown home, and taken to this nursing home which is also a 'safe house'. He died without regaining consciousness, so he was never able to tell us anything. You, Philip, have filled in the story for us.'

'Why didn't you tell me this in the beginning?' Philip's voice was hoarse with emotion. He could scarcely believe what Sorel had said – that all this time Peter had been alive, in England, within reach. 'Why? I could have gone to him.'

'It wouldn't have done any good. He was an appalling sight. You wouldn't have recognized him.'

'You might have given me the chance. I *was* his brother. And Zara, she is – was – his wife. Surely she had a right – '

'We couldn't take the risk. As few people as possible knew, only those whom we could trust completely.'

'And that didn't include the family?'

'No. Your father or Zara might have betrayed the secret by accident. As for you, Philip – ' Sorel gave a wry smile. 'You were an unknown quantity, an ex-convict found guilty of a particularly heinous offence. Can you blame us?'

'Not at first, perhaps, but later – '

'The Brig did consider telling you later, but decided against it for the same reason that applied to your father and your sister-in-law, and also for fear you might be forced to reveal what you knew if you got into Otto's clutches.'

Philip nodded reluctantly. He recognized the logic of what he was being told, and the stupidity of anger. There was no point in wasting regrets over what couldn't be undone. It was better to look ahead.

'Earlier you mentioned the future,' he said. 'Some time ago you made it clear that the authorities intended to cover for Peter. Are you still going to? And do I assume I'm to have some part to play in it?'

Sorel said, 'We'll need your co-operation, yes. Our stories must agree. What's going to happen is this. First, the Brig is going down to see your father and Zara. They'll be told an approximation of the truth, that Peter was killed in an automobile accident in Amsterdam and his body is being air-freighted home. With air-freight there can be no awkward questions about seeing the body; the coffin has to be sealed. There'll be a funeral, naturally, and in due course a flattering obit will appear in *The Times*. That will at least satisfy your father and make him happy.'

'But it won't satisfy Zara,' Philip protested. 'She knew that Peter had disappeared and I was taking his place.'

'The Brig will tell her that was a deception because Peter was doing some important secret work. He'll say you didn't know this at the time, and it's important that no one else should ever know. If you'll support that, I'm sure she'll accept it.'

'I expect so.' Philip sighed. 'And I suppose a few more untruths don't matter.'

'There'll be some real true news for your father and Zara too,' said Constant. 'Tell him, Greg.'

'The Brig is going to explain that fresh evidence has emerged, and it's now known that you were completely innocent of the charges against you, that the heroin was put in your bag by mistake and without your knowledge, and that when the formalities are completed your name will be publicly cleared. I hope that will please you – and your family?'

'Yes, indeed – if you mean it.'

'We mean it, but – '

'I thought there'd be a catch.'

'Philip, it would look very suspicious if this was done immediately, on top of what was accepted as Peter's involvement in that business with Sylvia Brelado at Heathrow, the bombing of the Rover and the announcement of his death. However, I can assure you that we are committed. Not only will your family be told at once, but Charles Sinclair, who always distrusted my motives for getting you released from his prison, has already been informed – and that should convince you. I might say he was delighted at the news, though appalled to think of the years you spent with him.'

'They could have been worse.' Philip shrugged. 'Charles Sinclair's a good man, very fair, and I quite enjoyed working in the prison library.'

Sorel continued. 'That brings me to the practical, business aspects of this affair, as far as you're concerned. Philip, in normal circumstances, you could sue for false arrest, but as it is would you consider an ex gratia payment of £350,000 as reasonable monetary compensation for imprisonment, and for all you've done for us since we got you out?'

Philip was taken aback. He had never thought of compensation. He bit his bottom lip to prevent himself from laughing. The sum of money he was being offered was both far too little and far too much. It was absurd in every respect, and anyway he wouldn't need it. Then he thought for a moment. Some could be used for Patrick's education and keeping up the house. Suddenly he remembered his godmother's money that had been withdrawn from his Oxford account. He was sure now that Peter had taken it, but it no longer mattered.

'That would be fine,' he said.

'You'll also be on our pay-roll for the next six months. The Brig thinks you need a real holiday. Go wherever you like,' Sorel said.

'You could go round the world,' said Constant, his face bright at the idea, perhaps seeing himself as a companion.

Sorel was more practical. 'It'll give you time to decide what you want to do. You've a degree, Philip. You could get a doctorate and have an academic career, start a business, train as – as – '

'A librarian?'

As soon as he had said it Philip wished he hadn't spoken so cynically. They didn't understand. Why should they? He would never be able to explain to anyone the true effect on him of those years in prison. He grinned at them. It hadn't been their fault.

'I don't need time to consider what I want to do with the rest of my life,' he said. 'I decided that long ago – in fact, before I returned from that holiday in Europe with Peter. Prison seemed to make any hope of achieving my aim impossible, though at the same time it reinforced my desire. Now, once I'm publicly cleared – or sooner if Brigadier Aubyn would co-operate – I can do what I've always wanted.'

And he laughed aloud at the amazement on their faces when he told them he intended to become a Benedictine monk. They knew of his faith, of course, but, 'A monk?' they exclaimed.

'Well, you did suggest I might become an academic,' Philip said. 'The Benedictines are a teaching order, so just think of me – if you think of me at all – as a schoolmaster. After this business it will be a nice, quiet life – and in my opinion considerably less strange than yours.'